HESSIANS AND HELLHOUNDS

MANNERS AND MONSTERS BOOK 6

TILLY WALLACE

ISBN: 978-0-473-58235-7

Published 2021, by Ribbonwood Press, New Zealand

Version 27.06.21

To be the first to hear about Tilly's new releases, sign up at:

www.tillywallace.com/newsletter

1

Love wrought a magical change in Mireworth, and the old house came to life—rather like a corpse hooked up to a galvanism device and hit by a lightning bolt. Conversation filled her rooms, and the echoes of footsteps raced along her halls. The very air seemed to warm, and the atmosphere became less gloomy.

The outward physical appearance of the house had not altered, and every day Hannah added two tasks to her list for every one she completed. But the *soul* of the house revived. The old lady shook herself free of a deep slumber and welcomed her new lord and lady. Or so it seemed to Hannah. Perhaps it was as simple as her good mood spreading to every corner, as she refused to let obstacles dampen her optimistic perception of the world around her.

One change, however, saddened Hannah—with her parents' arrival they lost the easy camaraderie of mealtimes. While they embraced a more casual dining environment at Mireworth, Seraphina's presence at the table proved too much for Mary. The maid's bravery didn't quite extend to meals with the dead mage. Even the robust and short-sighted Helga blanched at the idea of sitting at the same table as her employer's noble mother-in-law.

In search of an alternative, Hannah peeked into the long forgotten formal dining room and promptly shut the door again. The dark space was far too crypt-like, with evidence of its Tudor origins in the low ceiling, dark panelling, and small windows with thick glass. She also didn't want to disturb a colony of rather gigantic spiders that spun webs over the stags' antlers hung on the walls. Even if they lit a fire in the enormous hearth that could roast an entire cow, the room still couldn't compete with the warmth or charm of the kitchen.

Next, Hannah ventured into the servants' hall, where once the butler would have presided over the table at mealtimes. She tried to imagine lively conversations between the maids and footmen, but the long table spoke of all the silenced voices and staff let go as the estate fell on hard times. The two large dining rooms of Mireworth seemed sad and dim compared to the good cheer spreading elsewhere.

In the end, she decided that restoring formality could wait. The family continued to eat at the worn oak table in the kitchen, and the men found a square table and chairs to set up in the conservatory. Drenched in sunlight and warmth, the staff had a cosy spot to take their meals away from their employers. Outside of mealtimes, it also made a comfortable spot for Hannah to study the journals she found in the library.

The morning after her parents arrived at Mireworth, Hannah sat in the kitchen with her breakfast as her father wheeled her mother to the table.

"Good morning, Mother, Papa. Did you sleep well?" Hannah reached for the coffeepot and poured for her father.

"Like a babe," Sir Hugh Miles replied as he took a seat.

Mrs Rossett took a plate and dished up an enormous breakfast from the pots warming on the range, and placed it on the table in front of him. Then she took her cup of tea and a plate of toast and adjourned to the conservatory, Barnes trotting behind her on three fingers and dragging the latest edition of a housekeeping magazine with his thumb and forefinger. The odd couple made Hannah smile. Barnes had taken a shine to Mrs Rossett and took every opportunity to prove himself *handy* to the no-nonsense woman.

"Being here reminds me of the early days of my marriage to Seraphina, when we travelled all around England. We slept in many a different place, always on an adventure. I had quite forgotten how much fun it was." Hugh winked at his wife before picking up his cutlery.

"I apologise for the unusual accommodation. The workmen will begin repairing the roof this week. I am grateful to Hannah that Mireworth will be watertight once more before winter, and we will be able to reclaim the upstairs rooms." Wycliff glanced at Hannah with a mix of gratitude and love simmering in his eyes.

"There is no need to apologise. In fact, you may need to keep a stretcher for Hugh in the parlour—he rather enjoys playing forts like a boy draping a blanket over a table." Seraphina reached out and touched her husband's hand.

"There is something about this place that is invigorating and invites one to strike off and explore the nooks and crannies." Hannah's father waggled his eyebrows at her mother.

Hannah grinned into her hot chocolate. Neither time nor death could diminish the affection between her parents. How blessed she was to have found such a love with Wycliff.

"There is an energy about this house. I think Mireworth harbours many secrets—some running deeper than the mysterious tower. I believe they have constructed it over ley lines." Seraphina picked up an empty teacup with a silver rim, decorated with purple pansies and a blue butterfly.

Mimicking her father, Wycliff attempted to waggle his eyebrows at Hannah—a comical action that nearly made her choke on her drink.

"I will bow to your knowledge of ley lines, Lady Miles. Regarding the tower, Hannah is intent on uncovering those secrets, but she will have to wait until Frank finishes knocking down the wall and carting away the rubble," he said.

Hannah blew out a sigh. "He won't even let me peek! Honestly, ever since I nearly drowned, Frank and Wycliff have fussed over me like mother hens. I am quite recovered, and capable of stepping over some rubble."

"I believe he wishes it to be a surprise, Hannah, to repay the kindness you have shown him and Mary. There are plenty of other areas we can explore while you wait." Wycliff's lips twitched in humour.

"Why don't we have a closer look at the entrance foyer today, Hannah?" her mother suggested. "I am rather fascinated by the griffin newel posts. Or they might be sphinx, depending on other clues we may find."

"Very well. Then I would like your counsel about what to grow in the conservatory, and I shall show you the grave indignity that Wycliff's grandfather committed against the library." Hannah would appreciate her mother's opinion on how to go about restoring not only the library's physical form, but also its contents. It would take years before the shelves were filled again. The next time she went shopping in London, she intended to find rousing tales of pirates to appeal to the boy hiding inside Wycliff.

"Blast!" Wycliff muttered over his coffee cup. The newspaper in his hand shook.

"What is it?" Hannah enquired.

He folded the paper to highlight the article that had caught his attention and placed it on the table in front of Hannah.

She read the headline aloud. "'Bereaved man finds wife's brain missing.' Oh, dear." A cold lump dropped into her stomach as she read on. Not another rogue Afflicted dining on unsuspecting Londoners? The upper echelons of those in power were already muttering about the status of the Afflicted after one murderous spree. Any more deaths would see them all rounded up and quarantined like lepers.

"Read it aloud, please, Hannah, because that is a rather worrying headline." Seraphina gestured with her empty teacup.

Hannah scanned ahead and then began reading the article for the whole table. "'Mr Sennett, grieving the death of his wife, became further distraught when the pallbearers stumbled and dropped her coffin. His brother-in-law demanded the lid be removed, so that they might ensure Mrs Sennett rested peacefully within and had not been disturbed. On opening the coffin, horrified onlookers saw the top of her skull had been sawed off and her brain was quite absent.'"

Sir Hugh frowned. "Surgical removal of the scalp, or something more disorganised?"

"It would appear...surgical. Here, this part... 'It appeared some monster had stolen her mind and when the coffin was dropped, stitches were disturbed and the top portion of skull dislodged against the side of the coffin.'" Hannah passed the newspaper to her father.

Silence fell for a moment as Sir Hugh devoured the article again.

"It sounds like a donor to Unwin and Alder, but

surely the husband would have known and been paid for the brain?" Wycliff mused out loud.

"He might have been approached and in his grief, did not recollect it? Or what if another relative authorised the removal and pocketed the coin without his knowledge?" Hannah tried to imagine scenarios where the woman's body might have made its way into the hands of Unwin and Alder without the husband's consent.

But there was another possibility, one she didn't want to consider. What if they had an Afflicted mimicking the work of Unwin and Alder?

"He might have been trying to save face," Seraphina suggested. "With many people gathered for the funeral, it would be difficult to explain why your wife's brain had vanished. Perhaps he went with the easier option of expressing horror and was carried along as events unfolded?"

"If it's an Afflicted involved in the removal of brains, then Sir Manly will no doubt send word. The bigger problem is if word should get out about the true nature of Unwin and Alder's enterprise. It is one thing to claim the business need to peel back the scalp to perform their *phrenology* study, quite another to explain missing brains. Many people are uncomfortable with the idea of pieces of themselves being removed after death, and some cling to the notion that their body must remain intact after death for them to be admitted through the Pearly Gates." Wycliff reached for the coffeepot and refilled his cup.

"Another possibility might be Unwin and Alder performing unauthorised extractions. Although a fellow would hope they wouldn't jeopardise a lucrative business by trying to skimp on paying the bereaved." Sir Hugh passed the newspaper to Seraphina, but she waved it away.

"I will send a message to the Ministry today seeking further information." Wycliff glared at the newspaper as though it had deliberately broken the cheerful mood growing at Mireworth.

A little of the shine rubbed off Hannah's contentment at the idea of having to return to London for another investigation. But that was a worry for another day. It would take at least two to three days before Wycliff received a response, even if Sir Manly dispatched the secretary Higgs in his owl form.

After breakfast, Hannah wheeled her mother into the gloomy entrance hall with its double curved staircase and Juliet balcony where the two sides met.

"Do you think there is any way to clean the light dome, Mother? It is in a rather sad state, but the roof is not safe enough to send anyone up to work on it. I would so love to see whatever the design is." If they could clean the glass forming the dome high above, light would once more flood the entrance hall.

Hannah struggled with an uncharacteristic bout of impatience to tackle all the areas of Mireworth that needed repair. If only it were as simple as asking her mother to cast a magical spell to restore the house to her former grandeur. Unfortunately, magic didn't work like that. As her mother explained, such a large-scale spell was too vague. There was simply too much that needed fixing and too many different components and materials involved. Magic, somewhat like builders and architects, required detailed plans to follow. Spells worked best when they were narrowly focused.

The mage glanced upward at the smears of dark red and brown. "Yes, I think with a gentle approach, we could wash away years of dirt. Any such spell I construct will not deliver an instant result, though, Hannah. Do you think you can wait a week, as it scrubs away a layer at a time?"

"Since I cannot go up there to hurry the process along, I shall be patient. Besides, there are many other things I wish to tackle with your assistance—such as what is in the bottom of the tower emitting a purple mist." Although even that would have to wait, since Frank guarded the project. He left Barnes at the doorway when he carted out the debris to stop Hannah from entering. The hand waved a finger at her in an *oh no you don't* gesture and she didn't have the heart to simply step over him. Not when he took his guard duty so seriously.

"Let us have a change of focus from looking up, and look down instead," Seraphina suggested. "I think there is some pattern to the tiles in here, but I cannot discern it."

Hannah stared at her feet. Under their layers of grime, some tiles held a blue tinge, others a dull brownish-green. One, that seemed all on its own in an ocean of murk, had flashes of yellow.

Her mother waved to the stairs. "Why don't you go up to the balcony, Hannah, and I will cast a light. Perhaps that might make the pattern visible."

Seraphina wheeled herself to the middle of the foyer while Hannah trotted up the stairs and stood on the little balcony. When she was in place, her mother created an orb of glowing, creamy light and set it free. The rotating sphere rose upward past Hannah, until it hovered some twenty feet in the air like a celestial candelabrum.

The intense light and higher perspective helped. It also brought into stark relief the spiders staring back at her from the corners, and the intricate webs they had spun along the walls. Ignoring the smaller residents of Mireworth, Hannah leaned over the balcony to study the tiles.

"I think there may be a strip of blue running across the room, with green and yellow on either side?" No matter how hard she squinted, Hannah couldn't discern any further details from the vague placement of colours.

Seraphina wheeled herself to the middle of the room and gestured with her arms. "Which way does the blue seem to run from up there? Is it this way?"

"Yes, sort of diagonally in front of the staircases. I wonder what it could be?" She rejoined her mother below.

"If you are not averse to a little hard work, I can

concoct a potion to strip this back to the original colours. It would need to be scrubbed on and then wiped off," her mother said.

"Oh, yes, please." Hannah stared at her hands, the skin already red and chafed from the amount of manual labour she had undertaken lately. A visit to Mr Seager in the village might be in order, for some of his famed hand cream.

Her mother set to work, assisted by Mrs Rossett, and brewed her potion in the kitchen. The two women used a copper pot large enough to hold an entire suckling pig. Hannah thought they looked like witches plucked from a storybook as they cackled over the pot. The mixture bubbled until after lunch, when the mage declared it ready.

"We must dilute it in buckets of water," Seraphina said.

From the storeroom, Hannah and Mary found three sturdy metal buckets. They poured the thick orange liquid into each, then filled the buckets with water and stirred. A faint orange steam with the tang of citrus rose off the surface.

"Is it safe to put our hands in?" Mary asked with a tremble to her bottom lip.

Seraphina waved away her concerns. "Perfectly safe, Mary, and no worse than doing laundry. Hannah tells me the apothecary in the village has a most excellent cream for ladies' hands, and I shall treat you all to a pot each when you are done."

Hannah, Mary, and Helga each took up a thick

bristled scrubbing brush and a cloth. Then, carrying their pails, they headed to the entrance hall. The light orb still spun above them and illuminated their work. Among the three of them, they soon had the liquid rubbed into all the tiles. It bubbled a dirty brown and let off a nose-wrinkling odour not unlike the smell the puppy made when she ate something that disagreed with her.

"Gosh, it smells awful." Mary pinched her nose and waved a towel in front of her face.

"Why don't we prop the front door open to help dispel the odour?" Hannah suggested.

With Helga's help, they prised the large doors open and let a breeze swirl away the fumes.

Next they fetched clean water and fresh cloths, and undertook the much slower task of wiping all the liquified grime from the tiles. With the first sweep of her damp cloth, Hannah gasped. Beneath years of dust and dirt, she had revealed a portion of what appeared to be bright green grass. With more passes of her cloth, the murky blue patches turned into the deep blue and aqua of water.

Piece by piece, the larger picture battled the dirt and emerged victorious.

"What is it? A meadow?" Mary turned her head, looking one way and then another.

Hannah ran up the stairs and stepped on to the balcony. Excitement leapt up her throat. The blue tiles were a river, and on either side were depicted rushes, reeds, and the unmistakable flowers of lotus. When viewed from up high, what had seemed to be mottled grey patches turned into basking crocodiles and a hippopotamus. The bright green growth of the fertile banks gave way to the rich yellows and reds of sand as it reached the edges of the space. The griffin newel posts stood at the edge of a desert.

Hannah gripped the railing as ideas spun in her head. "Not a meadow, Mary. I believe it is the Nile flowing across the entranceway and running straight to the bottom of the tower."

2

FOR ALL HER GENTLE DEMEANOUR, Wycliff discovered that his wife contained a ravenous beast—curiosity. A hungry demon arose within her that demanded to be fed information. It took Frank two days to knock through from the small sliver of a room to the tower beyond, and to tidy up the space to his satisfaction. Two long days in which Hannah paced and tried to concentrate on other tasks.

It caused Wycliff some amusement that Frank refused to let the lady of Mireworth through until he had removed the debris, wiped down the dust, and ensured there were no sharp edges that might harm her. When Hannah tried to sneak in, the stitched-together man growled at her and placed Barnes as watchman. His wife developed a sudden interest in gardening and when Frank caught her peering in the window with a weed grasped in her hand, the large man nailed up a board to block her view.

In the interim, Wycliff marvelled at the change in the enormous entrance foyer with the tiles restored to their original sharp colours. While most houses of the Georgian era had floors patterned in simple geometric designs, yet again an odd departure had been taken with Mireworth's decoration. A painted landscape of life next to a fertile Nile spread between the two griffins. Or were they sphinx, after all?

The tiles had always had murky tones when he was a boy, and he never gave them any thought, except for how they gave away his boot treads when he was trying to sneak up on Lisbeth. In hindsight, he wondered if someone had deliberately obscured the pattern. The layer of grime that Hannah, Mary, and Helga had removed was so thick, old, and evenly dispersed over the entire space that they speculated someone had deliberately painted it over.

"Are you sure you don't know the history of this house, Wycliff? I don't know if she could be any more obvious in her clues pointing to Egypt. All we are lacking is the reason." Seraphina worked to construct a magical bridge across the tile river. The gentle arch could either be crossed, or it would shimmer and reform behind anyone who strode through its delicate sides.

A weight pressed inside him. "I did not have a good relationship with my father. I suspect he knew, but kept the information from me. When I discovered the tower he was...displeased and made it clear I was never to go there, nor ask about it again. Whatever information he had about Mireworth's history passed with him."

Hannah scoured the journals, looking for any reference to the history of the house and the origins of the family. While Wycliff had sold off the books he'd inherited, his father might have edited the collection of diaries and such. For all he knew, they could have been consigned to a bonfire years ago.

"There is one possible source we could consult to learn about Mireworth's origins," Hannah said from by his side. She stood next to the image of a lounging crocodile, as though she didn't want to stand on the painted animal.

"Who is that?" he asked. The only servant left from the early days was Mrs Rossett, and she didn't have any whispers or rumours to share. Mr Hartley had said he had collected stories about the estate, but they found none when they searched the journals in his cottage.

"Lord de Cliffe." Her eyes blazed with the ideas sparking in her mind.

"He's dead." Wycliff doubted even bones would remain in the family crypt after five hundred years.

"And you are a hellhound. Imagine if you could find his soul on the other side and ask him directly what exactly he got up to in Egypt that created such a firm grasp on this parcel of land. Or alternatively, we find an aftermage who can communicate with spirits, and see if he would come forward for a chat." She had such an earnest expression that he swallowed his rebuttals and doubts.

"You will have to write a list of all the souls I must seek out when I follow the inky path." He was saved from any further discussion about when he might take that one-way stroll to Hell by the arrival of Frank.

The monster shuffled out from under the stairs. "Ready," he intoned.

Wycliff expected Hannah to squeal and rush to be first. Instead, she seemed frozen to the spot like the crocodile. He took her hand and whispered her name. "Hannah? Why are you not racing me to the tower?"

She turned and placed her hand on his arm. "I need a moment to reflect. I have so many questions. Will they finally be answered, or will we find only a manger for wintering animals? I'm not sure I could live with the disappointment if we find only fossilised excrement."

He wrapped one arm around her waist and walked her to the narrow room they had dubbed the waiting room. "I doubt a purple mist arises from long-dead animals, even if the place had been full of donkeys with stomach complaints. Your mother has already confirmed it is of magical origin."

He let her go first through the door to survey Frank's hard work. The monster had removed the boards from the windows and sunlight streamed into the space. He had cleaned out the demolished wall, sacrificing the built-in seat in the process. Now, the space beyond revealed the secret it hid.

Frank had created an eight-foot-wide opening to allow light to reach the tower for the first time in over a hundred years, and greatly increased the space of the original waiting room, where once Wycliff could touch both walls with outstretched arms.

Hannah let out a soft gasp at the light-filled and spacious room. The curve of the tower drew the eye and its stone glowed a soft pink. The tower was enclosed in a corner of Mireworth with an eight-foot gap at the widest point between tower and wall. Then the space narrowed on two sides of the ancient fortification, where its curves butted up against its prison walls.

"Why don't you go first?" Wycliff suggested.

She let go of his hand and stepped into the tower's presence. No one spoke as they filed in behind her, Sir Hugh pushing Seraphina in her bathchair. Hannah walked around the available circumference, one hand stroking the stone as she went. When she reached the far corner, she turned and walked as far as she could back the other way. Wycliff watched her careful inspection.

"Bother. No door," she muttered when she returned to his side.

Half of the tower's circumference was blocked, due to being located in a corner. Wycliff didn't need his wife to voice her next question. He had resigned himself to more holes in Mireworth's battered body.

"There could be a door somewhere on the other side of it, if we could approach it from outside?" Hannah rested her hands on a block and tried to peer into the tiny space between tower and exterior wall.

"I draw the line at knocking down external walls," Wycliff said.

"Perhaps I might be of assistance." Seraphina wheeled herself closer. "The stonework is quite exquisite and I'll not have anyone taking a sledge-hammer to it. Let me see if the mortar will cooperate with me."

She raised her hands and placed them on a spot illuminated by a ray of sunlight. The mage bowed her head, and soft words whispered around the room and brushed over them. At first nothing happened. Then a faint crackle reached Wycliff's ears. The block under the mage's palms wriggled and the mortar holding it in place jiggled. Tiny pieces dropped to the ground with soft pops. Once all the mortar around the stone had separated itself from its neighbours, it marched to the edge and leapt to the floor like lemmings from a cliff. Then the stone itself slid an inch out of place.

Wycliff took hold of the stone and pulled it free. A whoosh of escaped air blew through the hole. He caught a whiff of old dust and turned his head to cough. He placed the stone on the ground in a corner as Lady Miles worked on another.

Piece by piece, she urged the mortar to surrender its grip on the stones. Then Frank or Wycliff would remove the block. Hannah fetched a broom and swept up the litter of chips. Soon, the men had a pile of blocks stacked to one side. The mage had worked her magic to create a slender opening, somewhat like the tear in the air when Wycliff summoned the void.

They gathered around Seraphina, which then blocked the sunlight streaming over their shoulders. But they saw enough of the rounded interior to see something large squatting in the middle of the room.

Hannah placed a hand on his arm, keen excitement burning in her eyes. "I think, given how long the tower has been bricked up, it might be prudent to use your hellhound vision before we enter, Wycliff? We don't want to anger any long-imprisoned spirits."

He nodded, and the group stepped back. Sir Hugh pulled Seraphina away, and they clustered by the opening to give Wycliff space.

Wycliff closed his eyes and sought the ember within him. Blowing upon it, he let the flames flare into life and then grabbed hold of them as he opened his eyes. Because of where the mage had created the gap, sunlight burst through and into a room that had lain in darkness for six hundred years.

He stepped into the bottom level of the tower. The brightness created a vivid red bolt that pulsed in the centre of the room and seared into his brain. He narrowed his eyes against the light and looked around the room. The musty odour was much stronger now, with the faint richness of earth and mushrooms— though the room seemed dry, with no fungi growing in the corners.

He ignored the enormous shape hunkering down in the middle of the space and searched for any entombed souls. Had the original de Cliffe walled up a trouble-some wife? Or perhaps he trapped a rival for his lady's affection, quietly done away with? Nothing moved within, not even the scuttle of a mouse running from sudden exposure.

Emboldened by the silence, Wycliff walked around the curved wall and used his peripheral vision to search for any spirit residue. When he completed a circuit, he turned to the central object. Made of granite, it appeared to be a sarcophagus some eight feet long, three feet in both height and width, and with a lid two inches thick. The purple mist filtered through the stone lid and drifted upward. Whatever it was, or whatever was hidden inside, he had found the source of the odd light.

He let go of the ember inside him, thought of winter snow, and extinguished the internal fire. He shook his head as his vision adjusted to the mortal realm again. Walking to the jagged tower doorway, he addressed the expectant faces beyond. "There are no souls or demons lurking in here. Nor is there any door other than the one Lady Miles just made. The mist the hound perceives is coming from what appears to be a tomb."

Hannah edged closer, and he held out a hand to her. Her fingers trembled as they slid into his grasp. Wycliff stayed by her side as she approached the granite construction.

"Do you really think it's a tomb?" she whispered.

"Yes. I doubt this tower was a vegetable cellar or that this object is a linen chest." He wondered whom de Cliffe had buried in the tower. *Someone he couldn't bear to be parted from—even in death*, a voice in the depths of his mind answered. People did odd things in the throes of grief. Perhaps this was his ancestor's tribute to a great love.

Hannah knelt and ran a hand along the smooth stone. Sunlight flickered into the base of the tower and caressed the sarcophagus for the first time in hundreds of years. Hannah studied each side. "Its sides are plain, but the ends both have a square in the centre carved with hieroglyphics."

"So your ancestor looted more than a few pretty tablets from Egypt, eh, Wycliff?" Sir Hugh chuckled as he pushed his wife into the room.

The older couple halted next to the tomb. Seraphina examined the engraving on one end. Roughly a foot square, the very middle had a tall oval shape containing a few symbols, then the whole was surrounded by rows of hieroglyphics.

"Definitely Egyptian," Seraphina murmured. Then she placed her hands on the lid and sucked in a breath. "The mist Wycliff can detect is a faint magical trace. I cannot see it as he does, but I can sense it. Whoever rests here once possessed a great deal of magical ability in life. In ancient Egypt, mages and aftermages were the priests and priestesses in their temples, and they treated magic with some reverence. Given that this trace has endured for centuries, I believe it most likely that this tomb contains someone who was once a mage."

"De Cliffe stole the body of a mage from a temple

during the Crusades?" Hannah turned wide eyes on her husband.

Wycliff held up his hands in a defensive posture. "I had no idea, but I wonder if my father knew the associated story. All I can offer is more questions—the primary one being *why*? If this were some looted trophy, why brick it into a tower? And why hide the tower during the construction of the new house?"

Seraphina patted the stone lid. "We will have to dig deep to uncover any other clues that might answer all our questions."

Sir Hugh shuffled around the tomb, staring at his feet. He stopped at one point close to the wall. Then he kicked at the centuries of dust and dirt that had accumulated. "There is something here."

Wycliff and Hannah joined him. Sir Hugh bent down and used his handkerchief to clear away the spot he had worked loose with the toe of his boot.

"There's something carved into the floor." Wycliff glanced up. "This is the very corner of the house and might once have been the outer corner of the original fort."

"It's hieroglyphics again, Mother," Hannah said.

"Help me down, please, Hugh." Seraphina held out her arms.

The physician plucked his wife from her chair and carried her over. Then he edged away to let the sun brush the surface. The mage incanted the spell to make the symbols reform into letters and then translate themselves. She muttered to herself and tilted her head to read the script.

"*One of mine, for one of yours. A bargain struck, the tower endures,*" Seraphina whispered.

The words sent a chill over Wycliff's skin, and his stomach lurched. *One of mine for one of yours.* What sort of exchange had his ancestor made that the rest of the family had tried to cover up? "I wonder if, over the years, my ancestors tried to tear down the tower but were unsuccessful, and so it was encased instead. But what was exchanged as part of this bargain?" With all the clues pointing to Egypt and the underworld, part of him could take a guess. But he didn't like the answer his brain supplied.

Sir Hugh placed his wife back in the bathchair, and she wheeled herself over to the tomb. "I am only speculating, but if whoever lies here came from Egypt and is the *one of mine*, then following that logic, the *one of yours* would be a descendant of de Cliffe."

"To what end, though?" Hannah gripped Wycliff's arm and leaned closer to his side.

He pressed against her warmth to dispel the chill creeping over him. He searched his memory for any snippets he could remember from childhood, but that particular cupboard in his head was bare. "I don't know, Hannah. Most men bring back trophies from war for either money or power. If this is a mage, perhaps de Cliffe brought the person here to perform some task. Then when they died, they could not be returned to Egypt and so were entombed instead?"

"If that were the case, what I find rather curious is that from my recollections, there is no mention in the mage histories of any Egyptian mage visiting English shores. Yet such an occasion should have been recorded —if the mage were living. Which lends more weight to de Cliffe's bringing back a mummy as a curiosity." Seraphina traced a finger around the carved oval inside the square on the sarcophagus.

"We are going in circles. I cannot see a looted mummy creating a scandal or necessitating being walled up in a tower. From what we find here, I think it is not a coincidence that the hellhounds targeted Wycliff." Hannah met his stare and gave voice to the cold lump in his stomach.

"Perhaps whomever de Cliffe struck the bargain with took six hundred years to collect on what he was owed." Seraphina crafted a single lotus bloom from the air, the edges a deeper pink than the rest of the flower, and laid it on the tomb.

"That's a rather unfair bargain. This de Cliffe got whatever advantage in the twelfth century, and then Wycliff here gets bitten by a hellhound and turned into one of them." Sir Hugh shook his head.

Wycliff stared at the tomb. A purely financial motive didn't sit well inside him. Nor would a mummy as a trophy have generated the secrecy around the tower. There was a deeper reason here, one ordinary men couldn't fathom. He glanced at his in-laws. A man who continued to love his wife beyond death...

"We'll keep looking for answers, Hannah. There

are so many clues, we have only to put them all together."

"Well, Wycliff, you have simply the most fascinating skeleton in the family closet. I cannot wait to see what you and Hannah discover next," Seraphina said.

3

THEIR DISCOVERY CHURNED up new emotions in Hannah. Excitement flared within her at finding another link to Egypt and the origins of the Afflicted curse. Then she plunged into worry at what bargain had been struck that could reach through the centuries to ensnare Wycliff. A tingle of curiosity crept along her limbs at how their paths were intertwined. Her mother's ability truly was magical in how it had guided her to insist Wycliff be included among the guests at Lizzie's engagement ball. How different would Hannah's life be today if he had not attended?

She tackled the worn and hard-to-read family journals with renewed vigour, determined to find some snippet to advance their quest. She took a stack of musty books to the conservatory and placed them on the table. With a fresh pot of tea at her elbow and Sheba asleep in the sun at her feet, Hannah pulled a journal from the pile.

A history of some sort must have passed from father to son that resulted in the Lord Wycliff of a hundred years ago enclosing the tower when he constructed the new house. After two hours of squinting at terrible handwriting (which made her imagine that the lord in question had spent more time outdoors than in the schoolroom), her next clue was found in the same hard-to-read journal as the first reference.

"'The tower is this family's greatest shame,'" she read aloud.

Wycliff's ancestors had a habit of dropping lines like that with no further explanation. It was infuriating. Given that they had written the journal expecting their words to endure for future generations, would it really have been so difficult to include a few explanatory background notes?

She pondered the sentence and wondered if it were the tower that was the great shame, or its contents? There was nothing particularly secretive or scandalous about building a tower with a lady's solar on the upper level. Unless it had been used for secret trysts. No, the circumstances surrounding the inhabitant of the tower had to be the source of the secrecy. But had de Cliffe returned from Egypt with remains or a living mage? Or perhaps he had propped the dead mage in a chair at the table and addressed the person as though they were alive? That would be decidedly odd and make the family look askance at him.

A mage, her mother had said. One who had come to

England, yet whose arrival the British mages had failed to mention, their absence in the mage histories rather like the blank spot on the Mireworth house plans. When others sought to conceal something by failing to acknowledge it, they instead drew attention to the omission.

What if the mage were a woman and de Cliffe had fallen in love, brought her back to England, and in doing so incurred the wrath of some higher power? Hannah snorted at the fanciful fairy tale she constructed. She could imagine how a woman mage would have upset the English mage council. They feared and loathed women mages, and used to snuff out the lives of babes if they were what they considered the *inferior* gender. What would they have done in the twelfth century if confronted with an adult woman mage who challenged them? *Burned her at the stake, or entombed her.*

Hannah waved a hand to dispel the ideas. Already she chased too many threads without imagining that Wycliff possessed an Egyptian mage in his lineage. Instead, she concentrated on how a family would pass down a terrible secret. An oral retelling was the most obvious, but what if a father got some detail wrong, or succumbed to a horrid accident before he could tell his son? If she were the cautious type in possession of such a secret, she would ensure there was a hidden account that a son could find to learn the true history of the tower.

Her mother interrupted her intellectual pursuit of

a possibly concealed journal containing all the missing explanatory details.

"Do you have time to discuss plants, Hannah?" Seraphina said as she wheeled around the central pool.

"Of course. I feel a headache coming on from trying to read this rather shocking handwriting." Hannah closed the aged book and placed it on the pile. "I would appreciate your touch to revive the conservatory. It would be lovely to fill this space with greenery, rather than staring at empty beds."

Seraphina reached out and placed one gloved hand in the fresh soil. "I do long for a creative project and soil between my fingers. I cannot remember the last garden someone asked me to design."

She fell silent, and a pang of sadness rippled through Hannah. Her mother loved working with Nature and creating gardens, or forests such as the one at their home in Westbourne Green. But since her demise, those commissions had dried up and blown away. She couldn't help but recall Mr Seager the apothecary's words: *Dead things should fertilise gardens, not give advice about them.*

"I thought perhaps a mixture of edible plants to feed the household, and something purely decorative to feed the eyes and soul," Hannah said as she pushed back her chair and stood.

Seraphina swivelled her bathchair and moved along to another raised bed. "Oh, yes. We have the space for delicate ornamentals to brighten the tables inside. If you are keen, I could work a little magic on a spot right in front of the glass with the southernmost aspect, and ensure it is warm enough to grow a pineapple."

"A pineapple? Goodness. I never dreamed to be wealthy enough for pineapple. Or perhaps, if we grew one, we could sell it to fund the renovations?" Hannah gasped as her mother painted the conservatory with her magic. A selection of deep green plants burst into life, along with bright flowers and in one spot, the spiky pineapple. Behind it, tomatoes climbed supporting wires and dripped with heavy red spheres. A tall pot held an orange tree with perfectly round fruit waiting to be plucked.

"Renting is more lucrative, from what I hear. Many a hostess secretly rents the pineapple to place in the centrepiece of her table." Seraphina waved her hands, playing with the placement of hanging plants that dangled like tassels, and more delicate orchids that needed to be cosseted away from any draft.

"It would be nice to have something planted before we leave. I fear Wycliff's work as an investigator will soon call him back to London. Particularly if the scandal sheets have any more stories of missing brains." Hannah reached up and touched a magical fern frond that curved over the path. The illusion shimmered as her fingers passed through it.

"I will also have to return. While I can set free other rumours from here, it is easier to control the spread of gossip when I can place my spells more exactly. That requires the help of Kitty Loburn, who hears so many society whispers." The mage clasped her hands and settled them in her lap.

"There is always a pull on our time," Hannah murmured as the surrounding greenery dissolved like a dream upon waking.

"Speaking of which, we must perform the renewal spell. I dislike venturing too far past thirty days between them." Seraphina swirled her hand through the dirt.

Hannah let out a sigh and seated herself on the bricked edge of a raised bed. "What if I do not want to perform the ritual?"

"Hannah..." her mother began.

Hannah held up her hands. "I am well aware of what will happen, Mother. My heart will still and I will die. From our observations of the Afflicted, we know it takes three to four days before they are reanimated. I can use that time to journey to the underworld with you and Wycliff to hunt for Dupré and a cure."

"And what if we cannot extract the cure from him? Or what if he isn't even there?" Seraphina wheeled herself closer and took Hannah's hand.

Hannah stared at their clasped hands. Would she need linen gloves or could she keep her flesh from rotting? Miss Knightley showed only very faint signs of the curse. If Hannah followed a similar regime to that of the other young woman, she too could almost pass for a living being. "If we fail to find either Dupré or a cure, then I will carry on, as you have. There is plenty to occupy me here, and I am sure Unwin and Alder will deliver to Dorset what I would require to sustain me."

Seraphina turned her head and pressed one gloved hand to her temple. "Do you know how it pains me to hear my daughter talk so calmly about her impending death? Your father and I sought to save you."

"You did save me—when you asked Lady Loburn to invite Wycliff to Lizzie's engagement ball. I have found a man who will love me beyond death, and that eventuality no longer holds any fear for me." Only a very slight tremor raced over her skin at the idea of dying. She would exhale her last breath surrounded by those who loved her and, she had no doubt, would reanimate to find Wycliff waiting for her.

"Very well. Your course of action makes me despair, but I take some comfort in knowing you will not be alone on your journey. I only ask that you discuss this with Wycliff first. Your decision affects us all, but he will bear the worst of it. He will hold you close as your life ebbs from your body." The words rasped from Seraphina as though the mage held back tears and remembered her own death.

Hannah nodded her agreement and swallowed the lump in her throat. "Now, shall we make a list of seeds and cuttings we require for the garden? Then we can ensure everything is waiting for you to plant and nurture on your next visit."

She grasped the handles of the bathchair and positioned her mother at the table. Next, Hannah fetched pen and paper to make notes as her mother dictated.

On her way back to the table, she passed the pool with its statue of Ma'at. "I believe this is a fountain. It looks as though water should trickle from the scales she holds." When she had cleaned out the conservatory beds, Hannah found a set of brass scales that attached to the woman's hand. A small pipe lined up with a hole in the rod, and its brass length concealed a tiny spout at either end. She hypothesised that water would trickle into one side until it filled the pan, then it would tip to empty the contents into the pool.

"Oh, how lovely. That only requires a simple spell to circulate the water. Why don't you ask Frank to fill the pool, while we make our lists? Then when he is finished, I can activate it," her mother suggested.

OVER DINNER THAT NIGHT, Hannah raised one idea with Wycliff that had sprung into her mind earlier in the day. "Do you know of any hiding places at Mireworth?"

Wycliff lowered his cutlery. "Do you mean like a priest's hole?"

Hannah shook her head. What she sought this time wasn't as large as a concealed tower, or a place to hide a hunted man, or even a nook for a boy playing hide and seek. "Nothing that large. A small nook where documents or valuables could be concealed?"

Wycliff blew out a sigh. "I imagine there are innumerable such spots in the house. Nobles are a suspicious lot and there is at least one place to store jewellery, deeds, and such. Why do you ask?"

Hannah took a sip of her wine before replying. "I have not found any history of the tower in the early accounts of Mireworth. Given what we have discovered so far, I wondered if information surrounding a mage's being here was kept away from prying eyes."

Wycliff stared at her, and a light flickered in his gaze. "I think you might be on the trail of something there, Hannah. But how would we find such a small and hidden space? We would have to knock on every panel and bit of wainscoting."

She had some inkling of the enormity of the task she had set herself—assuming a spot hoarding the secret history of the tower even existed. "I have given that some thought and believe we should start with the most likely rooms. The library, the master's study, and the private family rooms. If they reveal nothing, then we work outward to the other rooms and corridors."

Barnes trotted along the table and sat before her, waving his fingers in the air.

"Are you offering to assist, Barnes?" Hannah asked.

He made the nodding *yes* gesture with his index finger.

"Brilliant, thank you. Your perspective would be much appreciated." Hannah patted the hand. He really proved himself an invaluable member of their household.

"Tomorrow, I will show you the apartments for Lord and Lady Wycliff. We might as well start our search there, and we can discuss what needs to be done to wrest them back into usable shape." He said the words with a faint tinge of sadness.

Hannah stared at her plate. As Lady Wycliff, she possessed her own suite. Noble spouses spent much of their lives apart, seeing each other mostly at the dining table. A husband was expected to make brief conjugal visits to his wife's rooms and then retreat to his own. She glanced at Wycliff's profile. Propriety be damned. When at their private residence in the country, she would make her own rules to live by. Hannah brushed her thumb over the stem of her glass.

"A dressing room would be wonderful, but I have no need of a separate bedroom," she murmured. Then a blush crept up her neck at having declared in front of her parents that she preferred her husband's bed.

"We can work on making both suites habitable, then you will have a private place if you wish to avail yourself of it when not...elsewhere." Wycliff's gaze heated and left her in no doubt as to where he imagined her spending her nights.

Her father spluttered into his wine and turned beetroot red.

"Are you all right, Hugh?" Seraphina asked.

He waved aside her concerns and gulped his drink. "Merely thinking of all the rooms Mary will have to clean. You will need more staff eventually—and you should consider getting yourself a valet, Wycliff."

After a long dinner and pleasant conversation, Hannah and Wycliff said their good nights. She sat in bed and pulled her knees closer to her body under the blankets. She had promised her mother that she would discuss her course of action with Wycliff, however painful that conversation would be. Already the words tightened in her chest.

"I have made a decision," she began.

Wycliff stripped off his waistcoat and tossed it on the fort of wooden boxes in one corner of the study. He turned as he undid his shirt and pulled it over his head to join the other discarded item. "What about? Not more holes in Mireworth, I hope."

Hannah started to say the words, choked on them, and then cleared her throat. "When you journey to the underworld, I will accompany you."

Wycliff froze, about to remove his trousers. His eyes widened as comprehension rushed through his mind: In order for her to join him, she first had to be dead.

"No." The denial rasped from his throat.

"I am determined, and will not renew my mother's spell this month." Her fingers clenched in the blanket. She discovered that despite her assertions to the contrary, a sliver of fear at giving up life lingered inside her.

He ran a hand through his hair, and his chest heaved. "Hannah...no, please. You must remain suspended in time until there is a cure."

Tears burned behind her eyes, but she refused to cry. If ever there was a time for boldness, it was when confronting death. Hannah held out a hand and Wycliff moved to sit on the bed. He pulled her into his arms and rested his cheek against the top of her head.

"The last time Mother renewed the spell, she said the curse had changed inside me. She thinks it is testing her work. We knew her spell would be a temporary measure. It cannot last forever," Hannah spoke into his chest, unable to meet his pain-filled gaze.

"That is no reason to abandon hope," he whispered against her hair.

"Indeed I have not. There is much to achieve when you and Mother travel to the other side. You may need my help, too." Her heart felt heavy and weariness crept through her limbs. "You will not lose me, Wycliff. I have found a rare love that will endure beyond death and I am no longer afraid." Hannah reached up and cupped his face in her palm.

Tears shimmered in his dark gaze. "You cannot expect me to accept your impending death without a single protest."

She managed a weak smile. "No. But my mind is made up."

He closed his eyes and kissed her palm, then touched his lips to her wedding ring. "*Together, beyond death*," he murmured, repeating the words inscribed within it.

Then he pressed her to the mattress and showed her how desperately he loved her.

4

Wycliff had little time to enjoy life at Mireworth with Hannah. As he crept from bed the next morning, the weather cube balanced on the fireplace mantel drew his attention. Within its confines, crimson clouds swirled and where they clashed, the edges turned the deep hue of blood, with tiny slivers of lightning the size of sewing needles.

"Blast." He picked up the cube and shook it. Part of him hoped the clouds would return to their usual wispy cream, but the movement only made the red deepen.

A shard of lightning stabbed at his fingers.

"What is it?" Hannah asked, her voice still soft with sleep.

"I am needed in London urgently." Wycliff let out a sigh. He knew they had to return, but every evening he hoped for one more day. He carried the cube over to the bed and held it out to Hannah.

She stared at the weather formation, trapped by her

mother's magic. "Red sky in morning, shepherds take warning."

"I think the saying should be, *Red sky too early will make a hellhound surly*. I do not wish to go, but I must. Sir Manly would not summon me unless it was important." Wycliff took the cube from Hannah and returned it to its spot above the fire.

"It might be about the woman with the missing brain. Perhaps he has determined Unwin and Alder were not responsible and we have a rogue Afflicted to apprehend. Will you leave immediately?" Hannah flung back the blankets and found her robe.

He paced about the room retrieving the items of clothing that he had carelessly discarded the night before. "Yes. If I leave now, ride hard, and change horses frequently, I will make it to London by this evening. But there is one thing, Hannah. Please, I beg of you, have your mother perform the renewal spell."

She straightened her spine and he could see the denial making its way to her lips.

All he needed was a little more time to keep her alive. Time that might yet provide a cure for the dark magic poised to still her heart. "Let me deal with whatever calls me to London first. All I am asking for is a little more time. I—" He choked on his words. "I cannot go to London with—knowing—"

"You cannot go with my death on your hands?" she whispered as she wrapped her arms around him.

"Yes. I promise you that, once we resolve this case, we will all travel to the underworld together." He breathed her in and wished that keeping her alive were as simple as keeping hold of her. That had worked to save her from a selkie and drowning, but he could not battle this enemy.

She nodded and reached up to kiss him. "I will do as you ask, but I fear my time runs out, Wycliff. The curse inside me seeks a way to defeat my mother's magic, and I would rather die on my own terms."

He couldn't imagine her doing it any other way.

Wycliff pulled her tighter to his chest and stroked her hair. "I had hoped for more time here, away from the prying eyes of society."

She smiled up at him. "I am sure we can split our time between Mireworth and London, and that we can come to some arrangement with Sir Manly. Whether I am alive or dead, I would like to spend our first Christmas here, if you are agreeable?"

There at least was one glimmer of happiness in the sadness circling him. "Yes, I'd like that very much."

"We will certainly return to Mireworth before winter. There is the autumn harvest to help bring in and then celebrate, and I do not want to miss that. Mrs Rossett has so many more tales to tell me about the *rapscallion* that it will take several visits here before I have heard them all." Mischief sparkled in her eyes.

"Don't make me regret keeping her on," he murmured against her neck. How he wanted to linger and take her back to bed, but he didn't need Higgs smashing a window to gain his attention.

With reluctance, Wycliff dressed and set off on his

black mare. He left her stabled at a tavern, where he changed to a hired mount to keep up his frantic pace. Hannah would collect the mare on her return journey to London. Wycliff rode the hired horses hard, before he handed an exhausted animal over at the next stables and leapt on a fresh one.

Twilight hovered at the edge of the city as he reached London and rode directly for the Ministry of Unnaturals, leaving the sweaty horse at a nearby mews for a well-deserved rubdown and feed.

Higgs looked up from his desk. A tawny feather sprouted in his hair with the change of light outside. "Lord Wycliff. You have saved me a flight to Selham to fetch you. Sir Manly is still upstairs."

Ignoring his own desk and the stack of correspondence accumulated during his month-long absence, Wycliff took the stairs two at a time. The sooner he sorted this business in London, the sooner he and Hannah could retreat to the coastal village of Selham and Mireworth.

He rapped on the door and pushed it open on the command to enter.

Sir Manly sat with his back to the window and regarded Wycliff over the top of a sheet of paper. "Wycliff. Excellent timing, man. You must have ridden as though a demon from Hell pursued you."

"I gather the matter is of some urgency." Now that he stood still, his body protested the long hours in the saddle. He suspected he would awake in the morning to stiff muscles.

Sir Manly nodded and twiddled one end of his ornate moustache. "Quite. I say, the country air must agree with you. You look positively— Is that a *smile* upon your face?"

Odd. He was indeed smiling, despite riding all day with only minimal stops. Exhaustion should have been sweeping over him, but instead, he seemed energised. The sooner he dispatched whatever bother had arisen, the sooner he could carry Hannah back to bed in the old manor house. "Hannah and I have enjoyed our stay in the country and thought we might spend more time at Mireworth, once whatever matter you have for me is settled."

Sir Manly rummaged among the papers on his desk and extracted a page covered in a tight scrawl. "Well, we can talk about that later. I have a deuced odd case for you. Last night, several people saw a blue fire at Bunhill Fields, and a large dog. A Bow Street Runner by the name of Taylor was sent to investigate early this morning, and he found charred remains on a grave."

"Charred remains and blue fire?" Wycliff set aside the claims of a large dog. Many canines roamed London. He tried to think how flames might be turned blue, assuming the witnesses weren't simply mistaken. It could be a simple case of low light, making them appear blue, or some sort of spell. Charred remains were harder to explain away. He scanned the notes taken by the Runner, who had passed the case up to the Ministry. It appeared very little remained of whatever had been burned, but someone had identified bone fragments.

"Taylor promptly woke me up, muttering about how hellfire wasn't his area of expertise. They swept the remains into a box, which I've had dispatched to Sir Hugh's for examination. Someone was going to stay at the location until you had a chance to look at it." Sir Manly placed his pen in its holder and swept all the papers into a neat pile.

"I'll head there now, before the light fades." Wycliff nodded to his superior and trotted back down the stairs.

He rode to Bunhill Fields, the cemetery that had served London for hundreds of years. The name derived from *Bone Hill*; the site was littered with ancient bones from burials performed there in Saxon times. Wycliff dismounted and tied the gelding to a nearby tree.

When he stepped through the gates, a tingle ran up his legs. Whispers brushed over his ears. Some lost souls sought his assistance, while others hid from him. The dark souls who scurried away at his presence interested him the most. They were the criminals and miscreants who had escaped the void's clutches and who roamed the earth. Those were the ones he could catch and dispatch to their rightful place and the justice that awaited them. He could not help the others —the souls who had lived honest lives but who were tethered for some other reason to the earthly realm. What he needed was another similar to himself, yet able to send the lighter souls on to a better place.

He pushed the intrusions to one side and steeled his mind. Hunting the darkness could wait. Some souls had avoided their fates for hundreds of years. What was a few more weeks or months?

The Runner waited at the sexton's office, sitting on a worn bench outside. He leapt to his feet as Wycliff approached.

"I'm Charlie Taylor, milord. If you'll follow me." He took up an unlit lantern and gestured down a wide path.

Wycliff nodded. At least the man jumped straight to work.

A tall and muscular man, Taylor wore grey knitted fingerless mittens, as though he felt the bite of cold in July. Admittedly, it was the worst summer on record. That sent Wycliff's thoughts in an odd direction. Would Barnes feel the cold come winter?

"Everything all right, milord?" Taylor asked.

"I was admiring your mittens and thinking that a member of my household might need one come winter." They passed between two rows of gravestones, each topped by an angel in a different pose.

Taylor's wool-covered hand tightened on the lantern. "My nan knitted these for me because I've always got icy fingers. *Cold hands, warm heart*, she says. Your man would need a pair, though, surely?"

Wycliff huffed. "He possesses only a left hand." *And nothing else*, he added silently.

Taylor led him on a twisty path through the gravestones and toward a row of mausoleums encircled by large trees. These weren't the ostentatious buildings the wealthy constructed on their estates to house generations of the dead. These tombs were modest, for the lesser nobles or middle classes, who lacked large country estates to retire to for eternity. Or perhaps temporary lodgings for those caught by death while in London for the season.

An acrid tang lingered on the air that stirred old memories within Wycliff of the night his men had encountered the hellhounds. Burned flesh had an unmistakable aroma.

"It was here." Taylor stopped and gestured with his free hand.

The grave looked something like a sarcophagus emerging from the ground. The stone slab, seven feet long and four feet wide, was large enough to accommodate two members of one family side by side, and more if they were stacked on top of each other. The gravestone jutted ten inches from the ground, high enough to bang one's shins on. A diminutive iron fence enclosed it.

"Did anyone investigate last night?" Wycliff surveyed the blackened marks etched into the granite, with spidery fingers reaching for the edges.

"No, milord. Those that saw the fire were too scared and one sought me out just before dawn. I took my report direct to Sir Manly. Hellfire is Unnatural, and outside of my bailiwick." He glanced around him, staring at the trees that huddled together.

"I haven't ascertained what caused the fire yet."

Wycliff ignored the reference to hellfire and continued his inspection.

"The witnesses I spoke to reported hearing a howl of a large dog, around the time the fire broke out. Some said it was a hellhound with fiery eyes." The man stood near a gravestone.

Wycliff grunted, not yet ready to contemplate the involvement of a hellhound. He pushed the thought down while he conducted his examination. A flutter caught his eye. On one railing, a small scrap of black fabric responded to the light breeze. Wycliff retrieved the material. With a jagged edge, it looked to have been torn from some item of clothing. A feather embroidered in black thread and adorned with ebony beads created a border of some sort.

Keeping hold of the scrap, he walked around to the other side of the grave and found flowers scattered in the grass, their bright orange vivid against the dull lawn, almost like sparks from a fire. He picked one up and turned the modest flower in his fingers. A snapdragon. As a child, he had learned to squeeze the bloom to make it open and close its mouth.

A search of the grass revealed a peach-coloured silk ribbon, with a single snapdragon still tied within its length. It appeared to have been used to hold together the posy. From his jacket pocket, he pulled an empty envelope. Inside, he placed the strip of material, ribbon, and the snapdragon.

He carried on prowling the perimeter of the grave. Near the foot, the exposed dirt was scuffed and disturbed. Then a single undisturbed mark made him suck in his breath. He knelt down and his hand hovered above the impression—a large paw print.

"People are whispering about some hound from Hell rising up and burning sinners who deserve it," Taylor said. He glanced over his shoulder as if he expected fiery jaws to latch on to him and drag him into the shrubbery.

Another one? Impossible. Wycliff rose on unsteady legs and told himself it was simply the effect of the hard ride, and nothing to do with the thought of a hellhound stalking Londoners. He'd believed himself alone in the world. That the creatures who had created him had disappeared back into the murk from whence they'd come without making another.

He stood silent for a long time, gathering his thoughts. At length, the Runner coughed into his hand and Wycliff glared at him for the interruption.

"Will you be needing me for anything else, milord? It's just that I'd rather not be here after dark." Taylor stood taller and broader than Wycliff, yet the thought of a night in the cemetery made his mittens tremble.

Wycliff dismissed him with a wave. "Go. There is little more that can be done here. But leave me that lantern."

Wycliff had a few more things to do before returning to an empty bed in Westbourne Green. He pondered what had happened on the grave. At first he thought it might be a simple case of drunken idiots digging up a corpse and burning it. But that didn't account for the scuff marks in the dirt. Unless they had struggled with their burden? A mourner could have dropped the flowers, startled by the gravedigger's activities. The woman might have torn her skirt as she ran from the sight of a corpse dumped on the stone.

Pulling free his notebook, he jotted down the family name on the grave used as a fire grate—*Carlyle*. The last burial in the family plot had been 1815, when a young child had joined his grandparents. Next, Wycliff considered the mausoleum that overlooked the grave. As the last of the light faded behind the trees, he moved closer to peer at the name carved in the lintel above the door. *Albright*.

Memories flitted through his mind of the investigation that had brought Hannah into his life. A horrible series of murders had led to the happiness that now coursed through his veins. Briefly, he wondered if the mausoleum belonged to Lord Albright, whose wife had been struck down by the Affliction. A bitter man who made no secret of the fact that he would have preferred to inter his first wife and leave her to arise alone and with no escape.

There was one other thing Wycliff needed to do. Drawing a deep breath, he reached out to the hound and altered his vision. The world around him shifted to the dreamlike world the creature perceived.

Spectres watched him. Some peeked from behind gravestones, others gathered in groups like gossips at a dance. Some souls appeared fresh, their bodies distinct and their eyes wide with wonder. Others were decades old, their forms rubbed away by time until only the vague floating lights remained that some called *will-o'-the-wisp*.

He hoped a soul might linger near the grave and provide a clue as to whether the victim was recently deceased or had been dug up from elsewhere in the cemetery.

"Did any of you see who did this?" he asked.

A few souls drew back and hid from his gaze. More shook their heads. Getting a sensible response from some souls was like trying to discuss philosophy with a madman.

One soul stepped forward and pointed a finger at Wycliff. "Man," it rasped in a voice that hadn't been used for years.

"A man did this? One alone, or more?" He focused on the soul. It appeared to be male and somewhat elderly, with straggly grey hair that brushed his shoulders.

The figure gestured to Wycliff again and then floated backward into the protection of the trees.

"Useless," he muttered. The single word could have been a clue or simply the ghost making an observation about Wycliff.

He let out a breath, but on the inhale, he froze. Something in the air struck him as not right. He drew another slow breath. There. Under the tang of charred flesh, another aroma. One of decay and rot that registered as foreboding in his brain. Did he scent a rotting body burned on the grave, or the odour of something evil that had committed the crime?

With nothing more to learn from either the spectres clinging to the hallowed ground, or from his own investigation, Wycliff lit the lantern to navigate his way back to his horse. He could have used the hound's vision, but he'd rather not know what hid from him. Deep shadows flitted at the edges of his vision, and a strain of the void's music tickled his ears. Another night, he would hunt over Bunhill Fields and find those long overdue for their date with justice.

5

AFTER WYCLIFF'S DEPARTURE, Hannah made good on her promise and asked her mother to renew the spell keeping the curse at bay. Sir Hugh carried the mage up to the solar in the tower and then left the women alone. Hannah sat by a window and stared out at the rustling trees as her mother drew the chalk outlines and whispered to herself. A bundle of herbs burned in the fireplace and added a sweet fragrance to the air.

At length, her mother motioned her over. "All ready, Hannah. We shall see what happens—there is quite a charge to the atmosphere from the resident below."

Hannah gathered up her skirts and stepped into the outline of the coffin. "I wish I could see the mist that Wycliff observed. How unusual for magical residue to linger after so many centuries. Does it happen to all mages?"

"I had not heard of such a phenomenon before, but

we rarely have hellhounds examining our remains. I always thought that on death, all our powers were removed and gifted to the new mage," Seraphina mused out loud as Hannah lay down and crossed her hands over her chest.

"But you gained a different sort of power after death," Hannah murmured.

"Yes. Perhaps I have something in common with the ancient mage of Mireworth, but we will investigate that another day. Hush, child, while I reinforce the spell." Seraphina placed one hand on Hannah's head and the other on her heart as she began the ritual.

Once again, a spectral hand tightened around Hannah's heart as her mother spoke words of power. Just as the crush became unbearable, it peaked and fell away. She drew a shallow sigh and cracked one eye open.

Her mother placed both hands in her lap and stared at them, her head bowed.

"Did the magical residue affect the spell?" Hannah whispered as she sat up.

"No, or at least not directly. It swirled around us, offering itself if I wished to draw upon it. The phenomenon is most unusual. I must consult my texts for any information about the earthly remains of mages. As for the curse, it has altered a little, as though it seeks to reform itself into something that can slip through the barrier I erected." Seraphina called over a squat footstool and with a gesture, raised herself through the air to take a padded seat.

"It will yet be victorious. When Wycliff has concluded his new investigation, I shall ask you to remove your spell." Hannah stepped out of the chalk outline and shook out her skirts.

"I feel in my bones that we will find the answers we seek in the underworld." The mage straightened her shoulders and turned to Hannah.

"I will fetch Papa to carry you back downstairs. Then I must see to packing for our return." Hannah glanced one more time around the tower and then trod the spiral stairs to find her father.

HANNAH LINGERED as she packed to leave Mireworth. While she wanted to join Wycliff in London, the old house wrapped invisible strands around her and whispered for her to stay. The tower and its slumbering resident were a mystery she itched to solve. But given that the Egyptian mage had lain undisturbed for six hundred years, what was a few more weeks to uncover the secrets it held?

She heaved a sigh and closed the lid on her trunk.

"I'll have Frank fetch that, milady, now we're done," Mary said as she wiped her hands down her apron and surveyed the morning's work.

Piece by piece, they had turned the impromptu bedroom back into Wycliff's study—albeit one with a stripped bed and a pile of boxes in one corner.

"Thank you, Mary." Hannah picked up her bonnet

and paused in the doorway. Much had happened in the cosy room. The nature of her marriage had changed. Wycliff had whispered that he loved her. She had voiced her decision to remove the spell holding her in time, and would pay the price of death to walk into the next realm beside the hellhound she loved.

With a sad smile, Hannah closed the door. She marvelled at the landscape in the grand foyer and stepped over the shimmering bridge as the painted Nile flowed under her feet.

In the kitchen, Mrs Rossett packed two large baskets of provisions for their journey. Sheba watched with rapt attention and her tail brushed back and forth over the slate in anticipation.

"All packed, milady?" The housekeeper closed the lid on a basket.

"Yes. I am sad to go, but already look forward to our return." Hannah bent down to pick up the spaniel.

"I shall miss you all." A sad smile touched the older woman's lips.

Hannah reached out and took the housekeeper's hand. "Just you wait and see, Mrs Rossett. This old house will once again ring with laughter and be filled with light. Then you will wish we would all pack up and go to London for the season, and leave you in peace."

They walked out into the courtyard, where the two carriages were loaded with their luggage. The family gathered and said their goodbyes to Mrs Rossett and Mr Swift. Timmy climbed up to the driver's seat of one carriage next to Old Jim. Frank helped Mary up to sit with him atop the larger vehicle.

Sir Hugh lifted Seraphina into the family carriage, where she would start the journey with Hannah. They had much to discuss, from restoring the gardens of Mireworth to speculating how an Egyptian mage had come to be bricked up in a tower. Hannah had taken rubbings of all the hieroglyphics they found in the tower for them to pore over. Helga would ride with Sir Hugh, and Hannah suspected the two would probably nap, lulled by the rocking of the carriage.

As the horses pulled them away, Hannah leaned out her window for a final wave, not only to the staff they left behind, but to Mireworth itself. She made a promise to return. Perhaps on the next visit they could tackle the exterior. In many ways the house resembled Frank—fearsome and ghoulish, yet harbouring a gentle soul.

They passed the journey in conversation, short naps, and stops to stretch their legs and relieve themselves. At one tavern, Frank collected Wycliff's mare and tied her to the back of their carriage. Two long days later, as the sun dropped below the horizon, they finally reached the gothic mansion in Westbourne Green.

Hannah stepped down on the familiar packed earth behind the house and stretched her arms up over her head. A *pop* sounded in her neck and her muscles protested the prolonged sitting position. She imagined how good it would feel to drop into a hot bath, but she didn't want to bother Mary when the maid would be as stiff as she. She stared up at the house and wondered if Wycliff was in, or on business in London.

"I'll help Cook rustle up some dinner now we've all descended on her," Mary said. Then she scurried up the stairs to disappear into the house.

Hannah stood in one spot, soaking in the familiar atmosphere. Somewhere in the trees, Percy the peacock called out to his harem, gathering them to him before dusk fell. Around her, the men unharnessed the horses and moved them into the stables. Lights glimmered on in the house and a faint aroma of beef and garlic wafted from the open kitchen window.

"Are you all right, dear? You are supposed to be frozen in time, not frozen to the spot," her mother said from beside her.

"Just taking a moment to appreciate all we have and wondering what will come next." She rested a hand on her mother's shoulder.

Once Wycliff finished his current investigation, Hannah would relinquish her hold on life. In some ways it was romantic that her husband would stay by her side even after death. While they were no fairy princess and her champion, love flourished in the dark as strongly as under any light.

Seraphina took her hand and squeezed. "We face the future together, Hannah, as a family."

A wave of emotion surged up through her and moistened her eyes. "We might be an odd family, but I think we are all the tighter for being stitched together."

Frank unloaded their luggage to be carried inside, Barnes perched on his shoulder.

The sight made another thought occur to Hannah. "Do you think we could find a companion for Barnes?"

Her mother chuckled. "Let us keep an open mind on that subject. I think he was rather taken with Mrs Rossett."

Hannah peered into each room as she walked through the house, but did not find Wycliff. Assuming the investigation had detained him in London, she busied herself in the library until he returned. She assisted her mother in hunting out books about mages and the transference of their power to a new person. Then they searched for the magical rites and practices of ancient Egypt.

Darkness had settled over the landscape when the library door was flung open by her husband, his jacket buttons undone and his hair wild, as though he had lost his top hat on the ride home.

"Wycliff!" Hannah's heart leapt to see his sharp features, and she hugged the books to her chest as though they were armour to keep that organ in its place.

He stalked toward her, cupped her face in his hands, and kissed her thoroughly.

"I missed you," she murmured. "Does that make me silly, since we have only been apart for two nights and three days?"

"I missed you, too," he whispered before he kissed her again. "And no."

"You must tell me what has happened that Sir Manly needed you so urgently in London. Papa said there is a box of remains awaiting his examination in the morning." She loosened her grip on the books and glanced at the top one—*Tales of the Underworld.*

Wycliff took the books from her and carried them to a side table. "There has been an odd fire, which witnesses say burned blue and white. It appears to have consumed someone—those are the remains awaiting your father downstairs."

"Oh, a blue and white fire? Mother will know what might have caused that." Changing the colour of flames was a simple spell. Her mother had cast one to make the fire in Lizzie's bedroom burn in delicate shades of pink and green. Hannah preferred the enhanced autumnal tones of vivid red and brilliant orange.

"There is more. They burned the body in Bunhill Fields and next to the grave used as a fire grate, there were paw prints. Rather large canine paw prints." He held up a hand to indicate the approximate size.

"Another hellhound?" Hannah's breath caught in her throat. Was it possible that another such creature resided in London?

"That is what I fear. Although I am loath to rush to a conclusion on so little evidence. Nor does the appearance of the flames resemble what I saw the night the creatures slaughtered my men." He ran a hand through his unruly hair and attempted to finger comb the locks back into place.

"Well, let us gather the evidence and then theorise

about probable causes. There is one minor matter I can shed some light upon." Hannah walked to the desk and fetched the ensorcelled ledger that recorded donations to Unwin and Alder.

"Oh?" Tired lines pulled at his eyes.

"Do you remember the report of the funeral of the woman who had her brain removed? I found her in the ledger. Mrs Sennett was briefly at the premises of Unwin and Alder, and they paid her husband the usual fee for the minor inconvenience." She flicked to the most recent page and tapped a finger on the entry recording the woman as *O*, for ordinary.

"At least we know how her brain came to be missing. Perhaps her husband's behaviour was as simple as not wanting to reveal they'd paid him for what happened to her." Wycliff let out a sigh and reached for her hand.

Hannah dropped the ledger to the sofa and nestled against him. "I thought that since we are in London, I might pay Mr Sennett a visit and confirm that suspicion."

He kissed the top of her head. "A fine idea. I shall wash up before dinner and we can ask your mother about blue flames."

They ate a simple meal. Hannah pushed peas around her plate as conversation brushed past her ears. While she had spent her childhood in the gothic mansion and it held many happy memories, it dimmed when compared to Mireworth.

"Are you quite all right, Hannah?" Her mother

patted her arm and drew her away from her gloomy thoughts.

"Yes. Only a little tired, that is all." Hannah managed a small smile for her mother.

"Not missing Mireworth, then?" Humour infused Seraphina's words.

"Somewhat," Hannah murmured, and she glanced at Wycliff from under half-lidded eyes. "I have so many mysteries to chase now, I hardly know where to begin."

"Blue fire," Wycliff suggested. "The witnesses to the pyre at Bunhill Fields reported seeing blue and white flames."

"Coloured flames are a simple enchantment that even some aftermages can produce. There are two possibilities—either someone cast a change of colour spell over an existing fire, or a true blue flame was called forth," Seraphina said.

"Is it easy to produce a true blue flame?" Wycliff's hands stilled, knife and fork poised over his dinner as he waited for an answer.

"No. It is a different type of spell and more difficult to master. A high-level aftermage with an affinity for flame might be able to construct one, or a mage could create a potion for it." Tonight Seraphina held an empty wine glass. A simple enchantment swirled around the inside of the crystal and resembled phantom wine.

"Well, let us see what the morning brings. Although I peeked into the box and there is scant little to examine," Sir Hugh said from the head of the table.

After dinner and an hour of reading in the parlour, Hannah said her good nights. "I will move into Wycliff's rooms, if he is agreeable, and use my room as a dressing room."

"Of course, dear, whatever suits you best." Seraphina waved a hand, engrossed in a chess match with Sir Hugh.

In silence, Wycliff rose and shadowed her steps out into the hall. There he took her hand and pulled her closer. "We can move to your room, if you prefer? You have slept there all your life."

Hannah kissed his cheek. "Thank you, but no. I have begun a new phase of my life and I rather think the change of room is appropriate."

THE NEXT MORNING, after a quiet breakfast, Hannah assisted her father in his laboratory. They angled the mirrors to catch the light that burst through the tunnel near the ceiling and reflected it to illuminate the table. Sir Hugh carried over the box and prised off the lid.

What they did couldn't be called an autopsy—there simply wasn't enough for such an examination. With great care, they removed the remains from the container. The sad collection of charred pieces affected Hannah far more than an intact body might have. While it was efficient and saved space in the cemetery to have one's very self reduced to what one found in the bottom of the fireplace, surely there should be some marker to denote a life turned into ash? A small plaque could display the name of the person, even if no body decomposed in the ground.

"It must have been an intense fire, to reduce an adult to so few remains," Sir Hugh said as he sorted through them.

"Perhaps the blue flames were more than a colour effect and burned hotter, such as the crematorium uses?" Hannah used a pair of tweezers to sort lumps into similar piles. "More worrying is that Wycliff found large paw prints at the scene."

Her father paused in his work and met her stare. "Do you think another hellhound did this?"

Hannah moved a larger piece of bone to one side and a pile of ash to another. "Let us hope not. Wycliff does not seem to possess the ability to produce a blue fire to incinerate people. The colour of the flames might have resulted from an accelerant used, and the paw prints could have been made by any large and perfectly ordinary dog."

They worked in near silence, picking through bone fragments that, they hoped, would aid in discovering the unfortunate's identity. Although they had little to assist them. In all, there remained only a thigh bone, half a pelvis, and a lower jaw still holding teeth. The rest of an adult's 206 bones were reduced to rubble, charred lumps, and soot.

Sir Hugh picked up the left half of the pelvis in one hand. Hannah passed him a small brush, and he used gentle strokes to clear away the soot and dirt. Next, he dropped a magnifying lens over his eyes and peered at the bone.

"From the shape of this, I believe our victim was a woman," he said at length.

From the measurement of the thigh bone, her father performed a mental calculation to determine approximate height. Then the jaw received similar scrutiny. A gentle cleaning revealed a gleaming gold tooth.

"That could be an aid in finding out her identity." Hannah noted where in the lower jaw the gold tooth was located and drew a sketch of its exact placement. "We have no way of determining how the person died. We could have a murder, a terrible suicide, or someone might have desecrated a grave and burned a corpse they found."

They soon concluded their work. Hannah scoured the storage room and found an old piece of red silk that she used to line the bottom of the box. The bright strip of fabric reminded her of the lining of a coffin and, in her mind, turned a storage box into something more fitting as a final resting place for the unknown woman. She swept up all the charred bits and placed them in the bottom first. Then she laid the larger bones on top. Hannah draped the ends of the silk over the bones and closed the lid. She rested a hand on the top, hoping that whoever was contained within had attained a peaceful afterlife.

6

AFTER COMPLETING HER WORK, Hannah walked with slow steps up the stairs to find Wycliff and advise him of their findings. The door to his study was open and inside, he sat with a pen frozen in his hand as he stared out the window.

"Wycliff?" she murmured his name, not wishing to disturb him while he was deep in thought.

"Hannah." He half turned and held out a hand in welcome.

She grasped his hand, and he pulled her onto his lap.

"You seemed miles away." She peered out the window, wondering if something beyond had caught his attention.

"I was pondering hellhounds, and whether there might be another roaming London. Although I am not convinced it is a beast such as I. When I dispatch a soul, no fire is involved and my efforts to call forth a blue fire have failed. If I set something alight, it burns red and yellow as expected." A brief smile pulled at his lips. "What news do you have of our victim?"

"We found part of a pelvis, and there was sufficient bone for Papa to identify it as a woman of slight height, judging from the length of femur we found. There was also a gold tooth." She tapped her jaw to indicate where.

He tugged a piece of paper forward and added her findings to a short list. "I have a strip of fabric caught on the railing around the grave and flowers scattered in the dirt. Although they might not be related."

She let out a sigh. "Let us hope it is enough to discover the woman's identity."

"I will return to Bunhill Fields today, to ask the sexton if any graves have been disturbed. It is possible a grave robber dug someone up and, for whatever reason, incinerated the remains." He tapped the pen against the page with the little they knew written upon it.

Hannah imagined scenarios where a person could have dug up another to cremate them. "Perhaps the perpetrator sought to conceal another crime? It might be someone who was thought to have died of natural causes, but had really been murdered and they wanted to hide what they did."

He huffed a gentle laugh. "That hypothesis might be more difficult to prove, given how little remained. But I will first ascertain whether any resident of Bunhill Fields is missing."

"I will come into London with you, if that is convenient. I wish to seek out Mr Sennett. There is something about the salacious newspaper article that niggles at me." While she had confirmed the woman's brain had been removed under the strict conditions of Unwin and Alder, the discovery worried at her. For the entire section of skull to be dislodged would take some force.

"Very well. Old Jim could drop me at the cemetery and take you on to Sennett's house. Then perhaps we could meet at the Ministry offices to confer with Sir Manly?" He caught a wayward strand of her hair and stroked it between his thumb and forefinger.

AFTER DEPOSITING Wycliff at the gates to Bunhill Fields, it didn't prove too difficult to find Mr Sennett. Old Jim asked a person on the street once they were in the correct neighbourhood, and numerous people leapt to answer. Apparently everyone knew where to find the man whose wife's mind had gone walkabout. The old retainer halted the carriage outside a row of small terrace houses.

Hannah pondered what to say as she walked to the front door. Coldly announcing she wished to discuss a certain vanishing organ seemed inappropriate. But how to word her request to ensure she gained admittance?

Her knock was answered by a young girl of around ten years, with weepy eyes.

"Is Mr Sennett in?" Hannah asked, peering over the child's head into the dim corridor beyond.

"Yes, ma'am. He's in there." The girl gestured to an open door.

Hannah thanked the girl and walked into the small front parlour.

A man rose from a chair with a frown on his face. "Can I help you, ma'am?"

"Forgive my intrusion, Mr Sennett. I am Lady Wycliff. My husband is an investigator with the Ministry of Unnaturals, and with your permission, I should like to discuss recent events with you." Hannah walked to the middle of the room, a feat which took only three steps.

He swallowed and nodded before gesturing to a sofa covered in a worn green brocade. Once she was seated, he resumed his chair by the window. He leaned on a sideboard and a tremble made his fingers skitter over the surface.

"I didn't do it," he rasped.

"I am aware of that. What confuses me is that I know your wife briefly passed into the care of Unwin and Alder, yet the newspaper article reported you did not know how...the event...occurred." Hannah chose her words with care. No need to remind the man of what had happened while he still mourned his wife.

He looked away to stare at children in the street throwing a ball back and forth. "I didn't want to say anything. They said it was a condition of taking the money, that their research be kept quiet. You probably think I'm horrid, but with four mouths to feed, I did need it."

"I think no such thing, and cannot imagine how hard it is to provide for your family now that your wife has passed. I seek only to understand what happened, to ensure that Unwin and Alder are meeting the strict arrangements under which they are allowed to operate." It appeared that events were as they suspected. The bereaved husband had not wanted to announce he had sold his wife's brain when her coffin was jostled.

"What happened to her...brain?" He whispered the last word, casting around the room as though he expected something horrible to happen. His eyes were wide, the whites tinged red from either too much alcohol or a bout of crying.

Hannah didn't enjoy lying. Nor was she particularly good at it. She did, however, believe there were circumstances under which a small lie or an alteration of the truth was necessary to prevent a greater harm. Such as when Lizzie clasped both her hands, stared into her eyes, and made her swear she had never used the contaminated face powder. Another such situation arose before her now, with Mr Sennett demanding to know what had happened to his wife's brain. Hannah doubted he wanted the bald truth that the organ that once professed to love him had been sliced into thirty equal parts and floated in a herb-infused vinaigrette for consumption by an Afflicted woman.

"I am sure this is a terrible misunderstanding." Hannah clasped her hands together and constructed a likely story that skirted the truth. "In some rare cases, Unwin and Alder need to remove the brain to study the lumps. It is quite fascinating work. In some instances with particularly strong personalities, the indentations in the brain's surface affect the lumps felt on the scalp."

"But where is it now?" He leaned forward and clasped his hands between his legs.

"I can only speculate," she said, drawing out each word. She didn't need to speculate, having seen the items in their jars on a shelf. "Perhaps it was shown to the professors and didn't make it back to the premises before they returned your wife to you? Or it might have been retained as a teaching model, to further the advancement of medical knowledge."

His lip quivered. He must have loved her most devotedly. "But she won't be allowed into Heaven now. She has to be intact."

On this subject, Hannah could speak with more authority. "I believe God is far more lenient about that than we are taught. Admiral Nelson had only one arm. Do you think God refused him admission after the battle of Trafalgar and told him to go find his missing limb first?"

Mr Sennett snorted. "If anyone deserves to be sitting up on a cloud, it's Admiral Nelson."

"Precisely. I believe that no matter what happens to one's physical form, a person's soul remains intact. It is the soul that journeys to the afterlife to be united with its Maker." With his hound's vision, Wycliff had seen her mother standing upon the legs her father had had to remove—proof that the soul did not carry the injuries inflicted upon the body.

"Well, if it might help someone else, I guess they can keep it." The frown stayed on his face, but a few of the lines relaxed.

Hannah managed a weak smile. "That is very magnanimous of you. But I shall talk to them to ensure such a distressing situation doesn't happen again."

He sat back in the chair and waved a finger at her. "I blame Jimmy for what happened. It was his fault, really."

"Who is Jimmy?"

"Jimmy Kelly, my Kate's brother. He was one of the pallbearers. He tripped over a speck of dirt and nearly dropped her. Funny thing is, I don't think he even shook her that much for the top of her head to come off like that. Then he kicked up a right fuss that we needed to open the coffin there and then to check on her. When he did, that newshound happened to be in the cemetery and saw everything. Said he had been investigating something else, but Kate would be a front-page article for him." He screwed up his face.

"Really? How odd." Hannah tucked the coincidences away as the tiny kernel of an idea sprouted in her mind. "Thank you for your time, Mr Sennett. I am glad if I have relieved a little of your anxiety about this matter."

Hannah took her leave and mulled over the information as Old Jim drove her to Whitehall and the Ministry offices.

Higgs, the owl shifter, looked up from his desk and

smiled politely. "Good day, Lady Wycliff. His lordship is not here, if you are looking for him."

"We were to meet here after he made his enquiries at Bunhill Fields. Since I have some time on my hands, are there any small matters I might assist with?" Hannah peered over the counter at the long and tidy desk.

Higgs plucked a sheet of paper from a small pigeon hole, one of many that ran along the wall above his desk. "If it is not too much trouble, apparently one of the Afflicted has gone missing. Could I trouble you to find out more?"

"Of course." Hannah took the page with its neat script and froze on seeing the name at the top. "The former Lady Albright has gone missing?"

He nodded and kept his unblinking gaze on her. "Yes, milady. A Mrs Hamilton, who is her cousin, came in yesterday afternoon to report her missing."

"I am sure there is a simple explanation. She might have gone to visit a friend or another relative and decided to stay for a few days." Before they parted company, Wycliff had given her the envelope containing the scrap of fabric with its delicate embroidery, in case she recognised the work. Now the items in her reticule grew heavier and seemed to pull at her arm.

Hannah returned to the carriage and gave Old Jim the familiar address.

"Oh, dear," she murmured on the journey. Separate

clues were combining inside her mind and making a most disagreeable brew.

At her destination, Hannah stood on the pavement and stared at the modest townhouse where the former Lady Albright resided with her cousin. In her reticule was the scrap of material Wycliff retrieved from the scene of the fire, a pressed snapdragon, the length of ribbon, and her sketch of where in the jaw the gold tooth had been located. Nervous tension made her stomach flop like a landed fish. A large part of her was certain that the most obviously Afflicted member of the *ton*, apart from Lady Miles, had met a fiery end. It could have been someone else, or as Wycliff suggested, a horrible bit of mischief to disturb another type of deceased person.

But Hannah did not think so.

She rapped on the door and the maid showed her through to the parlour.

"Lady Wycliff," Mrs Hamilton said as she rose from the settee and bobbed in greeting. Then she gestured to the sofa opposite. "I do hope you have come with news of my cousin?"

Hannah took a seat and composed herself. "I am not entirely sure." That was her second fudging of the truth in one day. "Could you tell me when you last saw her?"

"It's been four days now. She's never been gone overnight before and rarely ventures out alone. I hope this is not my fault." Mrs Hamilton twisted her hands together in her lap, and her eyes shone with unshed tears.

"How could this be any fault of yours? Perhaps she is staying with another relative or a friend?" Hannah's gaze drifted over the locked cabinet sitting on a sideboard. Within rested a jar of what sustained Lady Albright. Once, Wycliff had demanded to see it.

Mrs Hamilton let loose a single sob and then placed a hand over her mouth. She drew up her spine before turning to Hannah. "We possess no relatives who would offer her shelter. That is why she has resided with me these past two years. But I am afraid to say we had words the last day I saw her. While I will do my duty by my cousin, having one of the Afflicted under my roof is...well..." Her voice trailed off.

Hannah could guess at what the other woman didn't want to say out loud. Living with one of the Afflicted was somewhat akin to taking in a leper. A subject of gossip and curiosity to others, but not necessarily someone they wanted to socialise with. Lady Albright's cousin would have found her invitations drying up and her friends not quite as keen to dine with her.

Hannah reached over and patted her hand. "Even the closest of cousins can rub against one another. I'm sure she did not take your words to heart, and there is some other explanation for her absence. Did she say anything before she left?"

"She said that if she was not wanted here, she would visit her kind. The maid picked a posy and then my cousin left clutching the bunch of snapdragons." Mrs Hamilton extracted a limp piece of cambric from a sleeve and blew her nose.

Oh, dear. Visit her kind—the deceased. "Orange snapdragons, by chance?" Hannah asked and then held her breath, waiting for the reply.

"Yes. How did you know?" A bright look of relief flashed over Mrs Hamilton's face.

"Is it possible she went to Bunhill Fields?" The icy dread swirled inside Hannah and a blast of bile shot up her throat as she could no longer ignore the sickening realisation.

"Yes, the Albright family crypt is there. You know that horrid husband of hers wanted her interred before she reanimated. Can you imagine waking, and discovering yourself nailed into a coffin with no escape?" Mrs Hamilton shuddered and rubbed her hands up and down her arms.

The idea of being buried alive terrified Hannah. Even her near drowning and the horror of battling the ocean didn't compare to the awful loneliness of being trapped in a coffin for eternity.

"Could you tell me what Lady Albright was wearing?" Hannah could take a guess. The former Lady Albright always wore black or very dark grey in mourning for the death of her marriage and herself.

"Black." A small smile pulled at Mrs Hamilton's lips.

"Was there anything to distinguish her gown? Can you remember the fabric and any ornamentation?"

With each question, the sense of dread expanded inside Hannah.

"A heavy cotton, with an embroidered hem. She used to stitch fanciful borders on her gowns. It kept her hands occupied as we sat here in the parlour. I think that particular one had feathers and some beading. Why do you need to know what she was wearing?" Worry pulled between the older woman's brows.

Hannah stared at her hands and wished Wycliff were beside her. He could blurt out the raw facts, whereas she found her dry throat wouldn't let the words pass. She fumbled in her reticule and pulled out the envelope containing the scrap. "Could this be from her dress?"

Mrs Hamilton took the fabric and stretched it taut between her hands. She peered at the line of feathers. "Oh, yes. I recognise her work. Where was this found?"

"At Bunhill Fields. It had caught on the metal railing around a grave in front of the Albright crypt." Next to the scattered orange snapdragons, but Hannah didn't see any point in revealing that piece of information.

"What are you not telling me?" Mrs Hamilton scrunched up the scrap in her hand.

Hannah drew a steadying breath and whispered her last question. "Did Lady Albright have any gold teeth?"

"Oh. Let me think." She leaned back and stared at the ceiling. "Yes! Here." She tapped the side of her lower jaw. Then Mrs Hamilton's face fell and her bottom lip trembled as she gathered up the trail of breadcrumbs Hannah had dropped. "Oh."

Hannah rose, moved to the settee, and took Mrs Hamilton's hands in hers. "Burned remains were found at Bunhill Fields. My father identified the person as a woman with a gold tooth. The slip of fabric and orange snapdragons were found nearby. I am so terribly sorry that what we have found points to its being the former Lady Albright."

"Burned remains?" One hand went to her chest as tears welled in her eyes. "The blue fire that the newspapers reported—is it true that some creature dispatched her to Hell?"

"She appears to have been the victim of a crime, yes, but I do not believe for one moment she went to Hell." Hannah recalled the sad figure of Lady Albright. Cut adrift by a society keen to witness her humiliation and fall, but none would offer her a hand in friendship or mercy.

"It was him, wasn't it? Lord Albright made no secret of how he wanted to dispatch her. Do you know he offered me money to keep quiet that she had risen? To let him bundle her into a coffin and nail the lid down?" The tears dried as her features hardened.

"Lord Wycliff will investigate, I assure you, and we will find the person who did this to her." Hannah rose to her feet to leave Mrs Hamilton to plan a second funeral for her cousin.

The other woman rose as well and kept her grip on the fabric, all that was left of her final glimpse of her relative. "I hope she haunts his every footstep, and he never finds peace."

Hannah rarely thought badly of others, but in this instance, she imagined that a temporary haunting might frighten Lord Albright into changing his ways and being more mindful of his fellow human beings.

7

Wycliff ignored the chill that washed over his skin and the insistent whispers in his ears as he stepped into the graveyard. He strode the path to the tiny cottage used by the sexton and kept his gaze fixed upon the rough stone exterior. Flashes darted past his vision, taunting him to blink and see the world with the hound's vision.

The sexton sat outside, oiling a shovel with a cloth. "Lord Wycliff. Here again about the odd fire, I assume?" He balled up the cloth, dropped it to the bench, and leaned the shovel against the wall.

"Yes. I am pondering whether the remains belonged to a deceased individual who was dug up and burned, or a victim brought into the grounds for that purpose. Do you have any recent burials with disturbed soil?" He could narrow his search somewhat, since they now knew the remains belonged to a woman. Although

death was too common among the large London population. How many died every week?

"Always busy here with comings and goings." He
waved for Wycliff to follow him inside to where they
kept large registers recording the names and plot
numbers of those interred at the site.

"Sir Hugh Miles identified the remains as those of a
woman." Wycliff resisted the urge to peer over the
man's shoulder.

The horrid odour of tripe and onions seemed
embedded in his clothing. His suspicion about the
man's breakfast was confirmed when he spotted the
pale gelatinous mass in a bowl on a corner of the desk.
A shudder ran down his spine. The stomach lining
appeared more brain-like than the objects suspended in
alcohol at the premises of Unwin and Alder.

"We've had at least fifty burials of women in the
last two weeks. Some will be in the paupers' mass
graves. Do you want to check them all to see if they are
still there?" The sexton puffed out his cheeks as though
the mere idea of the work exhausted him. Not that he
would do it himself. In a cemetery as large as Bunhill
Fields, the sexton commanded a few men with
callouses on their palms from digging the soil.

"I'll not unearth anyone at this point. I shall
exhaust other avenues first. What of any disturbances?"
If his enquiries went nowhere and he had to dig up fifty
women to determine their remains still rested beneath
the earth, then he would. Or rather, he would sit in the
shade while the gravediggers undid two weeks of work.

The older man closed the ledger and rubbed his neck. "None of late. Been right quiet, it has, and we haven't spotted a resurrectionist for some weeks now."

"I need you to inspect each grave and confirm they appear undisturbed, in case someone has slipped in unnoticed and covered up his tracks better than others." He would trust the man to do as he asked. How much easier it would be to monitor the cemetery if he could deputise a few of the more cooperative spirits to patrol at night.

"You're assuming the remains came from a recent burial?" The question halted his exit from the cottage.

Wycliff muttered a soft curse. He was a fool. The remains could have been decades old for all they knew. Could Sir Hugh determine how much flesh had remained on the bones by some sort of analysis of the volume of soot and debris? "An excellent observation. I shall ask further questions of Sir Hugh on that subject."

"Women and men alike have been buried here for over a thousand years. That's a lot of bones beneath our feet, milord." The sexton smiled and stared at his boots.

"Quite." The whisper of phantom voices sounded as though every single resident from the last thousand years demanded his attention. *How many souls fail to move on?* When he ventured to the underworld to find who controlled him, he should ask about payment terms. He had enough to do as investigator for the Ministry and landowner at Mireworth. If some shadowy deity expected him to fetch lost souls, that entity could damned well compensate him for his time and effort.

He walked out into the bright light and down the hill to hail a hansom cab. "Unwin and Alder," he told the driver, then sat back and watched London roll past.

Wycliff mulled over how the past six months had dramatically altered his life. Now that he was married to a woman he loved, his heart sat lighter in his chest and even old Mireworth struggled to pull herself from the gloom. The fortunes of the estate turned like a tide. The financing advanced by the Earl of Pennicott had funded the new sheep breeding stock, and the recent shearing had brought a good price for the fleece. Thanks to Lady Miles and her gift with Nature, the autumn harvest looked to be the best yet, enhanced by her magic. For the first time, he dared to hope the long, dark winter of his youth might give way to the warmth of spring.

In the warehouse district, he walked into the discreet office that reminded him of the rooms kept by his solicitor. The secretary looked up and a pained expression crossed his face as he recognised the person before him. "Lord Wycliff. How might we be of assistance today?"

"Is he in?" He gestured to the panelled double doors behind the secretary.

The secretary gave a long-suffering sigh as he rose and walked to the doors to rap upon them. "Of course, milord. We at Unwin and Alder are always keen to assist you in whatever way we can." He pushed opened the doors and waited for Wycliff to enter before closing them again.

Unwin sat behind an enormous polished desk and appeared to be playing with a small moveable model of the planets with a brass sun at the centre. The former grave robber turned affluent businessman pushed the series of globes on metal arms to one side. "Lord Wycliff. You want to discuss the Sennett case, I assume."

"Yes. Lady Wycliff has seen in the ledgers that the woman passed through here. Why did your employees not stitch the scalp back in place? Sloppy work to leave her head cracked open." A conversation with Sir Hugh highlighted how difficult it should have been to dislodge both scalp and the top of the cranium with a simple bump against the side of a coffin. That left Wycliff with the assumption that someone, probably in a hurry to get home to his supper, had failed to complete his job and assumed that no one would ever know.

Unwin pulled himself to his feet and scowled. "My workmen know better than that. Anyone who didn't perform the entire job would be out on the street. Our reputation hinges on donors being none the wiser about what is removed from their family members."

Wycliff studied the polished wood and the expensive rug for a moment. He would regret asking his next question, but he wouldn't let a bout of squeamishness deter him. He needed a full understanding of what happened in the building in order to figure out where things had gone wrong. "What exactly is your procedure for removal of the item?"

"I think a practical demonstration is called for, if you will follow me, milord." Unwin led the way out of the office and through a dark wooden door into the narrow hallway. The skylights above were criss-crossed with bars to stop anyone breaking in. Thick opaque glass allowed light to filter through, but no one, not even pigeons, could see inside.

Unwin stopped at a solid metal door with a symmetrical pattern of rivets around the outer edge and through the middle. He rapped three times, paused, and rapped two more times. From the other side came the heavy *clunk* of a bolt being drawn back, and then the door swung open.

"Mr Unwin. Is everything all right, sir?" A man wearing a thick canvas apron peered through the gap.

"Yes. Lord Wycliff here is asking about our procedure. Carry on—we will observe." The man retreated and Unwin followed.

Wycliff found himself in an unadorned room with whitewashed walls. A rectangular table on wheels sat in the middle of the room. A trolley by the head would have been ideal for holding tea and sandwiches, except this one held an array of tools and a large basin. Another steel door was directly opposite the one through which they had entered.

"Where does that lead?" he asked Unwin.

"The warehouse where *donors* arrive and are dispatched a few hours later. Carriages are drawn in and the barn doors rolled shut to give us complete privacy so that coffins are removed from the view of curious eyes." Unwin grinned as though pleased with the process he and his partner had implemented.

To be fair, they had been in business for two years now with London none the wiser as to the true nature of their operation. Shame a disturbed coffin had shone a light on their activities.

Wycliff returned his attention to the activity within the room. If he altered his vision, would the hound perceive a soul hovering over its mortal form, asking for an explanation for the act committed against it? He chased the thought away. He was here to watch and learn. At least what occurred within the clean room had none of the gore or sharp whiff of the battlefield.

A man lay on the table with a sheet draped over his body and tucked in under his chin. His gruesome and bloody visage appeared as though he had taken a cannon ball straight to the head.

Unwin stood next to him and gestured to the odd death mask. "My workers are most skilled and quick. As you can see, the scalp is cut around the back and peeled forward, leaving it intact at the forehead. They remove the top portion of skull with a small saw." Here he gestured to a blade sitting on the trolley beside the worker with specks of blood and pale matter embedded in its teeth. "Next the brain is extracted and placed in a container to be catalogued, sliced, and preserved in another room."

"Then how do you put everything back?" Wycliff asked as the worker picked up another instrument.

Unwin pointed to a clear jar with a pale aqua jelly inside. "We use a special paste to stick the skull back together, and then the scalp is stitched. We ensure there is hardly any visible sign of our work."

"Would the stitches become dislodged if the coffin were handled roughly?" Part of Wycliff watched with fascination as the worker put his hands into the dead man's cranium and removed the large pinkish mass from within.

"I find it unlikely that a pallbearer's stumbling would cause sufficient disruption to Mrs Sennett that the stitches and glue would give out, and the skull be dislodged." Unwin snorted.

If the skull hadn't become dislodged by accident, that left only design. Somebody had removed the stitches and loosened the skull, otherwise no one would ever have known when they checked on the corpse. "Who performed the procedure on Mrs Sennett?"

The worker placed the object, which didn't yet resemble cauliflower, in the wide shallow basin. "That would be Peters, Lord Wycliff."

"What happens when you finish? Does someone check your work?" From Wycliff's observations, the business premises resembled a church—quiet and with very few people about.

Unwin huffed and narrowed his gaze. "No one inspects their work. My men are trusted employees."

Wycliff assumed they ran on as few staff as possible. The more men on the payroll, the more potential leaks the business could spring. Not to mention the extra wages they would have to pay.

The worker gestured to the door behind him. "We wheel the body back through to the warehouse and place it in its coffin. That normally takes two of us. But smaller bodies we can handle on our own."

If Mrs Sennett had been on the smaller side, a man would have been able to lift her without assistance. "I'll need to talk to Peters."

"He's not here this week." The man wiped his hands on a cloth hanging from the trolley's handle before picking up the piece of skull.

"Where is he?" Wycliff glanced from one man to the other.

"Sick, apparently. Been absent for three days now." The worker dipped a brush in the aqua jelly, then he applied it to the edges of the piece he held.

Unwin scowled. "We prefer our men to stay away if they are unwell, but I will not pay Peters for missing so many days. I can send one of the men to check on him."

A familiar niggle took up residence in Wycliff's mind. The itch that said he was on the trail of a scent. "Give me his address and I will call upon him."

They left the worker to stitch the man's scalp back into place and returned to the office. The put-upon secretary looked up Peters' employment details and then wrote down his address. Wycliff tucked the card into his coat pocket and took his leave to return to the Ministry's offices.

There, he found Hannah had taken a new task upon herself, namely calling upon Mrs Hamilton about her missing cousin. He took a cab to the address but decided against entering the house. His last visit there had not gone so well. Wycliff stood by the carriage and waited for Hannah to cmerge. She walked toward him with tears shining in her eyes that answered one question on his mental list.

"Our remains are all that is left of the former Lady Albright?" He opened the carriage door and helped Hannah inside.

"Yes," she whispered.

"The Ministry of Unnaturals," he said to Old Jim, then hopped inside and slammed the door.

He sat beside his wife in silence and waited for her to continue. With the identity of the victim confirmed, at least the sexton wouldn't need to check every grave in Bunhill Fields.

"Four days ago, the former Lady Albright went to visit the cemetery. She clutched a bunch of orange snapdragons and wore a black gown with feathers embroidered around the hem and embellished with black beads. She also had a gold tooth in the same spot as the jaw we found and was short of stature." Hannah let out a heavy sob.

Wycliff pulled her against his chest and hoped his presence gave her some solace. The carriage rumbled along the road and drifts of shouted conversation from pedestrians filled the silence.

Hannah tilted her face to look up at him. "She did not deserve such an end. She suffered so much at the hands of her husband. Who could possibly have hated her enough to consign her to flames?"

His grip tightened on her. Once, he had thought all the Afflicted should be thrown on a pyre. Then Hannah had opened his eyes and his heart. "You have answered your own question. She was an impediment to one man—her husband."

"Her cousin was quick to make the same accusation. While I agree he is the most likely person to wish the former Lady Albright removed from this earth, I shall play devil's advocate and ensure we are not blinded to other options. A man should be found guilty by the evidence, not by our opinion of his character." Hannah took the handkerchief he handed her and dabbed at her eyes.

Wycliff kissed her cheek. "We will seek justice for the former Lady Albright. I shall pay her husband a visit. Now, how did your conversation go with Mr Sennett?"

"As we suspected, when the work of Unwin and Alder was discovered, he pleaded ignorance rather than reveal he had been paid for what happened to his wife's remains. While it is probably nothing, the circumstances surrounding the discovery of his wife's condition don't sit well with me. Mr Sennett said it was her brother, Jimmy Kelly, who tripped and jostled the coffin, though he says it was the smallest bump. Then Mr Kelly was most insistent the coffin be opened to see if they had disturbed his sister. When they prised off the lid, there just happened to be a reporter for the scandal sheets in the vicinity. It strikes me as too coincidental." A frown appeared between her brows.

They were of one mind on that topic. The whole affair made the itch at the base of Wycliff's brain flare—the same spot that had warned of an enemy hiding among the trees during the war. "I went to Unwin and Alder earlier today to ask about their procedure. Unwin was adamant that the way the skull and scalp are reattached would hold against any jostling and the woman's head shouldn't have come apart."

"And yet it did. In front of a reporter," she murmured.

His thoughts followed a similar line. A simple explanation was that the worker, Peters, had not completed his job as required or had made sloppy stitches that pulled apart easily. Then, perhaps realising he was about to be exposed after the newspaper article, he invented a sickness to remove himself from the premises and to escape questions. "The man who worked on Mrs Sennett, name of Peters, has been absent for some days. I shall pay him a call and ask a few questions."

"While you tackle Lord Albright and Mr Peters, I shall visit Mrs Sennett's brother, the man who took the unfortunate tumble that precipitated these events," Hannah said.

The warm, contented feeling in Wycliff's chest spread. Investigations went more efficiently when they shared the load, and each used their skills to interview those involved. She was the light to his darkness. If only Hannah's touch could release the good souls trapped on the mortal plane.

8

Old Jim turned the carriage into their drive later that afternoon. Hannah felt drained, yet her mind conjured different scenarios for how the former Lady Albright might have met her fate. She took Wycliff's arm as they walked up the back stairs. In the rear vestibule, they stopped before the stained glass window depicting a peacock with his tail spread to strip off gloves and hats.

Her father wheeled her mother along toward them.

"Why are you torturing your gloves like that, dear?" Seraphina's voice cut through Hannah's dense thoughts.

She looked down to find the soft leather wrung between her hands as though it were laundry. With a sigh, she shook them loose and tossed them to the table in the dappled blue and green light from the window. "The remains are all that is left of the former Lady Albright."

"No! She is a lost, but gentle soul. What a horrid way to end one's time on this earth." Seraphina wheeled herself closer and leaned forward in her chair.

Wycliff stuffed his gloves into his hat but kept hold of it, rapping his nails against the short pile.

Hannah could imagine the outrage flashing in her mother's eyes at discovering one of the Afflicted had suffered in such a way. She took command of the bathchair and wheeled her mother along the hall to the library. Such conversations as they were about to have needed to be conducted surrounded by soothing books.

Sheba ran ahead and sat on the rug before the fire, Barnes nowhere to be seen for a change.

Sir Hugh shut the door and stood by the sofa. His arms were crossed and his attention on his wife, but he asked his question of Hannah. "You are certain it was she?"

Hannah dropped into a seat and picked up Sheba to hold the spaniel's comforting warmth in her lap. "As certain as we can be. Mrs Hamilton, the cousin of the former Lady Albright, reported her missing. She was last seen heading to the cemetery as twilight fell some four days ago, wearing a dress with embroidery around the hem that matched the scrap Wycliff found. She also carried a bunch of orange snapdragons and had a gold tooth in the same location as the one in the jawbone downstairs."

"Who would do such a thing to a harmless woman?" Sir Hugh rubbed a hand over the back of his neck.

"Who indeed?" Wycliff murmured as he took up a position by the fireplace and leaned on the mantel. "One can almost imagine a drunken night at a club and one husband in particular shouting, *Will no one rid me of this troublesome wife?* To misquote Henry the Second."

"Lord Albright." Seraphina spat the words out with such vehemence, the veil puffed away from her face.

"If we were making bets, that is where I would place my money," Wycliff said.

"I am taking a contrary stance, to ensure we remain objective." Not that Hannah wanted to defend the horrid man, but any person was presumed innocent until proven guilty. Sheba reached up and licked her face, as though offering her own kind of support.

"As satisfying as it would be to storm his house and drag him out to be tossed on his own pyre, let us ensure we have correctly identified the victim first. It is possible I could detect some trace of the curse in her remains, thus confirming it is one of the Afflicted. Would you take me downstairs, please, Hugh?" Seraphina wheeled herself over to her husband.

Hugh rested his much larger hand over that of his wife. Worry pulled at his eyes as he gazed at the love of his life. "Are you sure you wish to see what little remains of her?"

The mage sat silent for a long minute. "Fire is the only way to put an end to us. If the choice of victim and method are deliberate, rather than opportunistic, that is information Wycliff needs to find the person responsible."

Hannah shuddered, remembering the nightmare-inducing deaths of the secondary Afflicted she had witnessed on the grounds of the Repository of Forgotten Things. They had been tied to stakes, as though they were witches feared by men. Her mother had cast an enhanced white flame that burned more intensely and ended their suffering quickly.

"There is another issue the identification of the victim raises. She would have to have been restrained in some way. If they targeted the former Lady Albright, this wasn't a spontaneous crime, but one that required forethought and some preparation." In Hannah's mind, the horrible event unfolded.

"Yes. Most methods of rendering a victim unconscious wouldn't work on one of the Afflicted, with no respiratory system. The attacker needed something that would work on both the living and undead." Sir Hugh waved his hands in the air as he spoke.

"A spell, most likely. Magic is intertwined with this crime," Seraphina murmured.

"First things first. Let's confirm it is one of the Afflicted, if Sera can find any trace left of the curse." Hugh picked up Seraphina in his arms and Hannah preceded them out the door. Wycliff brought up the rear.

"Stay, Sheba," Hannah said to the spaniel as she opened the door in the panelling to reveal the dark stairs that led to the basement laboratory.

Barnes appeared, jumping down the main stairs like a frog in a hurry. At the bottom, the hand reached up and tugged on a lock of fur to divert the spaniel's attention as they slipped through the door. Below the house in the cool laboratory, Hugh settled his wife on a stool while Hannah fetched the wooden box holding all that remained of the woman they believed to be the former Lady Albright.

"Her cousin has asked that she be returned, to give her a final burial," Hannah said. She placed the box on the table and then stepped to Wycliff's side. He took her hand and laced their fingers together.

Her father prised off the lid and kept hold of it. Seraphina peered inside and then withdrew the piece of the pelvis. She held the bone in her hands and bowed her head. After some time, she placed it back in the box and rubbed the grit between her gloved fingers. "There is an almost imperceptible trace of dark magic. Like finding a dirty crumb in a dark room. But it is there, lingering deep in her bone. This was one of my Afflicted sisters and when taken with all the other evidence, confirms it is the former Lady Albright."

Sir Hugh placed the lid on the box but left it sitting on the table. Hannah would return it to Mrs Hamilton.

"Now, take me to where this atrocity was committed," Seraphina said.

"That is Bunhill Fields, Mother. Are you sure you wish to go there as twilight falls?" Hannah thought they would make an odd group prowling the paths and graves with a dead mage and a hellhound. Perhaps they should take Barnes and Frank to make it even more disturbing. They might terrify any grave robbers into giving up their criminal ways.

Seraphina waved a hand and then pushed her stool away from the table. "I can think of no better place for a dead thing to be but in a cemetery at dusk."

Wycliff set off to tell Frank they were heading out again—the man was probably halfway through unharnessing the horses. Sir Hugh carried Seraphina back through the house to her bathchair. Then, they waited by the rear doors that overlooked the barn and forest.

Her mother stared at the smudge on her linen gloves. "I think we require a change of clothing. Cream linen is not appropriate to pay homage to the former Lady Albright. I shall emulate her example while walking this earth."

The mage sat still for a moment, then she clasped her hands and whispered. Words swirled over Hannah's skin and raised the familiar prickle. As she watched, the cream linen covering her mother deepened in colour. A murky brown dropped over the fabric as though someone had thrown a pot of tea at it. Then the brown edged toward inky black until she appeared in full mourning. Seraphina worked her hands in the air until a dark flash burst between her outstretched palms and she held a crown of twisted black feathers and gleaming black beads. She set the decoration on her head and declared herself ready.

Hannah shrugged on a warm pelisse and tied her bonnet under her chin as Wycliff trotted up the stairs and claimed his top hat from Mary. Sir Hugh picked up his wife once more so that Frank could tie the bathchair to its spot at the rear of the carriage.

In the vehicle, Hannah and Wycliff took the seats facing backward. Frank sat up top with Barnes beside him. Mary stood on the terrace and twisted her hands in her apron, worried whether the hulking giant would be safe. They travelled in near silence as the light dimmed outside the windows, arriving at Bunhill Fields as dusk settled like an old woman into bed.

Wycliff led the way. Sir Hugh wheeled Seraphina along the rough pathways until they reached the quiet corner under the trees with its row of demure mausoleums and raised graves. Hannah trailed behind. She found the older areas of the cemetery beautiful and peaceful. If she did not reanimate after the curse claimed her, she would like a spot under the shelter of a large tree for her remains, where she could become one with its roots. She glanced at Wycliff and observed the tight set of his jaw. Today was probably not the best time to discuss her interment if their plan failed. He carried a burden already on his broad shoulders, and she would not add to it.

Through another overgrown area, Hannah spotted one grave on its own in a tiny clearing. A monstrous metal cage enclosed the recently disturbed earth. A shudder worked down her spine. The metal spikes had been driven deep into the soil, and the solid bars were close enough that only a hand could slip between them. The purpose of the cage was to deter body-snatchers;

concerned families could rent the constructions from a blacksmith. Yet there was something about the haunting structure that made her wonder if its true purpose was to keep the resident inside the grave.

They walked along another winding path, where Wycliff directed them to rows of graves laid out before squat mausoleums with their backs to an unruly hedge. He stopped at a grave with a short metal railing around it. Hannah stood next to him and drew comfort from the warmth radiating from his form.

"A circuit of the grave, please, Hugh," Seraphina said to her husband.

Sir Hugh pushed the bathchair clockwise around the grave. They stopped at each side, as the mage considered the black marks staining the granite from different angles. At one point, she reached through the railing and swiped a finger across the stain, the soot near invisible on her black glove. She rubbed thumb and finger together and brought them closer to her face.

"This is as I feared. Someone used magic here. I sense an enhancement similar to the one I used to make the intense fire that shortened the suffering of the secondary Afflicted."

"But as I recollect, Mother, your flames burned pure white, while this was reported to have been blue and white." Hannah wondered if they used a different spell.

"If two people write the same sentence, does it look the same? There is a type of handwriting to magic. Two mages can cast the same spell, but there will be variations between them. This is the same spell, but the mage's handwriting is displayed in the colours of the flames."

"So a mage would have been present?" Wycliff asked.

Seraphina tilted her head and watched the last of the sunset paint fire over the clouds above. "Not necessarily. There were occasions when secondary Afflicted were euthanised and I could not be present. A mage can cast the spell directly, or it can be distilled into a potion that can be thrown into a fire as an accelerant."

"How many people know that?" Wycliff asked.

Sitting at the head of the gravestone, Seraphina resembled a monument, gazing at the person buried at her feet. "Only a few people know of the fate of the secondary Afflicted. Those who were present that horrible day at the Repository, whoever Sir Manly reported it to within the government, and the mage council were all privy to that information."

"Whoever did this didn't only consign poor Lady Albright to the flames, they knew to enhance the fire to make it burn hotter." Hannah stood opposite her mother at the foot of the grave and mentally added up those who had the necessary knowledge. Twelve mages, and perhaps as many more within government and the Repository.

"They also knew she had to be immobilised. No one stands still while they are immolated." Wycliff narrowed his eyes and glanced around.

"Whether by spell or potion, they would have

procured it from someone." Hannah reminded him of the slip of paper she kept in her stays that had rendered two Afflicted unable to fight back while being captured.

"There are mages who sell such spells, but who knows how many hands it might have passed through or when. Paper does not expire like fish. It could be a spell bought last week, or last year. Same with the potion. Someone could have acquired it at any time and kept possession of it for such an occasion." Seraphina cast a light orb as the dusk thickened in the sky, and it lit the clearing.

Wycliff huffed. "Lord Albright has stewed for two years, trying to either ignore his former wife or have her put away. He has had time to plan this crime. All he would have needed was the opportunity."

As her family discussed possible motives and the sequence of events, the Albright family mausoleum drew Hannah. On a plaque attached to the outside was engraved the names and dates of those who resided within. The light her mother cast flickered across the brass. Hannah reviewed the list, wondering which of these the unfortunate woman had set out to visit. And why snapdragons? While they were a charming flower, they weren't what one typically placed on a grave.

It wasn't the name at the bottom of the list that caught Hannah's attention, but the all too brief span between the years.

HENRY ALBRIGHT, 1800–1801.

A GASP CAUGHT in her chest and she reached out to touch the engraving. A son who had not lived to see a second year. A child who might have been amused by the odd flower that could be made to snap. She brushed her fingertips over the name, and it seemed that a wash of his mother's grief ran up her arm.

"What have you found, Hannah?" Wycliff's voice pulled her away from the tide of sadness.

"She gave him a son who did not live long. He died in 1801." Hannah turned back to the group. "It is so unfair that a woman should carry the blame when she does not provide an heir, or if that child is snatched away by some act of fate or disease."

"Laws are written by men to benefit men, my dear. Such will be the way of the world until women have a voice in how we are governed." Seraphina grasped the metal railing and stared at the scorch marks.

"Or for men to decry the practice and work to institute the change we need." Wycliff stalked to his wife and drew her to his side.

A tiny smile tugged at the corner of Hannah's lips, before it dropped away. "What do you see out here?"

He picked up her hand. "More souls than I would find at Almack's. Flashes dart at the corners of my vision and low words murmur in my ears. Some hide, knowing they have escaped justice. Others want my help to move on, but I cannot send them where they need to go."

"When you dispatch a soul, do you not have a choice of doorways?" Hannah asked.

He shook his head. "The void that opens is a place of punishment. There is nothing light or good within it."

Hannah mulled over his words. "That does not seem balanced. Surely if a hound can dispatch a foul soul in one direction, you should have the ability to send a lighter one to a peaceful place."

"Events are out of balance," Seraphina murmured.

Balance. The single word echoed through Hannah as though a tuning fork had been struck.

9

THE NEXT DAY, Hannah sat on the window seat with an enormous book open in her lap. She continued her study of the Egyptian underworld, while her mother worked on the hieroglyphics they had found at Mireworth. Today, Hannah read about the Duat, the valley of the dead where Anubis ruled and souls lined up to have their hearts weighed against a feather by the goddess Ma'at.

"It's a *name!*" her mother exclaimed from her desk.

Hannah set aside her tome and crossed to the desk to peek over her mother's shoulder. Before her lay the rubbing taken from the square inscription on the end of the sarcophagus.

Seraphina tapped a series of pictograms inside an oval shape. "This is the name of Wycliff's dead mage— Kemsit. A woman mage in a time when we were snuffed out in England. Although the ancient peoples were more enlightened than we."

"Kemsit," Hannah let the unfamiliar name roll around in her mouth. "Now that we know who she was, will that lead us to why she rests there and what bargain was struck with de Cliffe?" A shiver worked over Hannah's skin and with it came a certainty that everything was connected. Hundreds of years ago, events had been set into motion that would soon reach their conclusion.

"There is more. Not only do I have her name, but also her standing in Egyptian society. Here, these symbols identify her as a mage to Anubis. Or as they called her, a *shadow mage*." Seraphina extended her arm above her desk and in its wake, a figure appeared of a woman draped in a grey cloak made of shimmering spiderwebs.

Hannah sucked in a breath. "A shadow mage? I've not heard of such a title before. What do you think it means?"

Seraphina tapped her finger on the symbols. "I need to do more research, but I cannot help but wonder if there is also a *light mage*?"

"Shadow and light. Life and death. Everything in balance," Hannah whispered.

"I am a-tingle with possibilities, Hannah. The British mage histories are silent on such things, just as they prefer to ignore the fact I continue to exist and cast magic. They are like ostriches, sticking their heads in the soil so they can deny what happens around them." The tiny mage strode across the desk and knelt to touch the rubbing taken from her tomb. "I am most curious about her being a mage to Anubis, god of the underworld. While I am leaping to conclusions, I also wonder if Kemsit may have been similar to me. Dead, yet still powerful, drawing her magic from the afterlife."

Hannah placed a hand on her mother's shoulder. "Do you think that when we walk the dark path, we will find Anubis at the end rather than Hades, or the Devil, or any other incarnation of that god?"

"All evidence does seem to point in that direction." Her mother huffed a light laugh. "I have been thinking much of late about balance. It is odd that Wycliff can dispatch a dark soul to justice, but not release a light one to move on. The balance is missing. England used to have only twelve living mages, but now has one dead one to add to her tally. What if one shadow mage balances the twelve light ones?"

Her mother turned and grasped her hand. How Hannah wished to see the bright ideas burning in her mother's gaze! "Balance is at the core of the questions plaguing us. Even in this bargain struck between de Cliffe and someone unknown—must there not also be a balance in the exchange?" Seraphina said.

Questions crammed themselves into Hannah's head until she had to let go of her mother's hand and walk to the window. The soothing garden beyond rippled over her troubled mind. "We must make our journey soon to seek the answers, and yet we cannot until we know who committed this crime against the former Lady Albright."

Seraphina snapped her fingers, and the phantom Kemsit dissolved into the paper beneath her feet. "There is also the matter of Unwin and Alder. Someone attempts to pull back the veil with which I cloak their enterprise."

Hannah turned around and dropped to the window seat. "We could solve so many problems if we cured the Afflicted."

Seraphina huffed under her breath. "And put Unwin and Alder out of business. I doubt they would thank us."

"I am sure they could transition to provide for other needs Unnatural creatures have." The clock chimed once, the single note vibrating through the air and drawing Hannah's attention. It reminded her of the passage of time and all she had to accomplish. Wycliff had gone to London to question Lord Albright. Hannah had agreed not to visit Mrs Sennett's brother until he could accompany her. "I shall leave you to your studies, Mother. I have a chore to undertake for Papa and I must see how Timmy fares with his studies."

Hannah left the library and headed to the other end of the hall, where Timmy worked in his own airy space. When he grew older, it would become his study. Currently the room was a classroom, complete with fellow students. Barnes and Sheba rolled on the rug and appeared to be wrestling.

"How have you progressed this morning?" she asked as she stepped over spaniel and hand and stood by the lad's desk. He laboured on an anatomical drawing and added labels. His handwriting showed great improvement. "Oh, Timmy, this is such good work!"

The boy smiled and then ducked his head. "I'm finding it comes easier every day. It's like something inside me only needed to know the words, and now it can string them together and tell me all sorts of things."

On impulse, Hannah held out her hand. "Once, you saw inside me to my secret. Would you look again, please?"

His eyes widened, and then he nodded. Timmy took her hand, held it between his, and closed his eyes. Hannah stared out the window with its view of the rear yard and forest. She watched one of the chickens bathing in a dusty hollow.

"It's closer than I remember it being from the first time, milady." He drew the words out in a soft tone.

"Can you tell me anything else?" When she'd first rescued Timmy, he had touched her hand and seen the curse within her. The lad had been shocked that she balanced so close to the brink of death. Curiosity nibbled at Hannah as to how his perception of the dark magic might differ from what her mother saw.

"It surrounds your heart, like a darkness. There's a line holding it back, but it scratches at it, looking for a way through." He gulped and opened his eyes as he let go of her hand.

Hannah ruffled his hair. "Thank you, Timmy. That is most helpful. Now, why don't you run along—I'm sure your luncheon is ready."

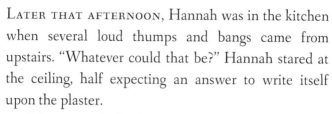

LATER THAT AFTERNOON, Hannah was in the kitchen when several loud thumps and bangs came from upstairs. "Whatever could that be?" Hannah stared at the ceiling, half expecting an answer to write itself upon the plaster.

The peacock feather wrapped around her little finger tingled and summoned Hannah to the library. She found her mother next to a massive, dusty trunk. The battered old thing looked large enough that Frank could have climbed inside during a game of hide and seek.

"Where on earth did that come from?" Hannah asked as she walked around the piece of luggage that had appeared since she'd left the library earlier. Two leather straps with buckles the size of her hands were secured over the top. She picked up the end of one and it tugged itself free of her grasp. She tried again, and the leather slapped her palm.

"Careful, dear, before it hurts you. It is ensorcelled so that only I can open it." Seraphina laid her hands over the buckles and murmured. The leather straps snapped against the thick hide of the trunk and then wriggled themselves free of the buckles to collapse flat on the rug. "Rather fortuitously, the trunk arrived today from friends in Europe. I asked them to find me any old books and scrolls about mages, and in particular, practices in Egypt. I thought it would aid our research into a cure for the Affliction. I am now hoping it might reveal a clue about the shadow mage in the bottom of Mireworth's tower."

That would explain the thumps Hannah had heard. Frank must have dragged the chest into the library. Perhaps it had struggled. But now, with the straps undone, Seraphina waved a hand over the lid and the trunk obliged, the heavy lid lifting with a groan and creak.

Hannah gasped in excitement at the contents—a treasure trove of knowledge. Books of all different sizes and bindings were crammed in among scrolls, some tightly wound and held with ribbon, others in small and stout leather tubes to protect the contents. "Oh, how marvellous."

She remembered the day she'd visited Lizzie as they planned her wedding trousseau. The modiste had arrived with a trunk packed full of samples of expensive fabrics, lace, and ribbons. Her friend had delighted in reaching in and plucking free a treasure. The trunk before Hannah, with its dusty pages and faded ink, generated a similar kind of excitement within her.

Hannah knelt on the floor and leaned close, but didn't touch the trunk. She glanced at her mother. "Is it safe?"

Seraphina nodded. "Yes. I have deactivated the hidden protection spells. My friends have searched Europe for more than a year now, hunting out rare and unknown volumes. Is this not the most fabulous thing, Hannah? There is a tingle in my bones. Something in here is calling to me."

Hannah lifted free the topmost book. A small volume, barely the size of her hand, with a deep green binding and faded gold lettering in a tongue she didn't recognise. An internal struggle erupted inside her. She wanted to take the book to the window seat and marvel over each page, yet at the same time she wanted to touch and hold every single object in the trunk. In the end, she set the book down on the rug and tried to decide which to select next. "What am I looking for in particular, Mother?"

Seraphina wheeled herself to the other side and lifted out a book with a worn brown leather cover. "Magical rituals and priestesses of Egypt. Let us see if we can find any mention of the mages who serve Anubis."

"Did you not learn about magic in other countries as part of your mage training?" Hannah asked as she scanned the odd assortment of books. No two were alike in size or binding.

Beside her, Seraphina fell silent.

Hannah chided herself for bringing up an unpleasant memory. The mage who had trained her mother had treated her poorly. He only took on the girl mage to draw the magic from the child for his own ends. When she turned eighteen and came fully into her power, Seraphina managed to remove the invisible shackles the old mage had placed around her. Kitty, who lived next door, aided her friend's escape. What a sight it must have been when the young mage appeared at court and demanded what was rightfully due to her.

"He told me little of our history, and then only his narrow view of it. Over the years, I have read what texts I could find in the possession of the mage council, but I find it has a similar bias. Everything is told from the perspective of mages' being Anglo-Saxon men. Mage-born women were seen as abhorrent."

Hannah paused in her search, an open book in her hands as she scanned its contents to make a quick decision whether it would aid their search or be put aside for another day. "And yet we know that to be untrue. The Druids roamed these isles for thousands of years before Christianity reached our shores. The Egyptians must have been the first to see the rise of mages. We know they had at least one woman among them. Is it so unusual that there might have been more?"

"If one were of a suspicious turn of mind, one might almost think the mage council had erased a vital part of our history. Which is why I asked my friends to find any history from beyond our shores," Seraphina murmured.

Hannah agreed with her mother. When men focused only on history that represented them, so much was lost to everyone. Hannah closed her eyes and let her mind guide her. If something in the chest called to her mother, did that mean it might have a very faint trace of magic she could detect? Back and forth, she let her hand follow the contours and shapes. One brushed against her palm with the tiniest tickle.

"You," she whispered, and closed her hand around it.

Opening her eyes, she freed her treasure, a small rolled scroll. A blood-red ribbon held it shut, and she tugged on it to undo the knot. A tremor rippled up her arm as she unrolled the thick paper to reveal the bright scene painted on it. Her gasp turned to an exclamation.

The scroll was twelve inches wide and six inches high. Tight rows of small hieroglyphics marched around the edges to frame a central scene. The picture stole Hannah's breath. The colours were so bright and fresh, it appeared the artist had just set down his or her brush.

In the centre stood Ma'at, the goddess of truth, before her golden scales. On one side she placed the pearly white ostrich feather, on the other a person's heart. Before the altar, a man was on his knees with his head curled over his body as he waited to hear the judgement. Anubis stood to one side, his obsidian skin glistening in the low light. The muscles in his torso had been drawn with great skill. Around his hips was tied a linen kilt with a delicate gold edge. More gold curled around his biceps and he held a staff. His jackal head had upright ears tipped in gold, and the Horus eye was drawn in gold around each of his eyes.

And beside Anubis sat a hellhound, the creature's smoky fur tipped in red and its eyes glowing. Droplets of fire clung to the tips of its monstrous fangs. A woman with long, ebony hair stood next to the hellhound, one hand resting on its head. The artist had drawn a serene expression on her face. She wore a simple linen gown bound with a gold cord.

"Who is she?" Hannah whispered.

Seraphina ran a finger along the line of symbols at the bottom of the page and muttered a spell to make the English translation reveal itself. "Anput, the wife of Anubis."

To the left of the scene ran a river of fire. Waves of glimmering red and orange flowed past the temple. Beside it hunkered an oddly formed creature with a body that was part lion, hippopotamus, and crocodile. Hannah knew a small amount about this god, her form constructed from the three largest man-eating animals known to ancient Egyptians.

"Ammit," she whispered.

The Devourer of the Dead. If the heart were judged impure, Ammit would snap it between her jaws and eat it. The dead person would never journey toward Osiris and immortality.

"What happens when Ammit swallows their hearts? Do you think it is similar to what happens when the void asks Wycliff to toss a dark soul into it?" Could her husband be the hound sitting beside Anubis?

"A soul that is consumed becomes restless forever. The Egyptians called it the second death, and those unfortunates will never find peace." Seraphina traced a fingertip over the fierce form of Ammit with her crocodile jaws.

Another figure stood in the background. A tall and slender woman in a linen gown with gold binding across the chest. She held her hands cupped together and between them, the artist had painted a glowing dark blue orb, as though she held the night sky. A silver crescent of the moon hung in the very centre.

"Do you think she is a shadow mage?" Hannah whispered.

Seraphina sucked in a breath. "Yes. The shadow mage of Anubis."

The scroll fell to her mother's lap. "Oh, Hannah! How much knowledge have we lost over the centuries? Erased by stuffy old white male mages."

Hannah rubbed her hands over her arms to dispel the goose bumps. "How do we find out if a shadow mage was dead?"

Seraphina picked up the scroll and turned it to one side. She muttered under her breath as she asked the symbols to yield their meaning. "She served Anubis, who rules in Duat, the underworld. The shadow mage draws her power from that realm, but walks the world of the living. As I do. The shiver in my bones tells me this is the piece I have been missing. In England, we have focused only on the light and life—we have upset the balance by shunning their opposites." Seraphina held the scroll at arm's length and the picture seemed to move over the papyrus. "It will take me some time to wrangle the meaning from the inscription on this scene. But there is another clue here. This is Kemsit, and unless there were other mages who bore that name or title, this might be the woman in the tower."

Excitement surged through Hannah. She leaned close to her mother's bathchair to stare at the scene of judgement. The shadow mage had a strong face, with sharply defined cheekbones and full lips of a reddish brown. There was something else she noticed about the possibly dead shadow mage. "If she is dead, then there is no evidence of rot about her in this drawing. Could she have been a vampyre?"

That caused a warning to surge up her torso. Had they left Mrs Rossett alone in the house with a blood drinker, who now had a convenient way to exit the tower that had held her captive for hundreds of years?

10

THAT DAY, Wycliff rode into London and headed for the smart townhouse occupied by Lord Albright and his second family. The man lived well and was the typical indolent noble. Albright spent his money on wine, women, and slow horses. The similarities to Wycliff's own father did not escape him—except that in Albright's case, his estate earned sufficient to keep pace with his spending.

He clenched his jaw as he rapped on the door. The man offended Wycliff's sense of honour and the hound whispered that it needed only seconds to latch on to his soul, wrestle it free of his physical form, and then toss it to the void.

"Is Albright at home?" Wycliff said as soon as the door swung open. He barged past the startled butler, who wordlessly gestured to a half-open door along the hall.

The man in question sat in a tastefully decorated

parlour, reading the newspaper before venturing out for the day. A brown dog stretched out in front of the fire and only twitched an ear at Wycliff's arrival. The current Lady Albright sat opposite her husband with an embroidery hoop in her hands. She froze to stare at him, whereas her husband didn't even acknowledge him.

"I bring news of your wife," Wycliff said. Without being asked, he took a chair in front of the window with the light behind him, equidistant between the two Albrights.

"My wife is quite well, as you can see." Albright looked up and gestured to the woman across from him.

Some twenty years his junior, she had a pleasing but somewhat bland countenance. A merchant's daughter, she had conducted a well-known affair with her husband while his other wife still possessed a pulse. The couple had married while the former Lady Albright lay in her coffin.

"I have news of your *former* wife," Wycliff bit out between clenched teeth.

The man before him was no gentleman, despite what society might say. He had abandoned his wife of many years once her heart stopped beating—had thrown her into the street with no more care than if she were the contents of a chamber pot. He had made it clear he would have interred her to scream unheard and bang on her coffin lid for decades, if he had known she would reanimate.

Albright folded up the newspaper and tossed it to

the sideboard with a loud sigh. "What on earth has Felicity done now? She is dead, for goodness' sake, and no longer my responsibility." His words were sharp and his narrow nostrils sucked in as irritation flared in his eyes.

"She is dead," Wycliff uttered the words, then realised they had fallen flat, given the lady in question had expired some two years previously.

Albright snorted. "You waste my time, Wycliff. See yourself out and don't come here again."

Wycliff counted to ten in his head. Admittedly, he did it as fast as he could and by increments of two, but he *had* paused to rein in his temper. "Let me rephrase that. Someone expunged the former Lady Albright from this earth. We found her remains at Bunhill Fields and Sir Hugh identified her through a gold tooth and a scrap of fabric, which her cousin recognised."

The current Lady Albright let out a soft gasp and dropped her needlework. The dog finally looked up to stare at its mistress. Then its enormous head fell to its paws again, followed by a loud snore.

"She's gone for good this time?" Albright jumped to his feet and rushed to his wife, where he took her hands in his. An odd look passed between the two of them.

Wycliff pulled out his notebook as he observed the couple. All of society knew of their affair, but had they conspired in other ways? Such as procuring what they required to dispatch an unwelcome predecessor? He wondered what the current, and now only, Lady Albright thought of her husband's treatment of his previous wife. Or was she one of those creatures who believed the advantages of increasing her rank and standing far beyond her birth were worth any price?

"Yes. Unfortunately, the former Lady Albright was incinerated and very little is left of her to inter this time. Where were you Tuesday night?"

"Tuesday night?" The man snorted and turned a hard gaze on Wycliff.

"Yes. I require you to tell me your movements that evening." The witnesses to the blue and white flames were next to useless. None had investigated the unnatural fire at the cemetery, superstition making them too afraid. By the time the curious crept out with the dawn, the perpetrator of the crime had long been gone. Not that Wycliff believed Albright would have done it. The man was too much the coward to do his own dirty work. Although Wycliff could see him hiding behind a tree to watch his former wife suffer a horrendous second death.

"What is the purpose of these questions?" Albright shot out, as though in a hurry to end the interview.

"A crime has been committed against the former Lady Albright, and I will find the person responsible." Wycliff wished he could drag the man off to Newgate prison now. How much proof did they need to throw him where he deserved to be?

Albright emitted a braying laugh that made Wycliff think of hyenas. "My former wife died two years ago, Wycliff. You surely cannot suspect me of murdering a dead thing? Although I am relieved she will no longer haunt our lives and Lady Albright and I can raise our children in peace. Felicity made a dashed nuisance of herself turning up wherever we went, draped all in black. Everyone knew who and what she was, and she put a dampener on every outing."

Everyone knew who and what she was... Albright was correct. The former Lady Albright was a familiar figure in London. Society lapped up her sad tale and how her husband had paraded his new bride before her. Her every appearance at soirées had been like a new instalment in a serialised drama. An idea flitted through his mind. What if this was not a crime against Lady Albright personally, but one which simply targeted an Afflicted—any Afflicted? That put a different spin on events. He tucked the thought away as unlikely. Her uncaring husband seemed the only candidate wanting to commit his pesky former wife to a funeral pyre.

"We have yet to ascertain if this was murder. No one can deny that she walked this earth and continued to live her life after her heart stilled. Or she did, until someone condemned her to the flames. A particularly gruesome way to expire. Perhaps Parliament will institute a new category of murder to prosecute those who extinguish the unfortunates whose hearts no longer beat." Wycliff measured his words and dispensed them with slow regularity.

Lady Albright's eyes widened as he spoke, and one hand went to her generous chest. Her already alabaster complexion paled further.

Lord Albright, conversely, appeared to grow more impatient and angry. He rose to his feet and paced by the fire. "Parliament cannot do that! It would be deuced unfair. How can one person be murdered twice? But anyway, I was home that night. My wife and any of the staff will confirm that. Little Tristan had a cough, and we sat by his bedside."

"I have not concluded this matter," Wycliff said as he stood. He'd question the staff on his way out, before Albright schooled them in any story.

"Yes, you have. The matter is closed as far as I am concerned. Done and swept into the gutter, I hope, like an unwanted burnt roast." Albright stalked closer to Wycliff, his shoulders tense and his hands clenched.

Intimidation didn't work on Wycliff. All the noble did was entrench his opinion about the man's guilt. Ignoring him, Wycliff nodded to Lady Albright and took his leave, stopping to ask the staff about their master's movements. Each footman and a startled maid confirmed the heir had indeed been poorly, and both parents devoted in tending him.

Blast it. He still could have found time to slip out, so Albright remained Wycliff's prime suspect.

He stalked away from the house, needing to pound the footpath before he struck someone. Lord Albright burrowed under his skin and irritated him. Part of it was the hideous reflection he held up to Wycliff. Once, he had possessed similar beliefs—that the Afflicted shouldn't be walking among Londoners. As he grew to know Hannah and her mother, they had opened his eyes. Most of his disgust was for the way Albright treated his wife. Legally, as a widower he was entitled to remarry. But he could at least have had the decency to ensure his former wife had a roof over her head and what she needed to sustain her. A little sympathy would have relieved much of the dead woman's heartache.

Wycliff exhausted his frustration after several minutes and returned to where the Albright groom still held his horse. His next destination was the home of the man who had removed Mrs Sennett's brain. William Peters lived in a modest house in a row of terraces. Unwin and Alder must pay their employees well for their unusual work…or for their silence.

Wycliff knocked on the door and a tired-looking woman answered. Strands of brown hair streaked with grey escaped from her cap. Wrinkles ruined her apron, as though she had spent much time balling it up in her hands. "May I help you, sir?"

"I need to see Peters. Is he in?" Wycliff peered over her shoulder into the hall, but all he saw was a set of stairs leading upward.

The woman gave a sob and rushed into a side room, leaving him standing on the doorstep.

Judging by the reaction, Wycliff wondered if the fellow had succumbed to his illness. If he had known in advance this visit would entail a weeping woman, he would have swapped with Hannah. With her gentle touch, his wife had a way of eliciting information from the more delicate individuals who needed questioning.

Wycliff pinched the bridge of his nose to stave off the headache pressing behind his eyes. Today was not progressing in his favour. Then he closed the door and followed the sound of crying. Inside a comfortable but modest parlour, he found the woman whom he took to be Mrs Peters in a chair before the fireplace, her shoulders heaving.

He waited for her to compose herself while he took in his surroundings. A bright rug in reds, oranges, and browns covered the floor and reminded him of fallen autumn leaves. A sage green fabric covered the settee positioned at an angle to the fire. Under the window and overlooking the road sat a small desk scattered with papers.

"He's been gone these three days now." The woman gasped between sobs. Then she pulled a handkerchief from her apron pocket and blew her nose.

"My condolences. Unwin and Alder told me he was ill, but they were unaware he had passed." Blast. Another dead end in his enquiry.

She blew her nose on a long, high note and then turned to stare at him. "Bill's not dead. He's *gone*."

The headache tapped on the inside of his skull. Lord save him from silly people. "I assume you mean physically gone, as opposed to dead?"

She nodded, and more tears dribbled down her cheeks.

"Tell me what happened." Wycliff took a chair and held in a sigh. This didn't make any sense. Peters had been absent from his job pleading illness. Or was the complaint self-inflicted? Perhaps he had got drunk and wandered off.

"He had a head cold. I didn't think it was that bad, really, but men do fuss when they're ill." She glanced up at him, as though expecting confirmation that he also took to his bed with the sniffles. Hardly. He had crawled through the mud after the hellhound ripped out his throat and hadn't uttered a single word of complaint.

"What happened three days ago?" Wycliff steered the conversation in the relevant direction.

"We were both sitting in here. He was going through the post when he leapt to his feet and said he needed to go out. When I asked where, he muttered something about fetching a tonic from the apothecary for his headache. But he never came back..." Her voice trailed off as her bottom lip trembled and the tears fell anew.

"Was he sitting there?" Wycliff gestured to the desk.

At her nod, he rose and relocated to the desk chair. Peters had been going through the post just before he went out and never returned. What had he found? Wycliff sorted through the invoices and letters from family. Had the man left behind a clue, or had he shoved a letter in his pocket and taken it with him? Nothing seemed to be an immediate summons, unless one missive were written in code. In which case he would need Hannah to lend her thoughts to uncover it.

He tugged a folded newspaper toward him.

Bereaved man finds wife's brain missing. He recognised the headline, the same article they had read in Mireworth about the missing brain of Mrs Sennett. He picked the paper up and held it closer. A squiggle in the margin caught his attention. Turning the newspaper sideways, he read, *Langholm, 10am.*

"What or who is Langholm?" he asked over his shoulder.

"It's a pub a few roads over." She waved in a westerly direction with her handkerchief.

"I shall make enquiries there about your husband and see if I can run him to ground." Wycliff tapped the paper against his palm.

She steeled her spine and met his gaze. "Thank you, milord. You send him running home and I'm going to give him a good talking-to for worrying me like this."

"I will need to know what he looks like, to aid in finding him." He pulled out the little notebook and jotted a brief description of the man as his wife spoke.

Wycliff left the terrace and rode in the direction of the Langholm. He found the pub three roads over and sitting on a corner. A squat building, it looked to have Tudor origins in its whitewashed walls and dark timber framing, though its name was Norse. He entered and wrinkled his nose as the stale odour of spilled beer and smoke assaulted his senses.

"Can I help you, sir?" a sturdy man behind the counter asked.

"I'm looking for William Peters. His wife said he was last seen here." Wycliff kept his hands to himself, not wanting to touch the sticky surface of the bar. An aroma of stale sweat circulated in the low-ceilinged room and he clenched his nostrils against it.

The man screwed up his face and stared at the lantern on the bar. "Don't think I've seen Bill these last few days."

Movement from one corner drew his eye, as the tall, broad Bow Street Runner joined him. "Lord Wycliff. Is there anything I can assist you with?"

Wycliff nodded at Taylor. "Yes. I'm trying to find a man called William Peters. He came here three days ago to meet someone and hasn't been seen since."

"I can ask around for you. He's not one of those Unnaturals, is he?" A worry line crossed the man's brow.

"Not that I know of. I need to talk to him about a matter related to his employment at Unwin and Alder." At least Wycliff could hand off one task. The Runner would have a better network with which to track the man down. Wycliff gave him the scant information he had about the missing man and his appearance.

"I'll put the word out on the street, milord. We'll find him for you." Taylor touched the brim of his bowler with a mitten-clad hand and set off out the door.

Wycliff returned to the stableyard at Westbourne Green, to be greeted by Hannah flying down the back steps toward him. A smile came unbidden to his face at the sight of her.

"Oh! Wycliff! I have such news," she exclaimed, her dark eyes sparkling like diamonds.

"Good. My day was particularly fruitless, and Lord Albright was as gleeful as you can imagine on hearing that his former wife had departed this earth." He placed a quick kiss on her lips, the small contact spreading warmth through his chilled body.

Her good mood deflated, and sadness dropped into her gaze. "I am not surprised to hear he couldn't even marshal sufficient common decency to mourn her final passing."

Wycliff handed his mare to Frank, and tucked Hannah's hand into the crook of his elbow. He leaned his head toward hers. "Tell me your news, I did not mean to ruin your excitement."

Her eyes brightened once more. "Mother had a trunk full of old books delivered today that fellow mages sourced in Europe and the ancient lands. Inside it, we found a scroll depicting the weighing of a heart in the underworld. And do you know what we found in the background?"

He took a guess. "A devilishly handsome hellhound?" He was only jesting a tiny bit.

"No. Well, yes. But the hound is standing beside Anubis. The scroll depicts a mage, called a *shadow mage*, who serves Anubis and her name is Kemsit. Mother thinks there is a chance it is the same mage who now slumbers in Mireworth's tower." She scanned his face, waiting for his reaction.

"Having found a resident of Mireworth who has been there longer than Mrs Rossett, I am glad we can give her a name," he said.

They walked through the doors to the vestibule, where Wycliff stripped off his hat and gloves. Then he shrugged out of his greatcoat, which Mary took. He didn't know what magic Lady Miles had wrought, but the house maintained a most pleasant temperature no matter what happened outside its solid walls.

"There is one other small detail." Hannah wrung her hands together.

"What is that?" A tiny warning prickled over his skin.

"Kemsit might be dead. I mean undead, like Mother. Although without further research, we are not entirely sure." Hannah worried at her bottom lip.

"Do you think that might be the secret my family has kept all these years—that they have imprisoned some sort of undead mage in our tower? I would suggest that we immediately free her, but would she be grateful to her liberators or exact pent-up revenge upon us?" Wycliff conjured a scenario wherein Lady Miles was trapped for hundreds of years. No, he would not want to be the one to take the lid off the sarcophagus. Nor did he ever want to do it, if the angry mage were to call down a fireball to flatten Mireworth.

11

OVER THE NEXT FEW DAYS, a growing sense of unrest pervaded London in general, and Hannah's home in particular. Even Barnes prowled the curtain rails and leapt to the light fittings as though he were trying to escape on some pirate adventure. In London, people gathered in the streets and whispered about the Afflicted, and how unfair it was that the toffs protected one another.

That morning, Wycliff gave a muffled exclamation from across the table and handed the newspaper over to Hannah.

"'Has your husband lost his mind?'" she read aloud. "'Bereaved widow Mrs Downing was horrified to discover her husband's mind had wandered as he lay in repose before the funeral.'" She scanned ahead, and the circumstances sounded similar to those of Mrs Sennett. During the wake, the coffin had been jostled and the top of Mr Downing's head had fallen to one side, revealing an empty skull. A scan of the byline revealed that Mr Nash had penned the article. The same man who had written the earlier salacious piece.

Hannah caught Wycliff's gaze. "One might be accidental, but surely two is deliberate? Have you found Mr Peters?"

"No. The man left for a meeting and didn't return. I have Taylor—a Bow Street Runner—keeping an eye open for him." He held his coffee cup but didn't drink. He appeared to be searching for answers in its depths.

"Someone works in the dark to bring attention to what the Afflicted need to sustain ourselves," Seraphina murmured.

Sir Hugh also stared into his coffee cup. "We've seen more people crammed into the seats during lectures at the hospital. I field many questions about the Afflicted as I conduct my rounds. One woman stopped me on the street, and asked how she would know if some monster had removed her brain."

Wycliff snorted at that one, and even Hannah stifled a laugh. It was uncharitable to make fun of those who didn't have the same medical knowledge that they possessed. "How did you respond, Papa?"

Sir Hugh winked at her. "I told her to run her hands through her hair. If her scalp was free of stitches, she still retained her mind. That reassured her, although she tore the cap from her son's head and checked his hair before doing her own."

"We cannot blame people for being afraid. It does not sit easy with them, which is why Mother has worked so hard to wipe away any rumours." Hannah had quite lost her appetite and now regretted chopping the top off her boiled egg. She placed her spoon on the plate, unable to scoop out the yolk.

"I am sure it is a mage working against me. No aftermage would have the level of skill required to unpick my work." Seraphina took up the paper to read the article. "I have requested a meeting with the mage council, but they dither over their decision, as though I am an unwanted suitor who has asked them to dance and they do not wish to offend by saying no."

"Do you think they will assist?" Wycliff stared from under dark brows.

Seraphina heaved a pantomime sigh. "For some reason, I make them uncomfortable. I have no ally on that council, but I thought a few of those men more open-minded than others."

"Wycliff, if you have time today, I thought I would call on Mrs Sennett's brother, James Kelly, to see what I can learn." Hannah outlined her plans to her husband.

"Yes, I shall accompany you. Then we should talk to Sir Manly and learn what is happening at the higher levels of government. I had asked for them to consider a special category of crime to account for attacks against Unnaturals." He pushed his half-consumed coffee to one side.

Later that morning, while Frank manoeuvred the carriage through the London traffic, Hannah pressed her nose to the window. A group gathered on one corner, waving placards and shouting that an Englishman had the right to keep his brain in his skull.

"Unrest grows," Wycliff murmured by her side. "Do you think you and your mother should retreat to Mireworth in case the situation grows worse?"

Hannah placed her hand in his. "No. I do not think there is any threat to us yet. People are only expressing their concerns."

"Very well. I will do what I must to protect you both." His hand tightened on hers.

A little of her worry lifted. She would not run to Mireworth, no matter how much she wanted to escape to pursue the mystery of the mage in the tower. A voice whispered through her veins, urging her to follow this investigation to an inky path and beyond. Whatever lay in the darkness ahead, she knew Wycliff would be at her side.

Frank drove the carriage to an address not too far removed from Mr Sennett's home. Hannah knocked on the door while Wycliff lingered on the footpath. Curtains twitched at the sight of the carriage in the street and the well-dressed couple on the doorstep.

A woman somewhere in her forties with greying hair opened the door. A clean white apron covered her dress, and she narrowed her eyes at Hannah. She didn't immediately speak, but glanced over Hannah's shoulder to stare at Wycliff. "Can I help you?" She clung to the edge of the door as though it were a shield.

Hannah stole a backward look. *Oh, dear.* Wycliff

was scowling at a cluster of nosy neighbours who gathered outside the house opposite to chat.

"I am Lady Wycliff and I should like to speak to Mr Kelly. Is he in?" Hannah plastered a smile on her face and tried to appear friendly. There was little she could do about Wycliff, whose features were pulled in a disdainful direction at those with nothing better to do but gossip.

"He's in the parlour, milady." The woman gestured for them to come in, standing well clear as Wycliff crossed the threshold. She waved her apron at the women across the street, as though to shoo them back inside, before slamming the door.

Hannah found Mr Kelly dozing in the parlour, his large body slumped on a settee and beefy hands crossed over his stomach. She cleared her throat and only elicited a vague snore from the man.

Wycliff's shoulders heaved in a sigh. He tapped the man's boots with his foot as he walked past and selected a chair.

"What is it, woman?" Mr Kelly sat up, glared at Hannah, then realised his wife had not awakened him. "Who—?"

"Lord and Lady Wycliff. We are here about the events surrounding the funeral of your sister, Mrs Sennett." Hannah adopted a brisk tone, and swept her skirt to one side as she seated herself on a chair next to Wycliff.

Mr Kelly jumped to his feet, bowed, and scratched both hands over his scalp. Then he descended more slowly to the settee, confusion written on his features. "Did you know her?"

"No. We are making enquiries about a more delicate matter." Hannah tapped one gloved finger against the side of her head and raised one eyebrow at the man.

The man's gaze darted around the room. He nodded and wet his lips. "Not much to tell, milady. It was all there in the newspaper."

Hannah smiled and hoped Wycliff would behave. He bristled beside her as though he had caught a whiff of something unpleasant. She carried on. "It wasn't entirely all in the newspaper, now, was it? For example, what made you stumble that day?"

Mr Kelly shrugged, and again a hand went through his thinning hair. "I can't remember now. Must have been a stone on the path."

"Really? When I spoke to Mr Sennett, he said you appeared to trip over nothing." Hannah tilted her head as she observed Mr Kelly.

He clasped and unclasped his hands and didn't appear able to sit still. The silence grew uncomfortable and the longer it stretched, the more he squirmed, rather as though he sat upon a secret that didn't want to stay put.

"Was it such a big bump that when you stumbled, you insisted the coffin be opened so you could ensure your sister remained undisturbed?" she asked.

The man's gaze shot around the room, alighting on a painting on the wall, then the door, then the fireplace. Anywhere except the people waiting for his answer. "It must have been. Yes. Yes, I think it was. There was a loud thump and then we all heard something pop. I was worried about her, you see."

Wycliff leaned forward and rested his forearms on his thighs. He waited until his prey glanced at him, then he held the other man's gaze. "How much were you paid to make sure they opened the coffin?"

Mr Kelly's eyes widened, and his mouth opened and closed. "How dare you!"

"You are not in any trouble, Mr Kelly." Hannah sought to reassure the man. "Nor will you have to repay the money. We simply want to understand the truth of the matter, and how events were set in motion." There were times in their past investigations where Wycliff's blunt approach extracted the information they required. Other times it made a mess of things that Hannah had to tidy away. Today he knew the exact question to ask and in a brisk enough manner. Hannah would have danced around the idea of payment for another half hour at least.

"Who paid you?" Wycliff leaned back in his chair as he took control of the interview.

Mr Kelly swallowed several times, then his body slumped as though his spine had stopped being made of bone and turned to pudding. "It was that scandal-sheet man—Mr Nash. He approached me and said he was investigating a story that some people were interfering with the dead, and he heard a rumour Kate might have been affected. She's my sister—of course I was worried about what might have been done to her. Her husband insisted on a closed coffin and wouldn't let us see her to say goodbye. That just made me more suspicious that he was hiding something."

Hannah chewed over the worrying revelation of a reporter following his own investigation about Unwin and Alder. No doubt his source told him which bodies to pay close attention to. Which meant the business had a talkative employee who was putting everything in jeopardy. When they were alone, she would discuss with Wycliff whether he thought the missing employee was responsible. "That is why the reporter happened to be in the cemetery as you opened Mrs Sennett's coffin."

"They took her...brain," Mr Kelly whispered the word and glanced over his shoulder. "What sort of horrid monster takes a woman's mind?"

"As I explained to Mr Sennett, there is a scientific group conducting a wide-ranging phrenology study. That's examining the lumps and bumps on our skulls," she added when he gave a blank stare.

"He knew then, the bugger? Pardon my language, milady, but that ain't right." Mr Kelly's hand curled into a fist.

"He most likely did not know they had removed her brain. Next of kin are asked to consent to an examination of the skull. He had no way of knowing any more than that." Wycliff smoothed over the more disturbing details. For once, and to Hannah's relief, he didn't state the horrible truth.

Hannah rose, since they had what they needed. Their next quarry was Mr Nash, the man who had penned the article. She suspected that interview would require Wycliff's talents to shake free the individual who had provided him with the name of the donor to Unwin and Alder. "Thank you for your time, Mr Kelly, you have been most helpful."

Wycliff gave Frank instructions to take them to the newspaper offices. Once underway, he clenched his hand into a fist on his knee. "Damned reporters."

"I am assuming the source of information for the reporter is the Unwin and Alder employee, Mr Peters?" Hannah hoped the business didn't have more than one gossiping employee.

Wycliff tapped his fist against his leg. "Most likely, and we still need to find him."

"The longer he is missing, the more concerned I grow about his safety." Hannah watched people hurrying about their lives on the street. Perhaps it was her imagination, but some women had their bonnets tied on with extra ribbons, as though they sought to protect their minds.

"Given that he betrayed his employer and has made enemies in the higher reaches of society, I wonder if they have paid him to disappear," Wycliff said.

Frank stopped the carriage in a busy road close to where the newspaper operated. Wycliff helped Hannah down, then kept her close as people flowed past them.

"Whatever is going on?" People tugged at her and for one horrible moment, she thought she struggled in the ocean against the clutches of the water. Only the solid presence of Wycliff stopped the panic from rising in her chest.

"They are gathering for some reason." Wycliff used his greater height to peer over the tops of heads and to stare down the street. Then he sheltered her with his body and ploughed across the pavement to the portico of the building.

A dull roar came from the end of the road, and Hannah wondered what entertainment drew the eager pedestrians.

"We can investigate that later, Hannah. Let us find Mr Nash first." Wycliff tucked her hand into the crook of his elbow and escorted her into the building.

A different sort of roar filled the room where the daily news was collated. Men yelled back and forth. Machines clacked and rattled. Chairs scraped against the wooden floors.

Wycliff stopped a lad rushing past with a clutch of papers in his hand. "Where do I find Nash?"

The boy pointed to a corner of the room. "Desk over there, sir." Then he ducked under Wycliff's arm and took off at a sprint.

Wycliff and Hannah wound their way through the obstacles of people and furniture to the far corner. Papers were scattered over the desk's surface, the chair pushed back, and a tepid cup of tea balanced on a stack of books.

Hannah glanced around, wondering which of the

men yelling at one another sought to expose the Afflicted.

"Where's Nash?" Wycliff asked the man furiously writing at the nearby desk.

He looked up and glanced around before he shrugged. "Must have stepped out. Always chasing a story, that one."

"He cannot be far—the tea is still warm." Hannah pointed to the cup.

"Or he could be avoiding us. Everyone saw us come in." Wycliff stared at each face, but without a description they had no idea whom they sought.

A lean older gentleman approached, of average height. His hair had gone bald in an odd pattern as though he had rubbed the growth away from years of worrying at it. He squinted at Hannah. "I say, aren't you Lady Wycliff, the daughter of the dead mage?"

A ripple raced through the room, and all eyes turned to stare at Hannah. She stiffened her spine. "Lady Miles is my mother, yes. We are looking for Mr Nash. Could you point him out for us?"

He glanced around. "Not sure I see him at the moment. Why do you want to talk to him? Is it about these missing brains? Last we spoke, he muttered that those dead Afflicted were eating them. But that can't be true, now, can it? Parliament would never let a bunch of dead women devour the minds of honest Englishmen. Or is it because we have a mad king and the nobles are looking after one another at the expense of the common man?"

Hannah reached for Wycliff's hand. She didn't like the direction the questions were taking.

"Nash might have information about a missing persons case I am investigating." Wycliff took a step toward the man and shielded Hannah from his view as he deflected the conversation.

The man's chilling gaze remained on Hannah, and she resisted the urge to shudder. "He's not here. Why don't you try later on tonight? Sometimes he turns his stories in late."

Wycliff nodded, and Hannah needed no persuading to leave the building. "I think we can safely assume the direction that Nash's next story will take," he murmured as they emerged on the pavement.

"I will discuss what to do with Mother. She needs to suppress the new rumours, even as someone seeks to unveil them." A roar from farther along the road drew Hannah's attention. "Whatever is happening down there?"

"We shall investigate, but stay close, Hannah." Wycliff kept her tucked against his side as they walked along the road and found a large crowd gathered.

They mob used the intersection of two roads as a square in which to assemble. In the middle of the cross-road stood an open cart. Using the vehicle as in impromptu stage was a man who resembled a ring-leader. He gestured with his bowler hat as he incited the crowd. Next to the man stood a forlorn-looking woman in a dirty shift, her head bowed.

A banner nailed to the side of the cart read, LONDON BELONGS TO THE LIVING, NOT THE DEAD!

"Stare at the face of death!" The man yelled as he put a hand under the woman's chin and tilted her head up. "This woman is a mind-devouring horror."

Hannah stared at the woman, trying to find anything familiar in her features. From this distance, it was impossible to tell if she were one of the Afflicted or an actor hired to portray one. People around them chanted and yelled. A woman screeched and swooned. Men rushed to prop her up while others yelled, "Disgusting things!" More shouted, "Should be in the ground. Go back to your grave!"

"Oh, dear," Hannah blurted.

12

Wᴙᴄʟɪꜰꜰ ᴡʀᴀᴘᴘᴇᴅ his arm around Hannah's waist and held her close. "Do you recognise her?" he said against her ear as he pulled her into the shelter of a shop's awning.

"No. But it is difficult to tell from this distance, nor do I know them all by sight. Many keep their lives private." Tight lines pulled at the corners of Hannah's eyes as she stared at the woman on exhibit.

"She hungers for your brain. Will she dine on yours tonight, sir?" The showman used a cane to point to a robust lad near the front.

People yelled and screamed. The man leapt back, as though he expected the woman to lunge and grab his head.

"I must get closer. I cannot tell if she is one or not." Hannah tugged on his jacket lapel.

Wycliff swore under his breath and took her hand before she darted away. "I don't want you wading through this lot. I will get closer and see what I can learn, if you promise to stay put?"

Concern flared under his skin. He needed to keep Hannah safe and away from the crowd in case the mood spilled over and turned violent. A backward glance revealed a group pelting the woman with rotten produce. How dared they behave like that toward another human being? Even the loathsome Unnatural criminals in the Repository were treated better.

Hannah swallowed the argument that flitted behind her eyes. "I promise. I will wait here until you return."

He kissed the tips of her gloves and silently prayed that for once, she would do as he asked. He pushed through the crowd, unwashed bodies rubbing against him and offending his senses. They were a mixed lot, from the poor in their rags to the more affluent working classes drawn from the surrounding businesses or street vendors. Even one or two gentlemen like himself watched from the outer edges. Wycliff used his greater height and lack of manners to shove his way to the front and close to the cart.

The woman kept her eyes downcast. Tomato dripped from one shoulder like pale blood. A smear of overripe pumpkin was caught in her hair. Wycliff took his time in examining her, searching for the telltale signs of the Afflicted. It was pointless to try to detect the faint odour of rot—the stench of the expired fruit and vegetables overpowered any such trace.

With an effort, he blocked out the noise around

him and focused. He started with the obvious—he didn't recognise her. Not that he knew all the members of the *ton*—he relied on their recognising and then avoiding *him*. Her gown appeared no different from the sturdy woven ones Hannah wore when assisting her father or working outside. The curse took nobles from various levels, but there was nothing about this woman's demeanour or appearance that hinted at her coming from the upper echelons.

As he watched her, tiny signs filtered through to him. The woman drew ragged breaths. The Afflicted didn't breathe, although some kept up the artifice in company to conceal their condition. More telling, in a tiny scratch on her arm no more than an inch long, a single drop of blood congealed. A well-fed Afflicted could easily heal such a wound and a droplet wouldn't even have time to form. If the creature didn't have access to her allocation of *pickled cauliflower*, then rot would bloom over her skin. Yet this woman had an unblemished complexion. She also possessed all her fingernails, one of the first things to slough off a decaying body.

Confident in his assessment that the woman was living, Wycliff turned to the man exhibiting his prize. "She's not Afflicted!" he yelled. "This woman is alive, and he deceives you!"

People around him stared, and a wave of chatter washed over the crowd. Whispers of doubt raced from person to person.

The showman dropped his arms and glared at

Wycliff with a narrowed gaze. "I assure you, she is indeed one of the Afflicted and undead."

"You lie. This woman is alive and breathing." People around Wycliff pulled back, isolating the nonbeliever in their midst. Yet at the same time, their whispers grew louder as others noticed the rise and fall of the woman's chest.

"The common folk have no dealings with the Afflicted. You must defer to my expert opinion in this matter." The man spoke to the crowd, trying to win them back to his side. He laughed, but only a few laughed along with him. He shot a murderous look at Wycliff for stealing his limelight.

"The Afflicted don't breathe and this poor woman does. But there is an easy way to settle this. The Afflicted can heal their wounds. Let us cut her and watch her skin reform around the wound. I'm sure those assembled here would like to see that." Wycliff gestured to those around him, and their eyes lit up at the idea of enhancing the spectacle by slicing the defenceless woman.

People cheered behind him. "Cut her!" an old woman yelled. Similar cries went up.

A nearby person pulled a knife from his jacket and rushed the platform. "Prove it! Cut her flesh and show us how the undead heal," he cried as he waved the blade.

The woman blanched. She sought Wycliff's gaze with panic in her eyes. "No, no, please," she whispered. The woman cast about her and looked ready to jump from the cart and leg it. Only the animosity rolling off the crowd stopped her. What was worse—staying put to be sliced or leaping into a crowd hungry to destroy an Afflicted?

Sweat dribbled down the showman's face and he reached out to take hold of the woman's arm. The man's brain fair smoked as he sought a way to wrangle the crowd back to his side. Then he stared at his prisoner and clutched one hand to his chest. "Why, I think this good man is correct! This woman does breathe and has deceived me!"

A disappointed groan rippled through the people, deprived of the next act in the show.

"But take this as a cautionary tale, my friends." Here he let go of the woman and leaned toward the audience, waving them closer. "The Afflicted look just like you, me, and this woman. We cannot tell them apart easily, except for the most rotten among them like Lady Miles."

Wycliff choked on a rush of indignation at hearing his mother-in-law used as an example of what to look out for. He toyed with telling her when he returned home. The showman might find himself turned into an exhibit should the mage give him a tail or webbed feet for the insult.

"We must band together to stamp out their scourge, before they feast on all our minds!" The showman sneered at Wycliff, pleased with his manoeuvring to turn events back to his advantage.

Wycliff didn't care. His goal had been achieved

when he'd determined the woman was not one of the Afflicted. He only hoped she received compensation for her ordeal. He drifted back through the unwashed tide until it spat him out at the edges.

Hannah peered from around the side of the sheltered doorway. "Is she truly alive? You weren't just saying that?"

"The woman breathes and has a slight cut on her arm that has not healed. Not that I think it really matters to that lot—they are hanging on every word. The articles Nash writes are fuelling them." He took her arm and led her away from the show.

Most of the worry eased from around her eyes. "How dare he call my mother the most rotten of the Afflicted. I had to remember my promise to you, but I was sorely tempted to rush out and demand he retract his words."

"I was also tempted, but nothing would be gained by letting them know who we are." The noise behind them lessened as they walked back to Frank and the carriage.

"I do not like how people are being rallied against the Afflicted." Hannah turned to him before climbing into the vehicle.

"Neither do I." Once he would have welcomed it. Now it made cold dread swirl through him. Where would it end?

WHEN THEY RETURNED to Westbourne Green, Hannah tore through the house searching for her mother and calling her name. She spied Mary carrying an empty tray along the hall.

"Where is Mother?" Hannah asked the maid.

"Outside, milady." The maid waved to the rear of the house and the forest beyond.

Hannah turned on her heel and ran across the terrace and down the steps. As her boots struck the dirt, the chickens squawked and scattered out of her way.

"Sorry, ladies." Hannah apologised for ruffling their feathers as she headed into the welcoming embrace of the trees.

Wycliff followed her, his long stride keeping pace with her. He rolled his shirtsleeves up to his elbows as he walked, having stripped off his hat, gloves, and coat while Hannah searched for the mage inside the house. He kept his anger contained, visible only in the faint ripple of invisible smoke across his skin and the dark fire in his eyes.

Hannah, on the other hand, felt ready to explode from the outrage pounding through her veins. Dots of red danced before her eyes. Wycliff reached up to hold a branch out of her way as she tugged on her gloves, but the leather refused to budge. Nor could she remove her bonnet—the ribbon appeared to have tied itself in a knot. Hannah burst from the trees to find her mother in her bower, enjoying the late afternoon warmth.

"Hannah! Whatever has you all flustered?" Her mother set down her book.

"A horrid man was exhibiting what he claimed was one of the Afflicted in the street. That newspaper man is intent on exposing us all, misinformed people are waving placards, and my blasted bonnet won't come off!" Hannah scrabbled at the ribbon and in the end she succeeded in pulling it over her chin. She threw the bonnet to the grass. The rough act dislodged a sizeable length of her hair from the arrangement Mary had carefully crafted, and it swung over one side of her face.

Hannah threw herself down next to the bonnet with a powerful urge to flail her fists in the soft lawn.

"My. That is quite a lot to absorb." Seraphina gestured to the bonnet, and it wriggled along the ground toward her like a snuffling hedgehog. "Tell me about this exhibition first. Was it truly one of the Afflicted?" The bonnet made its way into the mage's lap, where she picked at the ribbons, undoing the tight knots Hannah had pulled.

"No. Wycliff got close enough to discover she breathed and was a living person." Hannah finally peeled the gloves from her hands and clutched them as she sat at her mother's feet.

Wycliff took a seat at the other end of the bower. "The man was inciting the crowd with tales of how the Afflicted would dine on their brains and how the undead looked like any one of them." Wycliff crossed his arms and sank into the shadows.

Hannah heaved a heavy sigh. The situation intolerable, but how could they allay the fears of

Londoners when one man seemed determined to terrify them?

"Oh, dear. We feared this might happen, which is why I have always smoothed away any rumours about Unwin and Alder or how the Afflicted sustain themselves. Fortunately, the public have little evidence to fuel their fear." Seraphina set the bonnet free, and it floated toward Hannah.

"Only rational men require evidence. People in the grip of anger and fear seize on empty words." Hannah stuffed her gloves in the bonnet and left it on the grass. She hugged her knees to her chest and tried to figure out how to stop panic spreading among the population.

"The reporter, Nash, is fuelling the fire with his stories. Unfortunately, he was not at his desk when we went to speak with him. Nor would I wish Hannah to return there. The mood of the room was somewhat hostile toward the Afflicted—and she was recognised." Wycliff's gaze lingered on Hannah.

She rather liked his protective side, as long as it didn't become too suffocating. If he thought to keep her safe in the countryside while people gathered pitchforks and torches to seek out the Afflicted, they would have words.

"I will create new moths to find and erase rumours, even if someone else hunts them out and shoots them down. It would be an easier task if there were something to distract popular opinion. What we need is a bigger scandal." Seraphina drew in the air as she spoke.

Flashes of angry crowds turned into people watching a troupe of entertainers.

"If Prince George did something outrageous, that would give them all something to talk about, but he has been reasonably well behaved this season. I dislike this turn of events with a man exhibiting a fake Afflicted woman. What will they do if they get their hands on one of the genuine Afflicted?" A memory surfaced in Hannah's mind, of Emma Knightley cutting herself for the entertainment of society bucks so she could earn the money to pay for her allotment of pickled cauliflower. What if another of the Afflicted offered herself up, to ensure she had the supplies to keep her body from rotting? Or worse, what if the mob abducted one and kept her hostage until she starved and became desperate?

"I will return to London to look for Nash. He is key. Someone is feeding him information, and I suspect it is the missing Unwin and Alder employee. Have you received any answer from the mage council?" Wycliff leaned forward, the fire still flashing in his eyes.

"Of sorts. They will investigate the use of mage fire to destroy the former Lady Albright. However, they do not think it necessary for me to meet with them, as they claim the fire was most likely a potion sold by any registered apothecary. I disagree and have insisted upon a meeting. I would look them in the eye as they squirm before me." A flame erupted in the palm of her outstretched hand, the white so pure it appeared to dance silver, as though she held a captive moonbeam.

Hannah's rage seeped from her veins and flowed away with the gentle burble of the creek. Behind it, a wave of sadness washed in. How many lives would be irrevocably altered before they dampened the fear stalking the streets?

"I shall return to my study of shadow mages and the underworld. Do you require Papa to carry you inside, Mother?" Hannah rose to her feet and brushed twigs and loose grass from her skirts.

"Not yet, thank you, dear. I believe it might rain. I shall wait for it." Seraphina picked up her book and returned to her reading.

Wycliff took Hannah's hand, and they walked to the house at a much slower pace.

"We must find a way to end things, before people are hurt or...destroyed like the former Lady Albright." Hannah paused by a towering beech, the bark on its trunk an unusual purple tone tinged with silver. As a girl, she marvelled at how they soaked up the magic used by her mother to grow so fast and tall. Each held a tiny spark of that power, and created a truly enchanted forest.

Wycliff clenched his fingers on the bark. "You still intend to walk the dark path with me." His voice choked on the words.

Hannah slid her arms around his middle. "With the passing of each day, I become more convinced it is the only way to find the answers we seek."

Wycliff leaned back against the tree and pulled Hannah closer. Under her cheek came the steady thrum of his heart. When hers stilled, his would have to beat for her, too.

"Give me time to find Nash first. We might yet defuse this situation and in time, people will forget why they ever feared the Afflicted." He stroked her hair as clouds piled up above them and the light dimmed with impending rain.

"A few days, but no more. The time has come to make that journey—together." She stared at the sharp angles of his face that had come to mean everything to her. Any fear she held about dying dimmed, as curiosity grew inside her. They would find a solution in the underworld. She was convinced of it. And if not, well, the Duat did not seem such a terrible place, from all she had read of it. There were worse places in which to spend the afterlife.

Such as a coffin deep in the earth.

13

LATE THAT NIGHT, rapping at the window woke Wycliff from slumber and Hannah stirred in his arms. He slipped from bed and grabbed a robe from the back of a chair as he strode to the window. He yanked the tie closed at his waist before pulling aside the curtain. An enormous owl with mottled brown and cream feathers and black ringed around its wide and unblinking amber eyes sat on the sill and peered at him.

"Is it Higgs?" Hannah murmured as she roused.

Wycliff opened the window and the bird hopped onto a side table, an envelope clutched in its beak. He took the missive with a heavy heart. Midnight visits from the Ministry secretary meant an urgent matter, and he doubted he would return to his bed this night.

The owl hooted but held its spot, as though expecting some sort of response...or possibly a mouse treat.

Wycliff extracted the piece of paper with its

scrawled note and swore under his breath. He glanced at the owl. "I'll be there immediately. Have someone guard the place and keep nosy onlookers back."

The owl hooted again and took flight, swooping through the open window to disappear into the dark.

"What is it?" Hannah leaned against his side to peer at the note.

"Another blue fire and incinerated remains. This time at the rear of the Fiddler's Theatre." He removed his robe and tossed it to a chair as he snatched up his clothing.

"You go on ahead by horseback. I shall follow with Papa in the carriage." Hannah took down the striped gown she had left hanging over the screen in the corner.

He placed a swift kiss on her lips and then shoved his feet into his trousers. Hannah dropped a shirt over his head and he needed to take a calming breath to find the armholes. Once he pulled on his Hessians, he ran down the stairs, tucking in his shirt as he went. By the rear vestibule, he did up his waistcoat buttons and grabbed an overcoat and hat. Then he hooked a lantern on his finger and lit the wick with a touch of hellfire as he walked out to the stables. The horses nickered as he approached, the swinging lantern and his tread having woken them from a light slumber.

Setting the lamp on the edge of the stall, he worked quickly to saddle the mare. "Sorry, girl. None of us are sleeping tonight," Wycliff murmured.

Wycliff blew out the lamp before leading the mare from the stables and leaping up into the saddle. He put his heels to the horse and struck off into the night. On the main road, he reached deep for the hellhound and used its night vision to bring the darkness into sharp focus and to ensure they didn't stumble and break either a leg or a neck.

He slowed the horse to a trot as they neared the pleasure centre of London and the swirl of traffic around Covent Garden. Despite the late hour, it was as alive and vibrant as an early morning fish market. Lights strung above their heads cast a yellow glow on all that passed below. Laughter swirled and strains of music reached his ears. People either bustled with purpose, or lingered for slow conversations on the edges of shadows.

Avoiding pedestrians and carriages, he turned his mount to the Fiddler's Theatre, which sat a gentle stroll away from the main entertainments. The playhouse occupied a small brick building at the end of a lane. The troupes at the Fiddler's performed lesser-known plays for smaller audiences. Wycliff rode around back to find a cluster of people gathered at the iron gates. He dismounted and handed his horse off to a Runner who acted as an impromptu guard.

"Sir Hugh Miles and Lady Wycliff will be here soon. Make sure they are allowed to pass," he instructed the Runner.

A dirty white and brown terrier sat by the fence, perhaps drawn by the odour wafting from beyond. Wycliff growled at it and the dog let out a whimper and then shot through the crowd. Wycliff pushed through and entered the cobbled courtyard at the rear of the theatre. Red brick buildings encircled them, some two or three storeys high, others lower and half-timbered. A wide flight of stairs ran up to a door on the second level of the theatre. Another and much wider doorway lay in the gloom cast by the stairs above it.

In the middle of the courtyard were the smouldering remains of a fire. Lanterns suspended from wires running between the buildings cast their pale light on the scene. Smoke still hung in the air and swirled around the lanterns. Wycliff choked back the bile that rushed up his throat at the sickly sweet yet sharp aroma. He didn't have to ask if another unfortunate had met their end here. The evidence of that tickled his nose.

The familiar tall, broad figure of Charlie Taylor stood to one side, and he hailed Wycliff. The Runner clasped his mitten-clad hands together, tonight covered in a forest green wool. "I had your man send for you immediately, Lord Wycliff. This looks the same as what we found at Bunhill Fields."

Wycliff nodded. The Bow Street Runner had proven his worth in this investigation. He walked around the pile and searched for clues. Drifts of smoke curled from the deeper clumps and dispersed on the night air. All the while, he considered who might have been incinerated—and why here?

The former Lady Albright had been disposed of in front of her family mausoleum, and he had assumed her husband had been responsible. Now they had another fire in an entirely different, and far more risky, location. Did Lord Albright have a list of people he was working through, or was another responsible for this crime? If this proved to be another Afflicted, could there be some gentlemen's agreement to help one another dispose of pesky former wives who refused to stay in their graves?

The fire had charred a roughly circular patch on the cobbles, some four feet in diameter. A half-burned shoe lay at the edge, perhaps kicked off in a scuffle. The heel had been destroyed, but the toe with its ornate and bejewelled buckle, a remnant from a bygone era, remained intact. Once again there was little left to identify their victim. From what he could see without poking into the mess, there were a few bone fragments at most.

"Did anybody see who did this?" Wycliff asked Taylor, standing at his shoulder.

"No. There's no performances at the Fiddler's this week, and the theatre was empty. Several people saw the blue and white flames and being not far away, the nosier and bolder ones came to investigate. Someone said a large black dog with red eyes ran away down the lane." The Runner gestured in the direction the beast had taken.

Wycliff sucked in a breath. A hellhound, or just a large stray living on the streets of London like the terrier he'd seen earlier?

"There wasn't much left by the time a group of men got here. One chap recognised the smell and found me. I posted a guard to keep everyone out, woke your man, and sent for you. Handy, his being an owl. Much quicker to deliver messages, I imagine." Taylor hovered upwind of the snatches of smoke.

Wycliff grunted. The individual who recognised the odour had probably been a soldier. Some reminders of the battlefields were etched into their minds until their last breath. Time could not dull their effects. As he considered his next move, a small group pushed through the gates. Hannah had control of her mother's bathchair, and Sir Hugh walked at her side.

The doctor crouched close to the pile to conduct a visual examination. "There's not much to go on, Wycliff. But let us hope somewhere in this is a fragment that might hold a clue."

Wycliff glanced at Lady Miles as she wheeled herself closer. Faces pressed between the railings surrounding the courtyard and whispers grew as more people gathered to stare at the dead mage.

"She's one of them Afflicted!" someone yelled, and gasps came from the others.

Another faceless Londoner cried, "I'm not wearing a hat!"

"Move them on, Taylor, before they cause trouble," Wycliff said to the Runner.

The man drew a short baton from his waistband and advanced on the assembled people. "Sod off, you lot!" he called as he banged on the railing.

Seraphina stretched her hands out over the edge of the charred pattern. A long minute of silence followed, and even the curious onlookers who remained seemed to hold their breath.

She shook her hands as if she dispelled something stuck to them before clasping them together in her lap. "Mage fire, once again. It burns intensely, then once its fuel has expired, snuffs itself out. This is the same method as was used on the former Lady Albright. While I will need to hold any bone Hugh finds for confirmation, I suspect someone is indeed targeting the Afflicted."

Wycliff glanced from his mother-in-law to his wife. Who would be next if the arsonist sought out the most visible of that community? He clenched his hands into fists. First, he needed to convince Parliament a crime had been committed. As Albright had so succinctly put it, one cannot murder someone who is already dead. Many of the lords were uncomfortable with the way Albright had treated his wife, but silently some probably wished for a solution that would clear the Afflicted from the drawing rooms of London.

"We cannot assume the victim was one of the Afflicted until Sir Hugh has examined the remains. It could yet be someone else. As Hannah often reminds me, hypothesise, then strategise." He said the words, but the churn in his gut told him otherwise. He had a bigger problem looming on the horizon and it was gaining on them fast.

"Don't let that undead thing near your brain!" someone yelled from behind the railing.

Wycliff turned and narrowed his gaze. Laughter

rippled through the assembled people, but no one was brave enough to own their words. Taylor and his man tried to move them on, but there were too many people wanting to prolong their evening of entertainment.

Sir Hugh joined him and muttered under his breath, "Damned ignorant fools."

The powerful mage murmured a few words and arched her hands, then swept them to one side toward the railing. A purple light shivered along the metal and people gasped and jumped back. An ethereal curtain hung over the length of the fence and rippled with tiny dots of silver light.

Wycliff arched an eyebrow at her. Since no one was crying out or dropping to the cobbles, he assumed the spell was mostly harmless.

"I have blocked their view with a simple shield to stop their prying. All they see is a mirror reflecting their own faces. Nor can their words penetrate the shield, and we can work without their shouted nonsense." She wheeled herself toward her husband and gestured Wycliff closer. "I dislike this, Wycliff. Let us not forget the newspaper articles. While I set free my moth-like spells to disperse rumours, another works against them. Unwin and Alder have become a leaky boat and I find I cannot plug the holes anymore. If someone finds a jar of pickled cauliflower, I fear it will be the spark to a powder keg."

He cast around, staring at the confused faces who could no longer watch the spectacle. Did someone among them watch to see if the discontent and fear they spread took root? Did Nash linger out there, penning his next scandalous story?

"There is at least one man working against us, two if we include the missing Unwin and Alder employee. But I wonder if their strings are pulled by another. Let us discuss this fully back at Westbourne Green."

Seraphina nodded and wheeled herself to the smouldering remains.

Hannah returned from the carriage with a box and set it on the ground at the edge of the pile. "Could you make the ashes cool enough to handle, please, Mother?"

The mage held her hands before her face and whispered, then she opened them and blew over her palms. A white mist swirled toward the remains and then shook itself out until it resembled a blanket. Then it dropped over the patch with a soft hiss.

Hannah picked up what appeared to be a fireside set to shovel up the ash and bone. Wycliff retrieved the shoe and held it up to a lantern, turning it this way and that. Something about it itched at his mind. When he glanced at Hannah, the thought coalesced. She had pulled her skirts close to keep them clear of the soot. Doing so exposed her booted feet. The soft leather laced up past her ankles and overall, her shoes were much smaller than the one Wycliff held.

"I think this is a man's shoe," he said.

Sir Hugh let out a puff of breath. "More likely it is a large woman with big feet. There is only one male Afflicted we know of who resides within the confines of London and not...elsewhere."

Wycliff didn't need the reminder of the rotting beasts who prowled their iron cages deep under the Repository of Forgotten Things. Those sad creatures could not control their appetites and were prone to dashing open people's heads to scoop out their brains. If there was only one man who had the self-control to walk among the living, and this was indeed one of the Afflicted, he wouldn't have to look too far to identify his victim.

While Hannah worked, he took notes of the scene and gathered the names of those who had arrived there first from Taylor. Unfortunately, they had little information to aid his investigation. The fire had consumed most of its victim by the time people arrived in the courtyard, and they had only witnessed the flames extinguishing themselves. Nor could they offer any more detail about the large dog they had seen running away. Two men argued about every aspect of it, from size and shape to colour.

"It was a hellhound, I swear, with death in its eyes," one man said.

"Rubbish. It was a mangy mastiff," another contradicted his friend.

Wycliff scribbled down the differing accounts. If a three-headed flaming beast had sauntered past them with a soul in its jaws, surely it would have stuck in their minds despite the alcohol they had consumed?

Before they left, Wycliff approached Taylor. "Good work. My thanks for summoning me quickly. Haver you had any success in finding the missing William Peters?"

The larger man rubbed a hand over the back of his neck and stifled a yawn. "None yet, milord, but I have eyes on the street. If he's still in London, we'll find him."

Once they had retrieved all that remained from the fire, they returned to Westbourne Green. Back inside the house, they placed the box on the kitchen table. Sir Hugh prised off the lid and reached in to pull out a chunk of bone. Seraphina held it in her hands and then let out a heavy sigh. "Yes. It is one of the Afflicted."

"There is no point returning to bed—it will be light soon. Why don't I put the kettle on and we can discuss what to do next?" Hannah set about stoking the range and filling the kettle.

In contrast to the way they gathered at Mireworth, no one seemed comfortable sitting in the kitchen. Close to London, Wycliff felt the pull of society's conventions and constrictions. It simply wasn't the done thing to sit at the servants' table.

"Why don't I take our victim here to the library?" Sir Hugh picked up the box and set it on Seraphina's lap, then pushed the bathchair through the doorway.

Hannah set out a tray with a teapot, cups, and biscuits, and Wycliff carried it through to the library. Outside, dawn roused itself and the faintest blush of colour, like the work of a hesitant artist, crept over the horizon.

Wycliff took a quick sip of tea as he gathered his thoughts. "I agree with Lady Miles. What we have is more than an angry husband disposing of an inconvenient former wife. Unless there is a club of nobles intent on ridding themselves of Afflicted relatives, I cannot see it as a coincidence that a reporter is exposing the work of Unwin and Alder. We also have the mystery of their employee, Peters, who worked on both people featured in the paper and who has now disappeared."

"Someone wishes to expose all our secrets to the harsh light of day," Seraphina said.

Sir Hugh sat next to his wife and held a delicate teacup in one enormous hand. "The upper levels of society have always been divided. But enough lords have one of the Afflicted in their families to extend their protection to all of you. Soon, I fear, a title alone will not be enough protection. There are a growing number of young men at our lectures with many impertinent questions. They goad each other and laugh at our answers."

"What sort of impertinent questions?" A small marble of an idea rattled around the hollow inside Wycliff.

Sir Hugh pulled his bushy eyebrows together. "What stops the undead from rotting? How do they heal their wounds? What farm produces all the cauliflower—particularly out of season? What would happen if the Afflicted attacked an innocent person?"

"Such questions skate too close to many secrets we keep about the Afflicted." Hannah paused in sipping her hot drink. "Does Sir Manly know anything that might assist in finding the root cause of this agitation?"

Wycliff shook his head. If anyone secretly wanted action against the Afflicted, surely they would ask the Ministry of Unnaturals' sole investigator to round them up? Unless they knew his conflict of interest and didn't want to alert the most powerful mage in all of England to their plan.

"I smell a conspiracy. We see the marionettes moving upon the stage, but must follow the strings to reveal the hand that controls them," Seraphina said.

Blast. Wycliff preferred Albright as the disgruntled murderer of his former wife. Now he needed to cast a wider net. Although Albright might still provide crucial information. Someone had targeted his former wife and knew to watch her movements. They also knew her husband was the last person to raise a fuss about her being scorched from the earth.

14

Later that morning, the family gathered in the dining room for breakfast. A sombre mood hung over them after the previous night's discovery. Hannah tackled the issue of who might have owned the shoe and wracked her brain to identify the tallest among the women Afflicted who might wear such a size.

"'The Afflicted cannot escape God's judgement.'" Wycliff read the headline aloud and then tossed the scandal sheet to the table with a snort. "Another inflammatory piece from Nash to add fuel to the unrest."

"How does he know it was one of the Afflicted? Seraphina discerned it from the bone, but we said nothing anyone could have overheard last night." Sir Hugh stared at the paper from under bushy eyebrows.

Hannah picked it up. "This was written by the same man who wrote the articles exposing the work of Unwin and Alder. He is a reporter who does not rely on facts, but who crafts his own version of the truth." She glanced across the table to Wycliff, who ground his teeth. She suspected her husband planned an unpleasant interview for Mr Nash. Truth be told, she did not want Wycliff to temper his behaviour with the person who wrote such horrid things about the victims of the blue fire. "I shall refrain from attending when you speak to him. I think this matter is best discussed between the two of you."

Hannah read the article and then passed the paper to her mother.

After reading the article that detailed how the Afflicted were akin to demons polluting the London air, Seraphina waved a hand and the newspaper rose into the air before scrunching itself into a tight ball. Then with a *pop*, it exploded, distributing tiny specks of paper that hung in the air like dandelion fluff.

"Temper, Sera," Sir Hugh muttered as he picked a sliver of paper off his toast.

"He has written a load of utter rubbish that will provoke more fear in the general population and turn them against us. Nobles cannot afford to ignore the opinion of the people. Look what happened in France when the aristocrats did that." Seraphina drew her hands through the air and gathered up the dots of paper before directing them to an empty fruit bowl.

"Which is no doubt the reporter's intention. Or certainly that of whoever pays him to write such nonsense," Wycliff said.

"Perhaps I shall accompany Wycliff when he talks to the man," Seraphina mused. "I am sure between the two of us we can extract the truth of the matter." The dots of paper burst into a pure white flame and when it extinguished itself, only a black smear stained the porcelain bowl.

"We must not descend to the same tactics as whoever moves against us." Hannah glared from her mother to her husband. Never did she think these two would become accomplices.

"All this nonsense talk of Cerberus claiming escaped souls to send to Hell...honestly. Mark my words, this is nothing otherworldly. There is a very mortal hand at work." Seraphina bristled, the linen undulating over her body as she contained her rage.

"Several witnesses saw a large black dog run from the theatre last night, which adds more fuel to that fire. I don't know if it is another hellhound, a lycanthrope, or merely some ugly mastiff out for a walk." Wycliff poured more coffee into his cup and took a long drink. "The only thing the drunk mob agrees upon was that it had one head, not three. So it cannot be Cerberus."

"But it could have been a hound sent by Anubis." Hannah spent most of her time in the library, reading anything she could find about Duat, the Egyptian afterlife where souls journeyed to be judged.

Mary appeared at the doorway and then crept in, holding a sheaf of letters. "These arrived this morning, milady." She passed them to Seraphina.

The mage took the pile and sorted through them,

glancing at the handwriting and turning them over to see the sender's name. Then she broke the seal on one sheet and read the note. It was discarded, and she opened the next.

Hannah grew curious as papers littered the table. "Whatever is it, Mother?"

"Here. They are all similar in content." Her mother passed the letter in her hand to Hannah.

"'I beg of you, extend your protection to me. I have lived a good and honourable life and have done nothing to deserve the fires of Hell...'" Hannah's voice faltered. A circular stain smeared the ink. The author had shed a tear as she pleaded for help.

"They are from the Afflicted, afraid that something hunts us in the dark and will drag our souls to Hell. Or more likely, they are terrified to be consigned to the flames, unable to die but only to...cease to exist." Seraphina laid the last letter on the table and smoothed out a crease in one corner.

"Today I will try again to hunt down Mr Nash." Wycliff gulped the last of his coffee.

"I can assist there, with a finding spell. If you anchor one end at his desk, a red thread will appear that will lead you straight to him," Seraphina said.

"Excellent. I have a suspicion he is avoiding me." Wycliff turned to Hannah. "If you are able to confirm the deceased was indeed a male Afflicted, it shouldn't take too much time to discover the latest victim's identity."

"I'll assist Papa with the examination." Hannah

placed the sheet of paper in her hand on top of the others. Until they found whoever was responsible, she feared the pile would only continue to grow.

Sir Hugh stared at the stack of letters. "After Hannah and I have finished, there are a few gentlemen I will call upon this afternoon. One or two are highly placed in the House of Lords, and are sheltering an Afflicted daughter under their roof. I will determine what they are doing to ensure they can charge the perpetrator with some crime. They must act to dampen the panic spreading on the streets."

"I will construct a protection spell for these poor women to ease their mental torment. I think some sort of token that will screech if they are rendered insensible might work to alert anyone near them." Seraphina gathered up the letters and dropped them into her lap.

With their day planned, the family set about their tasks. Hannah followed her father down the dim stairs to his laboratory. She grabbed her apron from its hook by the door and then angled the mirrors to cast a bright shaft of light on the table. Once again, they emptied the box onto the table and undertook the tedious task of sorting bone fragments from the soot-like matter too far gone to aid identification.

They treated everything with respect, and Hannah ensured that not a single speck of ash dropped to the floor. Whatever she had gathered was all that remained of a person who had once walked the earth. Someone who perhaps loved and laughed. The shoe with its glittering buckle sat to one side and made her think of the tale of Cinderella. Whose foot fit inside the shoe? Though no prince awaited the owner, only the certainty of a name to carve into a tombstone and a family to mourn a loved one's passing.

Sir Hugh picked up the pelvic bones and brushed away the soot and charring. "Wycliff was correct about the shoe. Our victim is a man this time."

Hannah sucked in a breath. There were so few male Afflicted, and most resided beneath the Repository of Forgotten Things, unable to control their urges. It would take no time at all to determine if one were missing. "How odd that in both fires, sufficient pelvic bone remained to enable us to narrow down the identity. Do you think it was deliberate?"

Her father peered at her over the rims of his spectacles. "The pelvis is a large structure in the centre of the body. It might be the result of how the fire consumes— from the extremities to the core. If whoever did this truly wanted us to know their victim's identity, then a note with a name would be much easier, given how completely mage fire destroys an earthly form."

Hannah shuddered. Two horrors lingered in her mind, and she couldn't decide which fate was worse. One was to be consumed by fire, unable to either escape or die, but held captive in excruciating pain until enough of the body were irreparably turned to soot. The other nightmare was to awaken trapped in a coffin, to claw against the wood for hundreds of years.

That idea reminded her of Kemsit, the shadow mage. Did she pound on the lid of her sarcophagus, demanding to be let out, or had her soul travelled to the underworld centuries ago?

Her father cleared his throat and held up a charred tibia. "I say, Hannah, there is an old break here. Whoever this chap was, in life he broke a leg at some point. You can see how the bone has healed, but there is a misalignment. I wonder if it affected his gait."

"A male Afflicted, found burned at a theatre, who might have limped?" Hannah added together the three clues and sorted through her memory for a name. "There is only one person that matches such a description—Mr Oliver Berridge. He possesses all those attributes. I think he broke his leg in a tumble from the stage one night, as he was an actor."

"Let us finish our work here. I'm sure Wycliff can find out if he is still limping around his home or is missing." Her father fetched a fresh sheet of paper on which to record their few findings and to jot down the measurements of the remaining bone.

Hannah stared at the remains as she took up the pencil and handed her father the tape measure. Who would do this? Or indeed, how did they arrive at their potential list of suspects? The trouble was, many men were vocal that the Afflicted should be expunged from the earth by cleansing fire. Wycliff had even once professed such ideas.

HANNAH CHECKED the ledger of the Afflicted they kept in the library and confirmed that to their knowledge, only one male Afflicted resided in London—and indeed it was Oliver Berridge. Then she journeyed into London with Wycliff, he to chase the reporter to find who had slipped him the information on donors to Unwin and Alder, and Hannah to undertake two sad tasks. One involved the wooden box next to her in the carriage. She rested one hand atop it.

"I can come with you when you return the remains of the former Lady Albright to her cousin and to ascertain if Berridge is at home." Wycliff spoke in a low tone and the words whispered over her.

Hannah patted the box. "No. I will perform these visits alone, but thank you. You must find Mr Nash and I cannot assist with that task."

He nodded and rapped on the roof of the carriage to signal Frank to stop. As the carriage slowed, Wycliff placed a tender kiss on Hannah's lips. "Promise me you will keep Frank close. I do not like the mood on the street. I will attend Parliament this evening and will see you later tonight in Westbourne Green. But signal me if you require my assistance and I will meet you at the Ministry offices if I am able."

He referred to the way they could make the other person's wedding ring tingle if they thought of their spouse while stroking the gold band—a simple device Hannah's mother had created to enable a rudimentary communication between them. In the future, she hoped to allow them direct conversation over a distance. Ensorcelled paper was an option, but one hardly had time to sit down and pen a letter in the middle of a chase or urgent situation.

"I promise to use Frank as a shield." A sad smile flitted across her face.

Wycliff jumped down to the pavement and headed into the newspaper office. Hannah leaned back in the seat and stared at her silent companion. "I hope you have found peace, Lady Albright, and that you are reunited with your son."

Frank steered the carriage along the busy roads. At every crossroads, somebody shouted about the Afflicted and how they were a plague upon London. That made Hannah scoff. Only about two-thirds of the three hundred Afflicted purchased their product from Unwin and Alder. Rats were far more plentiful in London and carried a greater risk of disease.

A few pedestrians wore old-fashioned metal helmets, as though they were about to don the rest of their armour and ride a charger into battle against anyone who might steal their brains.

"I imagine blacksmiths are doing a brisk trade in metal headwear," Hannah murmured to herself as they passed. "How heavy a metal bonnet must be."

Protestors diminished as they moved into the quieter and more genteel neighbourhood where Mrs Hamilton lived. Frank helped Hannah out of the carriage and then picked up the box in his enormous hands.

"I can manage, Frank, thank you." Hannah took the object from him and tucked it against her hip. Hannah wasn't sure she should add a monstrous delivery boy to the burden Mrs Hamilton carried.

Fortunately, the maid opened the door as Hannah walked up the path and bobbed a curtsey as she entered the house.

"Mrs Hamilton is in the parlour, milady. Can I carry the box for you?" She held out her hands to take the container.

"No. It's not heavy." The mage fire left little to mourn or bury.

Mrs Hamilton pushed off the sofa to stand and her greeting never made it past her lips. Her eyes widened at seeing the object Hannah carried. One hand went to her chest. "Is that...?"

Hannah placed the box on a side table next to the sofa. "This is all that remains, yes. Please let me know if you plan any service. I should like to attend."

Mrs Hamilton gestured to the sofa and waited for Hannah to take a seat before resuming her own. "He was here. Asking about..." Her attention drifted to the wooden container.

With some difficulty, Hannah swallowed her ill feelings about Lord Albright, for that was who *he* must be. "Perhaps he wanted to pay his final respects?"

A loud snort came from the older woman. "He would tip her into a dustbin. I still think he did it. Who else would want to harm a hair on her head?"

A sentiment Hannah shared. "Lord Wycliff

continues his investigation, especially after another body was burned last night at the Fiddler's Theatre."

"I read about that in the newspaper. Is it true? Do you think that someone is targeting those unfortunates?" Mrs Hamilton perched on the edge of her seat.

The maid entered carrying a tea tray. She stared at the wooden box and chose a different table on which to set down the tray.

"I do not wish to think so, but I fear what will happen if the scandal sheets continue to turn public opinion against the Afflicted." Hannah clasped her hands in her lap and willed herself not to tighten her grip. People who acted out of fear abandoned any common sense. The hideous murders of six months ago that had stolen lives had been, unfortunately, committed by two Afflicted who could not control their hunger. Thankfully, the reporter had not got wind of the full extent of *those* horrors, or the homes of the Afflicted would be stormed by a frightened mob and women would be pulled from their parlours and burned in the streets.

Mrs Hamilton poured tea and handed a cup to Hannah. "It is such a dreadful curse to live with—being neither dead nor fully alive. My cousin wrote to another mage, you know, begging for a cure. I know your mother is trying her best, but she wondered if a living mage might be able to restore her heartbeat."

A blast of indignation swirled through Hannah. No mage worked harder than her mother to find a cure for the Afflicted. Then a strand of curiosity brushed aside the heated emotion. If one type of mage snuffed out a life, could their opposite restore it? If a living mage had created the curse that stole so many lives, perhaps what they needed was a shadow mage to rescue those souls from the twilight world in which they dwelt.

"Do you know who your cousin corresponded with?" Hannah sipped her tea. The hot drink soothed nerves she hadn't realised were on edge from having to undertake the grim task of delivering the charred remnants of the former Lady Albright.

"I don't recollect if she told me. Although the answer sent her into a right temper, which was so unusual for her. I might be able to find it among her letters." Mrs Hamilton put down her tea and walked to a small writing desk. Above it hung a painting of a rural landscape with a stream where weeping willows dipped their boughs into the water. The scene reminded Hannah of the day she'd strolled along the river with Wycliff after the summer shearing.

Hannah let out a sigh. She missed Mireworth, and they had only been home in Westbourne Green less than two weeks. How had the old estate squirmed into her affections with such ease and speed?

Mrs Hamilton took a seat at the desk. At the rear were wooden slots crammed with letters, notes, and cards. She picked up a pile and sorted through it, glancing at each before slipping it into the back of the pile and examining the next. "Not in here." When she had searched all the slots and the papers left on the desk, she turned her attention to the drawers.

Hannah drank her tea and found anticipation building inside her. What would the letter reveal? Who had Lady Albright turned to in her quest for a cure? Lady Miles had never mentioned any of the living mages studying the Affliction, but who knew what arcane magic they studied in their tall tower at the military base in Woolwich.

A drawer rattled but refused to budge. "This one is locked. Let me see...ha!" Mrs Hamilton extracted a small key from inside a slender vase on the corner of the desk.

Hannah placed her teacup on the table and edged forward as Mrs Hamilton took a bundle of documents from the locked drawer. Once again she sorted through them until she found a particular piece of paper.

"Here we are. Although I don't know how it might help you to discover who did this to Felicity." Mrs Hamilton passed over the letter.

Hannah glanced at the scant two lines of text, and then her eye went to the bottom and the signature that took up most of the page. A cold ocean poured into the space where hope and curiosity had been. With an effort, she dragged her attention back to the lines of text.

DEATH BEGETS DEATH, *and it is no surprise that woman cannot cure you.*

Your kind are a plague upon London that should be burned from this earth.
James Tomlin

"Oh, DEAR," Hannah whispered.

15

Wycliff hopped to the pavement with his own task to complete while Hannah visited Mrs Hamilton. With the ensorcelled thread in his pocket, Wycliff strode up the steps of the bustling newspaper office. This time he didn't stop to ask for Nash to be pointed out to him. He crossed the floor to the desk in the corner. Today the tea appeared stone cold and the papers in some semblance of order.

"He hasn't been in yet today," a man called from his desk.

Wycliff huffed. Nash must have put in an appearance to hand in the story about the burned body at the theatre. But what if he had written it in advance? If someone at Unwin and Alder had told him which funerals to stalk, perhaps another informant could have told him who would be consumed next by mage fire. Each day the number of people involved grew, which had to work in his favour. As the old adage said, the only way three people could keep a secret was if two of them were dead. Someone would talk. All he had to do was pull the right loose thread for it all to unravel.

The first one he would pull was the short length of thread in his pocket. In all regards, it looked ordinary, some eight inches long and dark red. How, he wondered, would it lead him to the reporter? Wycliff did as instructed and tied the cotton to something Nash had touched—the handle of the teacup. His hand slid back into his pocket to retrieve the paper with the odd inscription on it, and he whispered the words in the unknown tongue.

As he uttered the last word, the teacup rattled. The thread wriggled and jiggled to the point he worried it might untie itself. Then a spectral red light flared up and pooled by the ceiling like smoke unable to escape. Lady Miles had said only he would be able to see the tracking thread. The mist shimmered and congealed, then it broke into a tangled line like a ball of unwound wool. One end picked itself loose and drew circles in the air, rather like a bloodhound that went around and around until it settled on the scent. Then a red arrow shot across the room and out the door.

Wycliff took off after the phantom arrow and its tail. Down the stairs it flew and out into the street. Pedestrians walked through the line and it dissolved, turning into a red mist, but enough of it remained intact to show him the way. Across the street he trotted, along lanes, then zigzagging back to the other side of the road. He followed the trail of a crimson will-o'-the-wisp. Just as he wondered how far away it would lead him, it bounced up a set of stairs, snaked around an open doorway and into a lodging house.

Inside, Wycliff paused while his eyes adjusted to the dim lighting. From somewhere above came the scream of a fractious baby, and a woman yelled at a man. Furniture crashed, a door slammed, and a heavy tread raced along the hall. The tracking thread headed up the narrow stairs, weaving its way through the railings to avoid a man hurrying down.

Wycliff stepped to one side to let the fleeing figure pass. On the second floor, the thread dropped to the ground and turned into a caterpillar. It inched its way along the hall to the door at the end and slipped underneath.

"Got you," Wycliff murmured, then he rapped on the door.

A scrape came from within, then the door cracked open an inch and a bleary eye regarded him. Before his quarry could slam the door, Wycliff put his shoulder to it and forced it open.

"I've been waiting to talk to you, Nash. You're a hard man to pin down." Wycliff closed the door and leaned against it.

Nash was short and wiry, and reminded him of a hungry rodent that would put up quite the fight despite its small size. The man stalked across the room to put distance between them, and he spread his hands as though about to take flight.

"Lord Wycliff. I heard you'd been asking for me,

but I'm a busy man. I was on my way out, so we'll have to postpone our little chat." Nash picked up a battered leather satchel from the table and then gestured to the door and Wycliff, as though expecting him to move out of the way.

Which he didn't.

Wycliff drew in a slow breath through his nose and took in the messy surroundings. The room was on the large size for such lodgings, with an unmade double bed in one corner. Two armchairs sat before a cold fireplace. A square table had four chairs around it and books and papers piled to one side. The single window looked over the street and the drift of noise floated up. It was obvious a bachelor lived in the room. Clothes were strewn about, two drawers pulled open, and plates with the remains of congealed dinners were stacked in the middle of the table.

He'd start with an easy question. "What happened to Peters?"

"Who?" Nash held his gaze and didn't blink.

"The man who works for Unwin and Alder. Who slipped you the names of whose funerals to attend." While Wycliff didn't know for sure if Peters had met Nash the day he disappeared, it was a safe bet the two men had been in cahoots at some point.

The reporter's lips narrowed to a thin line, and he shrugged. "Don't know him."

"Shall we try another name? Like whoever is paying you to spread your salacious stories?" It was a long shot, but one never knew which question might elicit a response.

The reporter's hands twitched and tightened on the satchel, and he broke eye contact. "You married Lady Miles' daughter and reside under the same roof with the mage. What's it like sharing a house with one of those dead things? Do you wear an iron hat to bed, to make sure your brain stays in your cranium?"

Wycliff's lip pulled up in a snarl and he could feel the hound creeping over his skin, waiting for him to let it off the leash.

"I bet you know all about what they eat to sustain them. You're an investigator for the Ministry of Unnaturals—you should be hunting them to keep the rest of us safe." Nash grew bolder with the success of his attack. "But then, you lot all stick together. All those noble women dining on the brains of the common folk. It shouldn't be allowed. We should follow the French example—rise up and overthrow the toffs. Then all those dead women will be where they belong—six feet under. Or their ashes scattered on the wind at a crossroads."

Wycliff closed his eyes and allowed the hellhound the control of his features. He opened his eyes and the room around him shimmered with a grey mist, punctuated by a bright red shaft of sunlight from the window. "The Afflicted harm no one. Unlike your rabble rousing. I assure you, Nash, you don't want to get on my bad side."

The newspaper man sucked in a breath and took a

step back. Then he stared at Wycliff with renewed interest. "What are you? You're not dead like them. Wolf? You growl like one, and I know a few of your sort were made during the war."

"I will be your worst nightmare if you don't become much more cooperative about who is feeding you information." He let the heat drip over him and fangs extended in his jaw.

Nash swallowed and clutched the satchel to his chest. He trod backward until he bumped into the table. "You'll get nothing from me. Turn into a wolf if you want, but there are those I fear more than you. You can either join us or them, on a bonfire. We'll have a wicker man no one will ever forget."

Wycliff ignored the comment about making a wicker man of the Afflicted and stalked toward Nash, who compressed his spine and shrank before him. "You fear someone more than I?"

Part of him was insulted that the reporter didn't immediately divulge who had given him fodder for his stories. What could invoke more fear in the man than a hellhound about to snuffle out his soul from his physical form?

The answer flowed into his mind and swirled with the lava in his veins. "He's a mage."

Nash's eyes widened, then he ran. Wycliff had moved away from the door and given the man an opening. He sprinted for the doorway, flung it open, and scrabbled across the landing to make his exit.

Wycliff considered pursuing the man. He could

catch him on the stairs. But what would it achieve? Let him run like a startled rabbit. Since he now stood alone in the room, he would use the opportunity. Pulling out a chair, Wycliff seated himself at the table and began reading the scribbled notes and balled-up pieces of paper. Due to Nash's messy habits, it didn't take long to find the screwed-up missives. One note had the name of Mrs Kelly and the details of the funeral. Another piece of paper, in a different hand, mentioned Fiddler's Theatre.

Folding up the notes, Wycliff placed them in his pocket. At least two more people were involved. Three, if a mage had not written either note. He suspected the one about Mrs Kelly would prove to be in Peters' hand.

He descended the stairs at a slow pace, gathering his thoughts and his temper. Nash had fled, but where could he go? Wycliff now knew where he lived and worked. If he didn't turn in his stories, he wouldn't earn his pay, nor would he advance his master's plot against the Afflicted.

A mage. Someone within the mage council sought to erase the unfortunate women and men. He would need to tell Lady Miles. Could this be why the council refused to allow her to address them?

He wandered back through the busy roads, when a tall figure reached out a hand and tapped his shoulder, pulling him out of the dense mist of possibilities in his mind.

"Lord Wycliff? I was on my way to find you."

Taylor danced back a step to let a mother dragging two children go past.

"Taylor. You have news?" Wycliff would add to the man's tasks. He needed someone to keep an eye on Nash and tell him who the man associated with over the course of his day.

"Yes. We found Peters." The Bow Street Runner fell into step beside Wycliff.

There was one piece of good news for the day. "Excellent. I need to confirm a few things with him."

"There's a problem with that." The Runner's face performed a contortion. "We pulled him out of the Thames this morning."

"Damn it." This investigation was nothing but false leads and dead ends. "Do you know the cause of death? Did he have anything on him?"

"I had his body taken to a doctor not far away." Taylor waved down the road and the two men began walking in that direction. "There's nothing obvious as to why Peters died, or not that we saw from handling him."

"Do you know Nash, the reporter?" Wycliff asked.

"I know him. Seen him about a bit. He's the one penning those stories about the...Afflicted." Taylor bent his head closer to whisper the last word.

Wycliff hoped the Runner wasn't succumbing to the creeping fear that pervaded the streets. "That's the one. Can you have someone watch him? I want to know if he is talking to anyone unusual."

"Unusual? You mean like an Unnatural?" Taylor

rubbed his mitten-clad hands together. Today he wore dark grey ones that matched his long coat.

"I'm not sure who I mean. Watch for anyone out of the ordinary for a reporter to be sidling up next to. I believe someone else is behind the articles and I want to find out who. He was rather uncooperative when I spoke to him, and there was a glint of fear in his eyes when I asked who controlled him." It still astonished him that the man had expressed a greater fear of that unknown hand than of a hellhound.

Taylor snorted. "Not sure I want to meet the creature that can put fear into that one. Given what he does to get his stories, I didn't think he could feel anything."

They turned into a narrow lane, and then Taylor stopped at a gate in the stone wall and cracked it open. They entered the rear yard of a tall house, the ground before them bare, compacted earth. Washing was strung on a line that spanned the narrow space. Hunkered into the ground and huddled with its back to the stone wall sat a squat building like a root cellar or cool store. Taylor rapped on the door, and in a moment an older man pulled it open.

Wispy white hair was plastered to his skull and small gold spectacles perched on the very end of his nose. He peered over the rims to look first at Taylor and then Wycliff, before he stepped back to admit them. "I'm nearly done, Taylor. He can be collected by his family today."

"This is Doctor Thurlow, milord. He attends

people hereabouts and agreed to take a look at your man for us," Taylor said by way of introduction.

The cellar had been converted to a small autopsy or treatment room. The wall of shelves that should have held preserves contained bottles and vials such as an apothecary would stock. A single slab of stone sat in the middle of the room. Lanterns hung from the low ceiling to illuminate the deceased, and Wycliff had to duck to avoid hitting them as he neared.

A foul odour similar to that of rotting fish wafted off the man and assaulted Wycliff's nostrils.

"He's not fresh, so let's not linger too long over him, gentlemen," Doctor Thurlow said.

"Do you know how long he's been dead?" Wycliff wished they could have done the examination in the cleaner and brighter rooms of Sir Hugh, but appreciated that Taylor had acted quickly. Without evidence of Peters being an Unnatural or dying at the hands of one, Wycliff couldn't pull the death under the Ministry's jurisdiction and involve his father-in-law.

"Given the state of him, he's been in the water for a week," the doctor replied.

"Cause of death?" Wycliff asked as the doctor folded down the sheet.

A dark red scar spread across Peters' chest and then down his sternum to his navel, the two sides held together by regular stitches of black thread.

"Drowned. I found water in his lungs." The doctor stared at the man's form.

So he had been alive when he went in, then. "No

other marks or injuries?" Wycliff scanned the body, but the autopsy scar seemed the only major affront to him. A few bruises and scrapes could easily be explained by the action of the tide banging the body against obstacles under the surface of the murky Thames.

"Most of the scrapes are post mortem and happened after he hit the water. There is a slight bump on his head, but I can't tell when it occurred." The doctor pulled back a lock of hair to show it. "It's not a large wound and wouldn't have killed him."

"But could it have rendered him unconscious?" The ability to swim wouldn't have saved Peters if he had been knocked out before he was tossed into the Thames.

"Possible. Unfortunately, it's not uncommon for the Runners to haul a body from the Thames. Most people can't swim, and a few too many drinks and a tumble can prove fatal." The doctor picked up the corpse's hands and placed them over his chest. Then he shook out the sheet and spread it back over the man.

A flash of blue caught Wycliff's eye. "Wait." He put his hand on the sheet and leaned closer. "Here. What is this?"

On the back of the man's left hand was a blue squiggle.

The doctor lifted the arm and turned the man's hand toward the light. "Paint? He might have rubbed against a boat hull."

"It doesn't look like paint to me, and a week in the Thames would have washed it away." Wycliff stared at the mark. "It's a tattoo." An odd thing to permanently inscribe into one's skin. It seemed like the scribble of an artist testing his brush. It might be important, or it could be nothing. Wycliff pulled out his notebook and copied the curls and twists of the symbol.

"He might have belonged to a gang as a lad. Some of them ink themselves as a way of recognising each other," Taylor said.

"Perhaps. But I'm not discounting any clue." Wycliff tucked the notebook away. "Thank you, Doctor Thurlow."

He left the close atmosphere of the stone-walled room and stepped back into the light and comparatively fresh air of London.

Taylor pulled the door to the cellar shut behind him. "I'll go tell Mrs Peters and arrange for the body to be delivered to her. Then I'll set some of the lads to watching that reporter for you."

Wycliff nodded his thanks. The Runner proved his worth as an assistant daily. Now if only he could pull all the loose threads together and discover who sought to remove the Afflicted from London.

16

Hᴀɴɴᴀʜ sᴛᴀʀᴇᴅ at the missive in her hand. Lord Tomlin, the mage grandfather of gentle Timmy, had poured onto the page that he wished the Afflicted burned from the earth. Had he created mage fire to achieve his goal?

"Dreadful thing to say to a woman who only wanted her life back. I can understand why such a rude response provoked my cousin's temper." Mrs Hamilton picked up a biscuit and bit into it.

Hannah tapped the letter against her palm. "Lord Tomlin is not sympathetic to the plight of the Afflicted. Might I hold on to this?"

"Of course, if you think it would be of any assistance." The older woman passed the plate of biscuits to Hannah.

Hannah stayed a little longer and promised to attend the service to inter with her baby son all that remained of the former Lady Albright. The letter from

Mage Tomlin lay heavy in her reticule. She needed to speak to her mother. Who better to provide mage fire to their unknown attacker than the man who believed the Afflicted were a plague upon London?

But first, there was another task on her short list—to determine whether Mr Oliver Berridge was taking his tea in his home, or sitting in a box in her father's laboratory.

At their next destination, Frank climbed down from his perch and helped her from the carriage. Barnes clung to the seat in a lookout position. The spell binding the two remained in place, as the disembodied hand seemed to enjoy his outings to London. Or perhaps Frank preferred not to leave his rival alone in the house with Mary. Although Hannah suspected Barnes had become rather enamoured of Mrs Rossett during their time at Mireworth.

"Keep. Watch," Frank intoned in his slow drawl.

"Thank you, Frank. I suspect I shall not be too long." Hannah glanced up at the town house in the quiet street. Constructed around a square, all the homes looked over the central green space where children played, while a nanny sat on a bench under a tree. The street had a peaceful air as the last days of summer unfolded.

Hannah rapped on the polished black door and composed herself.

A footman opened the door, and the ghost of a smile flicked over his lips. "May I help you, ma'am?"

"Is Mr Oliver Berridge at home?" She hoped the

answer was yes, but the turmoil in her stomach predicted the response would be no.

The footman's hand tightened on the door. "No. I am sorry, ma'am, but he is not home at present."

At that moment, a man wearing a trailing robe in bright blue with gold embroidery appeared in the foyer. His eyes widened on seeing her. "Lady Wycliff!" he exclaimed. "Do come in."

Hannah knew the gentleman—Brandon Trayling, Mr Berridge's live-in companion. He clutched a hand-kerchief between his hands and his silver hair was dishevelled, as though he had pulled at it all night. Somewhere in his late fifties, he maintained a trim figure and possessed a face with excellent bone structure and few wrinkles. Hannah imagined that many a woman of a similar age would be jealous of how the dandy kept signs of ageing at bay. Not to mention his outstanding fashion sense that made the couple a much-loved addition to any evening.

"Good day, Mr Trayling. I am most concerned about Mr Berridge—"

Mr Trayling burst into tears, his shoulders heaved, and he sobbed into the handkerchief. The footman shut the door and took off down the hall, leaving Hannah to deal with the distraught man.

"It's him, isn't it?" Mr Trayling whispered.

"Let us go into the parlour to discuss the matter." Hannah took his arm and steered him into a tastefully decorated parlour. White walls were highlighted with deep navy and gold trim that perfectly complemented his robe. She guided him to a chaise upholstered in blue velvet and then sat beside him.

"Now, the footman said Mr Berridge is not in. When did you last see him?" Hannah had thought Mrs Hamilton would be the most distraught person she would see today. She hadn't imagined the depth of Mr Trayling's reaction, and she hadn't even told him about the contents of the box yet.

The horrendous noise increased in pitch. The man barely stuttered a few syllables before collapsing against the side of the chaise. Hannah wondered how to elicit the information she required from him. Then her attention alighted on a crystal decanter on a sideboard. She crossed to it and pulled the stopper free. A brief sniff made her eyes water and confirmed the contents would prove useful.

She poured a good dollop into a tumbler and took it to Mr Trayling. "This will help with the shock. I need you to tell me what happened before we can determine whether or not Mr Berridge has been the victim of foul play."

The older man's hand shook as he took the glass. He wrapped his other hand around it, stared at the amber contents for a moment, and between sobs, downed the lot in one gulp.

"Ollie left last night. To meet a patron. About a new play." He spoke in short bursts, between hiccups.

"Do you know whom he met with?" Hannah took the empty glass and placed it on a side table.

"He received a note and left straight after." Mr

Trayling pulled his spine erect and heaved a great sigh that ended in a hiccup.

"He was summoned to the theatre?" Hannah asked. Lady Albright had gone to visit Bunhill Fields after a disagreement with her cousin. No one could have known of her intention until she walked out the front door. Either a servant had told someone, or another watched the house waiting for a chance to catch her alone. If Mr Berridge had been summoned to his doom, then their attacker had progressed to selecting his victims in advance.

"Yes." A long pause followed as Mr Trayling blew his nose not once, but twice. "There was no show last night, and the theatre was empty."

Which confirmed the man had been at the Fiddler's Theatre at the time of the fire. "Do you have this note?"

"Ollie took it with him, tucked into a pocket." Then grief overwhelmed the man, and he threw himself back on the chaise, sobbing into his hands.

"I am sorry to have to ask, Mr Trayling, but could you tell me if at some time Mr Berridge had ever broken a leg? And what shoes did he wear last night?"

The last bit of her question broke through the man's grief. "Shoes?" He sat up and rubbed at his eyes. "He wore those horribly old-fashioned things with the heel and a big sparkly buckle. As much as I love him, he does still think he's a courtier from last century."

Hannah smiled at the mental image his words conjured. "I don't think any man should apologise for being well dressed. But did he ever break his leg? I seem to recall some tale about it."

Mr Trayling snorted—part laugh, part sob. "Yes. Some five years ago. The old fool fell from the stage and broke his left leg. Actors always tell each other to break a leg for good luck, but he took it literally."

Oh, dear. All the evidence pointed to Mr Berridge being the newest houseguest at Westbourne Green. Hannah clasped the other man's hand. "I am so sorry, Mr Trayling, but I believe Mr Berridge was the victim of last night's fire. We found an old-fashioned court shoe with a large buckle, and the person had a broken left tibia."

Hannah braced herself for a scream of anguish, but only silence greeted her words. Mr Trayling's eyes rolled up into his head and he swooned in a dead faint. Fortunately, he fell back on the rolled arm of the chaise. She pulled the bell by the door and waited until the footman reappeared.

"Milady?" The man glanced to his unconscious employer and not a flicker passed across his face, as though swooning were a common occurrence in the household.

"Mr Trayling is overcome at hearing some rather upsetting news. Do you have any smelling salts?" she asked.

"Of course, milady." The footman walked to a cabinet against the wall, opened a drawer, and retrieved a small green bottle. He uncorked the top and passed it to Hannah.

Hannah held the bottle under Mr Trayling's nose. It took only a few seconds for the noxious odour to do its job. He spluttered and sat up. His chest heaved with the deep and silent sobs of grief.

"A pot of tea, please," she said to the footman and then dismissed him. She couldn't leave Mr Trayling alone in such a state. "Is there anyone I can send for, to sit with you?"

He nodded and his fingers worked at the handkerchief as tears rolled down his face. When the footman returned, Hannah issued instructions for someone to fetch a dear friend of the couple who lived across the square.

Afterward, she dashed off a note for Wycliff at the Ministry and then sat alone with her thoughts as Frank took her home. She only hoped her husband's search had proved successful. They now knew the identity of their second victim and that a note had invited him to his end. They couldn't call it a murder, for he was already dead. That didn't sit right with Hannah. Mr Berridge had conducted himself in an honest fashion, much like the former Lady Albright. What was murder if not the extinguishing of a life, regardless of the state of a person's heart? But apparently that raised all sorts of legal ramifications about not being able to charge someone for murder, when another had already murdered that same person. Would it matter, then, if one person murdered the same victim twice?

As she stepped down from the carriage in the stableyard at Westbourne Green, she remembered her earlier call and the note Lord Tomlin had sent to the former Lady Albright. *There* was a man she could focus her anger upon. Pulling the slip of paper from her reticule, she charged through the house to the library. Hannah waved the note at her mother as she burst through the door.

"Did you know that the former Lady Albright wrote to Lord Tomlin to seek his help? Look at the horrid reply he sent her!" She stopped before the desk and held out the letter.

Her mother waved it away. "I don't need to read it, dear child, to imagine. Let me use my psychic powers." She placed one hand to her temple and bowed her head. "Tomlin makes a disparaging comment about the Afflicted in general, and me in particular."

Some of the hot air escaped from Hannah's lungs. Her mother didn't possess psychic ability—that was one of the few limits Nature placed upon mages. They could not peer into the minds of ordinary folk. What her mother possessed was a long history with the ill-tempered mage in question. "Yes, well, he said something along those lines."

Hannah dropped the letter to the desk and walked to the window seat. She curled up in a sunbeam and watched a sparrow sitting on a branch of a nearby tree. "What if he is behind this?"

The bathchair squeaked as her mother turned it to face the window. "We must tread carefully if we seek to accuse a mage of wrongdoing. Especially when Parliament cannot agree whether a crime has been committed at all. Sadly, he is not the only mage who takes a dim view of the Afflicted. Two others on the council openly supported Tomlin when he suggested a *permanent* solution to our curse."

Hannah sucked in a breath. "Why did you not tell me this before?"

"Because the knowledge serves little purpose. We are well acquainted with Tomlin's character and I suspect the others side with him out of fear—either of us or of him." Seraphina tapped one gloved finger on the arm of her chair.

"But someone uses mage fire to immolate the Afflicted. What if the attacker has not purchased it from an apothecary, but is being provided with the potion he needs?" She curled her hands around the edge of the cushion. The library door cracked open and Sheba rushed in and jumped to the window seat beside Hannah. Holding the spaniel helped to disperse some of the hopelessness that crept over her.

Seraphina wheeled herself closer. "We need proof, Hannah. Do you know the last time a mage was convicted of a crime?"

"No," she sighed. She didn't even know if such a thing were possible.

"Exactly. Kings and those in power will excuse any number of infractions to keep mages on their side. Besides, it would take mages to capture another and bind his magic to make him safe enough to be incarcerated in the Repository." Images formed and disappeared as Seraphina spoke. Mages encircled another, magic crackling between them. Then the one in the centre burst free and as he ran away, he turned to smoke.

Hannah slumped back against the window. "Mr Berridge is our latest victim. Mr Trayling said he received a letter last night summoning him to the theatre to discuss a new play. He wore the shoes we retrieved."

Seraphina bowed her head, and mournful music filled the library. "He will be much missed. Mr Trayling must be devastated."

Sheba rested across her lap as Hannah stroked the dog's fur. "Someone is targeting the Afflicted, and not only physically, with the destruction of their bodies. Someone seeks to alert all of England to what is used to sustain them, and the reports in the scandal sheets spread fear among the population. If popular opinion demands action, Parliament will have to act even if it means the end of their wives, daughters, and sisters who have borne this curse."

Wycliff and her father would attend the sitting of Parliament that afternoon, where the crimes and the articles would be hotly debated.

"I fear you are correct, Hannah. My knots of silence have been attacked and frayed. Worse even than that, the falsehoods are fertilised and sprout in every nook and cranny like weeds." Seraphina waved her hands and tiny soft yellow moths appeared, each a spell to seek out and silence a rumour about the

Afflicted. Even as Hannah watched, the light of the moths winked out and they fell to the ground.

"Which confirms it is another mage. No one else would be strong enough." Hannah still cast Lord Tomlin in that role, even though her mother had attracted many enemies during her life and more after her death.

Seraphina snorted. "I agree that Tomlin is the most vocal of our detractors. But we have so many enemies, how do you pluck out only one name to accuse? What I have seen could be achieved by potions or spells acquired from any mage, and I fear there is more than one hand behind this."

"We need to stop them before more Afflicted lose what little they have left. If London is turned against us, there will be mass pyres until none of the Afflicted remain." Or would they all be consigned to the Chelsea Crematorium, used to dispose of bodies from the hospitals? No, Tomlin and his ilk would demand a public spectacle, like the Smithfield fires of Tudor times.

"Do you still wish to remove the spell, my dear? To do so would make you a target alongside me." Her mother lifted her veil, something she did only for their most serious conversations.

Hannah never saw the discolouration caused by rot that could not be stopped. To her, Seraphina remained as she once was, with blue eyes as sharp as ever and undiminished by death. "How simple the solution would be if we could ask Lady Albright and Mr Borridge who attacked them. Or, we could stop someone else from being harmed by wresting the cure from its creator. My concern is that the longer we delay, the further this conspiracy will spread and the more people will be...extinguished."

Seraphina blew out a sigh and her lips pulled in a tight line. "I dislike what you are suggesting, but with each day I believe more that you are right and we must journey to the underworld. Besides, I have found little in the trunk of books about shadow mages. I think that I need to ask the source directly."

Hannah tried to smile, but events weighed too heavily on her heart. "We will go together."

"Except for your father, who cannot join us." Seraphina turned her face away from Hannah and pulled the veil back over her features.

The lump of fear inside Hannah grew a little denser. Her father would remain alone beside their still bodies. He had lost his wife once. How terrible for him to lose Seraphina again, along with his daughter, in the same day. "We will return, for Papa's sake."

Seraphina nodded. "Your father was telling me of a new bill being proposed in Parliament that will concern the Afflicted. Some agitators want us confined to a *secure location* for our own safety."

"Secure location? Do they intend to round us all up and inter us at the Repository?" Hannah slid off the window seat and Sheba jumped to the ground beside her.

"No. Hugh says the rumour is that they want us all confined to the Isle of Dogs. Those afraid of us seem to think we cannot cross water. They obviously forget their old wives' tales. Witches float like ducks." Seraphina wheeled herself back to the desk and the open scroll that depicted the weighing of a heart.

Hannah paced as she tried to determine what to do next. They had too many threads to chase. Someone worked to expose Unwin and Alder, another stalked the Afflicted to destroy their physical forms, and there were agitators in power. "There will be no Afflicted to quarantine if the unknown arsonist is left at large," Hannah murmured.

"Yes. First, we must find the hand holding high that torch and save our fellow Afflicted. Then we can smooth over the troubled waters at Unwin and Alder. When that settles, Parliament's concerns can be addressed."

There was one more thing Hannah would add to her mother's course of action. "You must confront the mage council and determine whether Lord Tomlin is behind this."

"Yes, and I am rather looking forward to it." Seraphina held out her hand and a pure white flame burst into life, dancing an inch above her glove. "The first shadow mage in England for over six hundred years is going to demand a few answers."

17

Wᴄʟɪꜰꜰ ʀᴇᴛᴜʀɴᴇᴅ to the Ministry of Unnaturals and dropped his coat and top hat in his office. Then he trod the stairs up to Sir Manly's office with a weary step. A sense of foreboding shadowed his investigation as he worried about who sought to remove the Afflicted from London. He had no doubt that Lady Miles would ably protect herself and her daughter should any Londoners arrive on their doorstep carrying pitchforks and torches, but what of others?

He barely waited for his rap on the door to be acknowledged before pushing into the calm office.

Sir Manly glanced at him and gestured to the sofa and chairs set before the fire. "Sit down, man, you look done in."

Wycliff dropped into a brown leather armchair and rubbed his hands over his face. "I don't like where this investigation is going, nor the unrest in the streets these reports are fuelling."

Sir Manly joined him, the former general quiet as he settled into the chair opposite and stroked a curled end of his moustache as though checking it hadn't moved during the brief journey across the office. "We are being pressured from above to put an end to these pyres and the rumours about the Afflicted. Apparently it will sully the reputation of certain ladies if it is known what they dine upon and their social invitations might diminish."

Wycliff leaned back in the chair. "We should be grateful that some months ago Lady Miles worked her magic to keep the more gruesome details of the murders committed by the Afflicted from the press." The work of Unwin and Alder sparked enough alarm, even though they obtained the consent of relatives and only took donations from the deceased. The city would have a panic-fuelled mob if Nash ever seized on the murders committed by Lady Gabriella Ridlington and her lover, and wrote about how innocents had been killed and their skulls cracked open.

"Have you found out yet who is behind this?" Sir Manly rested his elbows on the arms of the chair and tented his fingers.

The only thing Wycliff knew for sure was that Nash hadn't ambushed and overpowered the two Afflicted. The man resembled a weasel, with little muscle to him. Gut instinct whispered the man wrote his articles, but didn't dirty his hands with anything except ink. "I have a suspicion. The reporter turned in his article about the latest immolation before the fire had even died down. One could almost conclude he had it written in advance. When I cornered him about who had fed him the information, he said there was someone he feared more than a hellhound."

Sir Manly let out an audible sigh. "You let him see the hellhound and he still wouldn't talk?"

"I let it simmer to the surface, thinking a creature from the underworld who could consign his soul to eternal suffering might loosen his tongue. I am somewhat insulted there is a more fearsome entity on the streets than I." He tried to inject a little humour, although there was scant to laugh about in the case.

"It has to be a mage," Sir Manly huffed out the words and then stared at the ceiling. "No mage has ever been accused of a crime, let alone stood trial for one. Tread softly, Wycliff."

"I have no intention of setting the mage council against me. But the truth must be brought to light." He would find those responsible for extinguishing the two Afflicted first, then let someone else worry about the charges.

"That is probably exactly what this reporter claims. We both know the information about Unnaturals that is withheld from general circulation." Sir Manly waved a finger in the air as he spoke.

Wycliff snorted. Once, he'd thought everybody had the right to know what sustained the Afflicted. Now, he considered it nobody's business as long as they existed within the dictates of England's laws. "If the Afflicted commit no crimes, they should be left in peace.

Whoever is behind this has taken two lives, whether that is considered murder the second time or not."

"If the proposed amendment to the law does not pass, we may have to let this one go, Wycliff." The former general pushed off the arms of the chair to stand. Some years earlier, he had championed the pivotal bill that gave Unnaturals the same rights as all Englishmen. That bill had been bolstered by the wartime efforts of the Highland Wolves. Yet in times of peace, the deaths of those without a heartbeat fell between the cracks.

Wycliff's lips tightened into a grim line as he stood. Whoever had consigned the former Lady Albright to a bonfire might escape the law, but they wouldn't escape the kind of justice he could deliver. If the perpetrator dared reach for Lady Miles or her daughter, they would find themselves thrown into a torment that would make them long for the end delivered by mage fire.

He spent the rest of his afternoon tackling the paperwork stacked neatly in a wooden tray on his desk. Higgs proved invaluable in sorting and tallying his invoices, so all he had to do was sign them off. Then he laboured over the reports of his investigation. Hannah had sent a note that confirmed Mr Oliver Berridge was unaccounted for and had been summoned to the theatre the night in question. Wycliff was staring at his report of the charred remains found at the theatre, when a soft rap came as Higgs stood at the open door.

"It's nearly three thirty, milord," he said.

"Excellent." Wycliff pushed the paper to one side. He would finish the report tomorrow.

Parliament sat at four; he had time to make his way to Westminster for the session and find Sir Hugh. Wycliff's title of viscount entitled him to a seat in the House of Lords, but his work as an investigator gave him a handy excuse for missing the sittings that often lasted late into the night. He had better things to do than listen to long-winded aristocrats nitpick legislation.

Today was an exception, and he wanted to attend as the House debated a new category of crime that impacted those creatures defined as Unnatural. He needed to cast his vote, assuming he could stay awake that long. He set off at a brisk pace. Pedestrians mostly dodged out of his way and the few who didn't earned a glare as he stepped around them. A few people gathered on corners, waving placards calling for the removal of the Afflicted from London. A brief urge to call out their stupidity slowed his feet, then he berated himself. Nothing could be done for the simpletons who blindly believed every word in the scandal sheets. Change had to come from Parliament and trickle down to the streets.

The swirl of people around the Palace of Westminster slowed his pace, and the chimes struck to summon the politicians as Wycliff made his way to the chamber where the House of Lords sat. Sir Hugh stood with a group of men outside the entrance. His father-in-law could not vote, but he would watch from the gallery.

He hailed Wycliff and detached himself from the cluster. "Wycliff. I am told the House will consider a curfew for the Afflicted this afternoon. Damn fools. We don't even know who they all are. How the blazes do they intend to enforce a curfew?"

Wycliff grunted as they walked into the chamber. Enforcement would probably fall on his head. "While there is noise in the streets, for once we should be grateful for the rotten boroughs that have allowed a handful of lords to control the majority of seats in the House of Commons. They are at least voting in line with the Lords, and I doubt any of them want to tell their wives and daughters they can't go out at night. Balls, after all, must be attended."

The two men parted company, Wycliff to find his seat at the back of the chamber on a hard wooden bench. The more earnest and verbose lords crowded together in the front rows. Sir Hugh took the stairs to the balcony above. The gallery was placed high, near the ceiling, and he looked down on the politicians like a bird perched in a tree. Noise rolled upward to the spectators, as the Lords argued and shouted like angry schoolboys.

For once, the Lords dispensed with all the introductory posturing and leapt straight into debate. The Speaker announced the amendment under discussion —murder of an Unnatural, or other being, who lacked a heartbeat.

"This amendment is preposterous. You cannot murder a dead thing!" A lord in the front row leapt to his feet and turned to face his companions. "Dead is dead."

Cries of *hear, hear* went up from a clump of lords across the floor from Wycliff. The lord on his feet held his arms wide as though his declaration of *dead is dead* was the final nail in the bill's coffin. "What's next? Am I guilty of murder for tucking into my roast beef at dinnertime?"

Laughter greeted his comments. Then Lord Jessope rose and stepped to the middle of the floor. He paused before the other lord and with a withering glare, sent the younger man scurrying back to his seat. Then he clasped his hands behind his back and faced the Speaker. "I lost my wife to this dreadful curse that stilled her heart, but kept her mind intact and trapped in a dead form."

Silence, or as close as the assembled lords and gallery could manage, rippled away from where Lord Jessope stood. The earl rarely spoke of how the curse had struck his family, and those without an Afflicted family member hung on every word.

He walked down the space between the two sides of the assembly, speaking as he went. "Some argue that a life requires a heartbeat. That murder is when another steals the steady rhythm of that organ. But I stand here before you today to say that is not always the case. My wife maintains a devout and Christian existence, her days spent in prayer. The former Lady Albright was known to many as a kind and thoughtful woman—even without a heartbeat."

Heads swung to stare at Lord Albright, who had a deep scowl on his face.

"If it is not murder when an Afflicted is consumed by flames against their will, then how *do* we describe the snuffing out of a person's existence?" Lord Jessope stopped before Lord Albright as he asked his question.

The mean-spirited lord narrowed his gaze. "The Afflicted died. Those who peddled the infected face powder were charged and convicted. How can one person possibly be murdered twice? We make a mockery of our laws and reputation for fairness if we entertain this amendment."

Agreement echoed around Albright. He would push that a person couldn't be murdered twice, as he had long tried to rid himself of his former wife. Certainly he took advantage of her dead status to remarry with unseemly haste. Wycliff suspected he had a hand in the former Lady Albright's fate. All he needed was proof.

Another lord stood. "Where do we draw the line? If those without a heartbeat have special protection, what about those without their minds? What fate awaits them?"

"Those without their wits could always practise law," someone yelled across the floor.

Chortles of laughter erupted in the chamber. The Speaker banged his gavel. "Order! Order, my lords."

A large and dour-looking lord used a walking stick to stand. His hand shook on the cane as he supported his weight. "While you jest, my lords, our friend

Jessope raises a very real concern. If the Afflicted truly dine on the minds of Londoners, we should be less worried about attacks against them, and more concerned with the crimes *they* might commit. Murderers should not be given free rein, not matter who they are related to."

Having said his piece, he lowered himself back into his seat.

Wycliff curled his hands into fists on his knees. That comment veered too close to revealing that two Afflicted had murdered innocent people in order to consume the contents of their skulls. What direction would the debate take now?

"The Afflicted shouldn't be allowed to roam the streets and steal the brains of honest Londoners!" a voice shouted from the back.

"They should be rounded up and held somewhere, for their safety and ours." The lord who asked where they would draw the line added to his argument. "Surely that resolves two issues? They cannot be burned if they are kept secure, nor can they attack the rest of the population."

Wycliff heaved a sigh. He was going to regret making himself known, but he could sit in silence no longer. Standing, he faced the lord arguing for the Afflicted to be quarantined on the Isle of Dogs. "How exactly do you intend to capture and imprison all the Afflicted in England? Will you storm the homes of dukes and earls, and drag their wives and daughters screaming from their drawing rooms?"

Mutters came from sections of the room, no doubt men imagining the scene as they had to tell their female family members their nocturnal entertainments were to be curtailed, and worse, they were to be sent to a dreary spot without a single dress shop or millinery.

"Don't you have a list of their names?" Another lord tossed out his question.

Wycliff tried to discern where the voices came from in the crowded room. "No. We know a few, but not all. Many nobles refuse to make it known whether or not they have an Afflicted relative."

"Isn't that part of your job, Wycliff? What do you do all day funded from England's purse? Perhaps you are following in your father's footsteps." That voice he recognised—Albright.

For a moment he contemplated letting the hound loose at the implied insult that he frittered away his salary. Like many bullies, Albright felt emboldened with his cronies around him. The pressure from all the shouted questions and retorts built in Wycliff's head. Nobles and politicians tried his patience, and the House of Lords combined the worst of both.

"There could be some three hundred Afflicted, not to mention how many other types of Unnatural creature, residing in England. I am one man, and there are only so many hours in the day. Contrary to what you think, Albright, I do not rest until I bring a perpetrator to justice, no matter where he might hide. Perhaps the Lords could support a bill to greatly increase the funding for the Ministry of Unnaturals, thus increasing the number of investigators. Twenty of us might be able to perform half the duties you expect of me."

Having said his piece, he sat down. The debate wore on as the sun fell outside. One faction argued with another, then they veered off into religious quarters, arguing whether a heartbeat, a brain, or a soul gave a person life.

As the clock neared midnight, the Whig leader thumped on the back of the wooden bench. "Too long have bloated Tories feasted off the backs of the common man. Not content with snatching our hard-earned coin, they now they let their wives steal our minds. We demand they curtail their Afflicted relatives. Let us have a curfew while these other matters are debated, so at least they do not creep up behind some poor Londoner!"

Cries of agreement bounced off the walls. Wycliff shook his head. There would be no progress on the bill this night. A curfew would relieve some fears and keep the Afflicted safe from whomever roamed the streets clutching his vial of mage fire. But it would be a nightmare to enforce.

The Speaker seized on a simpler matter that might be resolved. "Let us take a vote on the matter of a curfew. Those in favour of a dusk to dawn curfew for the Afflicted, say aye."

A roar of ayes charged across the floor.

"Those against?" the Speaker asked.

Shouts of nay, including Wycliff's, went up but the volume alone was far less than the ayes.

"The ayes have it." The Speaker banged his gavel on the desk. "From today onward, all Afflicted must be in their place of residence between dusk and dawn. Any caught on the street are to be incarcerated in a secure location."

A groan came from some men present, no doubt anticipating the chilly reception of such news.

Wycliff slipped from the House of Lords after midnight and met Sir Hugh out in the hall. The large surgeon shook his head. "I don't know how I feel about a curfew. It will keep the women safe from the attacker, but it's the first step out on thin ice."

"My feelings exactly," Wycliff murmured as they headed out into the sharp night air. "Next they will propose they all be moved to a secure location. How convenient to have all the Afflicted in one place if someone decides that a permanent solution should be applied to them."

"But without the amendment, no crime has even been committed. Except, perhaps, interfering with a corpse if they insist the Afflicted are dead." Sir Hugh led Wycliff across the expansive courtyard and through the tall iron gates.

Wycliff stared up at the moon, hanging clear now that the clouds had scudded away. London lay awash in its silver light. "We cannot rely on support from Parliament. We must find a solution of our own." Such a solution resided in the underworld, but he had promised Hannah he would not go without her.

Was he ready to watch her die, in order to save her?

18

HANNAH WOKE the next morning to Wycliff's warmth surrounding her. She rolled over and placed a hand on his face. "I never heard you come home. How late did the Lords sit?"

He kissed her palm. "You sleep soundly and hardly stirred. Your father and I left a little after midnight once it became obvious nothing would be achieved."

"I sleep soundly because I am safe, and in that I am very fortunate. But what do you mean nothing was achieved? Did they not agree that the snuffing out of an existence is a type of murder?" She sat up and gathered the blanket to her.

Wycliff blew out a sigh. "No. The argument devolved. The only thing the House voted on was a curfew. The Afflicted are to remain in their homes between dusk and dawn."

A number of different arguments as to the absurdity of such a proceeding crammed Hannah's mind. "A curfew?" she spluttered. Indignation flared in her torso. The bill before Parliament was intended to recognise the Afflicted's right to exist, and that no one could snuff out.

Wycliff rose from bed and gathered his clothing. "Yes. I voted against it, but I can see some merits to it, so please hear me out before you explode. It will at least keep the Afflicted safe in their homes while we figure out who is behind the fires. It might also dampen some of the fear in the streets."

Hannah fetched a robe and shrugged it on. She would meet Mary in her old bedroom down the hall to dress. "It also casts the Afflicted as criminals who need to be monitored."

He softened his tone. "If the amendment does not pass, no crime will have been committed against the former Lady Albright or Oliver Berridge."

"Mr Berridge was *lured* to the theatre. Mr Trayling said he received a note from a patron who wanted to discuss a new play. Unfortunately, he had it in his pocket when he left. If we possessed the note, either Mother or Lady Alice Shaw might have been able to locate the writer." Hannah wrapped the robe's cord around her finger and then let it go again.

Wycliff sat on a chair to tug on his stockings and Hessians. "The former Lady Albright made her own way to Bunhill Fields and was most likely followed, but Berridge was summoned to his demise. The difference in approach may tell us something about the person behind this."

"Did you learn anything from Mr Nash?" Apart from a note Hannah had left for Wycliff at the Ministry, they had had no chance to share what they had each learned the previous day.

"No. Only that someone directs his activities and he refused to disclose whom, even when I let the hellhound become visible to him." Wycliff tucked his shirt into his trousers and then buttoned up his waistcoat.

Hannah sucked in a breath. "He showed no fear of the hound?" She didn't either, but for entirely different reasons. Wycliff would never harm her no matter what form he took. The sort of person who penned horrible and inflammatory articles about the Afflicted should have some concern for his immortal soul. If he possessed one.

"Why don't you dress and we'll discuss everything over breakfast with your parents?"

"Very well. I'll not be long." Hannah hurried to her room and found Mary waiting. In no time she was clad in a blue-and-green-striped gown and headed downstairs. She sipped a hot chocolate as her father wheeled her mother into the room.

"Did you hear about this ridiculous curfew, Hannah?" Seraphina said as she took her place.

"Yes, although I see Wycliff's point that the Afflicted should be safer from this attacker if they are at home." Hannah took a piece of toast and dropped it to her plate. The edges of the bread were somewhat burned, and the charring made her stomach turn.

"I found Peters yesterday. He is—was—the Unwin

and Alder employee we suspect of not completing his job and telling Nash what funerals to attend. Unfortunately, he was pulled from the Thames and won't be telling us anything." Wycliff downed his first coffee in a few gulps and then poured another.

"Someone is tidying up after themselves," Seraphina murmured.

"I suspect a mage is behind this. Who else could Nash fear more than a hellhound?" Wycliff met his mother-in-law's gaze.

Hannah couldn't eat and worried the edge of her cup with her teeth. One name squeezed over her lips. "Tomlin."

"There is no doubt he dislikes your mother, but surely even he wouldn't stoop to such a crime against the Afflicted?" Sir Hugh paused for a moment before returning to his plate of sausage, eggs, and toast.

"Do we know for certain that Lord Albright is not involved?" Hannah had to ask the question, as deep down she suspected the horrible man guilty of something. However, she couldn't see how he might be the connection between the death of Mr Berridge and that of the former Lady Albright.

Wycliff tapped his long fingers against the side of his cup. "I know nothing with certainty, except that Peters won't be leaving bits of skull off any more donors to Unwin and Alder. That should see an end to Nash's stalking funerals, although it makes me suspicious that he has another source yet to be tapped."

Hannah pushed her plate away, the toast uneaten.

"Parliament's lack of action does not mean we must likewise stagnate. We must continue to investigate who is behind this. If they do not cease, then neither shall we."

"Exactly, Hannah. The legal system is only one form of justice. Wycliff and I can both access another sort to ensure the guilty party is punished." Seraphina tilted her head at Wycliff and he nodded in agreement.

THE NEXT FEW days dragged as they sought to make progress with the investigation. Protests in the streets continued. The imposition of a curfew upon the Afflicted was taken by many as proof they were dangerous and shouldn't be allowed to roam free. Wycliff prowled the streets at night, ordered to enforce the curfew but left to determine for himself who was, or wasn't, one of the Afflicted.

That evening Hannah accompanied her husband, fascinated by how he allowed the hellhound to see through his eyes. If a soul resided within a person, he had told her, they emitted a pale yellow glow of the living, whereas the Afflicted were shadowed by their souls, attached to them by a silver strand. He scanned the mass of people, looking for souls trailing behind their bodies.

Hannah stayed close to Wycliff as they navigated the evening traffic. London at night became an entirely different place than its daytime counterpart. Shadows smudged away the dirt and grime. Laughter and music replaced the cries of children and the poor, who sought a few coins from passers-by. Women wore more vibrant colours as they spun and danced with friends. Even the daytime odours of horse manure and coal smoke were overlaid with the sweeter hint of ripe fruit and wine.

"You should not be out here," he muttered as he kept her hand tucked in the crook of his elbow.

They strolled the streets, doing what little they could to ensure the Afflicted remained safe in their homes. Since the imposition of the curfew, at least no one else had been destroyed by mage fire.

"The women of the *ton* barely rise by midday and entertainments don't start until after dark. It's as though men in power know nothing about their wives and daughters." Righteous indignation partly fuelled Hannah's determination to accompany Wycliff. Why should a woman be stuck at home because a man could not control himself? "Not to mention how ridiculous it is to expect one man to monitor three hundred Afflicted —even if we knew all their identities. It is only because the Ministry allows it that we have the ensorcelled ledgers from Unwin and Alder. We cannot violate the Afflicted's privacy by using the ledgers to make their identities known. Even then, what about those who have their needs met elsewhere?" Such was the height of her passion on the subject that she let go of Wycliff to speak with her hands. An oncoming group side-stepped to avoid her.

"It does seem a rather poorly thought out plan,"

Wycliff agreed. "Although I do understand the underlying sentiment of the Lords—they want to ensure the safety of their loved ones."

Hannah's anger deflated somewhat at his tone. Safety had been her husband's primary concern as he had tried to convince her to stay at home only this evening. "They order their wives and daughters to stay at home during the height of the season, and then hide when it comes to enforcing such a ludicrous rule. Do they expect Runners to stalk noble women and drag them back inside if they disobey?"

"People are afraid, Hannah, and when they act from a place of fear, others will be hurt. Nash has roused the population against the Afflicted and they are a powder keg needing only a spark." Wycliff steered her along another road.

People clustered on a corner, and angry words drifted toward her. "They should all burn," someone in the middle said in a strident tone. People agreed and shouted, "Burn the dead!"

She shuddered. Part of her was disgusted that people were so ignorant or so lacking in their own minds that the untruths written by a reporter could sway them. What had become of society that people grabbed burning torches because of a few salacious paragraphs and didn't stop to question for themselves?

"We still do not know who is behind all of this, though we suspect a mage who is cloaking his actions," she murmured. It was not beyond the realm of possibility that a mage might try to strike out at Seraphina. It had happened before and ended in her assassination. The bastion of white male mages did not take well to an outspoken dead woman in their midst.

An approaching figure drew Hannah's eye. The woman was trying to avoid attention, a grey cloak clutched around her, the hood drawn and pulled over her forehead. As she glanced up before crossing the road, the hood fell to one side and a lamp burning above illuminated her face.

Hannah gasped. She recognised the furtive pedestrian. She tapped Wycliff's arm and gestured with her head.

"An Afflicted. Her soul follows closely behind," he murmured in confirmation.

They changed course to intercept the other woman.

"Miss Knightley, it is not safe for you to be out." Turmoil erupted in Hannah's stomach. She hoped the woman had not agreed to meet a party of bucks again, earning a few coins by letting them slice her flesh to watch her skin heal before their eyes. An agreement with Unwin and Alder now met her needs. Hannah monitored the other woman's remarkable condition as they tried to ascertain what kept her free of any signs of rot.

Miss Knightley pushed back the hood and relief washed over her features. "Lady Wycliff. How fortuitous to meet you here. I know it is not safe, but your note said it was a matter of some urgency."

Hannah swallowed her next words, stuttered,

then managed to say, "My note?" She glanced at Wycliff, in case he knew anything about such a communication.

Miss Knightley searched in her pocket. "Yes. You sent it this afternoon and asked me to meet you in the booksellers' lane at midnight." She held out the slip of paper and Wycliff took it. Hannah was still frozen to the spot.

"This isn't your handwriting, Hannah." He glanced around them and then angled the sheet for her to see.

Hannah peered at the short missive in the moonlight. It urged Miss Knightley to meet her at the booksellers' after dark, claiming to have made a discovery that would cure her symptoms. Hannah would never endanger the other woman by arranging such a meeting, nor would she engage in subterfuge if they had a cure. But she could imagine who would.

Miss Knightley's eyes widened. "But if you did not send it, who did?"

A cold lump settled inside Hannah. "Those who seek to eradicate the Afflicted."

Miss Knightley gasped and one hand flew to her mouth. "You mean I am being lured to my...end?" She whispered the last word.

"Let us move away from here. Put your hood back up, Miss Knightley. We need time to think." Wycliff ushered them along the road and up into a hansom cab. He gave the driver instructions to where they had left Frank and the family carriage in a quiet area near Bond Street.

"You mean there is no cure?" Miss Knightley whispered as they shared the cramped seat.

"I am sorry. No." Hannah could imagine the depth of the woman's disappointment. But imagine if they had not met her by chance. The magnitude of Hannah's horror at having another person's horrid demise on her conscience knew no bounds. "We need to go ahead with the meeting. It is our chance to unmask them, Wycliff."

He stared out the window, his hand balled into a fist on his thigh. For a moment, she thought he might not have heard her and was about to launch into an argument as to exactly why they had to carry on, when he raised a hand.

"I heard you, and I agree. Give me a moment to work out how to dangle my wife as bait without endangering her very existence." He spoke with a heavy and somewhat resigned tone. Then he picked up her hand and kissed her gloved knuckles.

"I can borrow Miss Knightley's cloak, and we are of a similar height and build. We also have both Frank and Barnes waiting at our carriage, although I am not sure what assistance Barnes might provide." They would need a safe location in which to secrete Miss Knightley until they could escort her home and out of the reach of the unknown assailant.

"But Lady Wycliff, you cannot do this. It is too dangerous." Worry lines pulled at Miss Knightley's eyes.

Hannah dug deep for a brave smile for a woman

she considered a friend. "We must find the culprit before another innocent life is snuffed out. Besides, I think Wycliff and Frank will hover close to me. My concern is ensuring *your* safety."

"Stop here!" Wycliff called out.

Hannah stared at the buildings, trying to recognise the area. A light burned above a shop front. As she squinted, she made out the items arrayed in the window at street level. A gentleman's tailor. One who didn't sleep and who would fuss over Miss Knightley—Daniel Brae, vampyre.

"If you would accompany me, Miss Knightley, Daniel Brae will keep you safe until we return." Wycliff offered his hand.

Miss Knightley removed her cloak and bundled it up before passing it to Hannah. "Thank you, Lady Wycliff."

Then she stepped down to the road. Wycliff escorted the other woman up the stairs. More lights came on in the upstairs rooms and after a few minutes, Wycliff returned alone. "Brae will ensure her safety. I left the two of them exclaiming over the latest issue of *La Belle Assemblée*."

At least one Afflicted was saved from the mage fire this night. "I'm glad she will be safe. Now, what have you planned?"

They met Frank at the family carriage, where Wycliff outlined his plan. "He will try to grab you, to use whatever immobilisation spell or potion he has. That will give Frank and I a chance to capture him."

While she knew both her husband and the monstrous Frank hid in the dark, a shiver of fear still crept along her limbs as she turned into the narrow lane. The buildings on either side leaned inward and narrowed the dim light of the moon and stars to a strip down the middle. Hannah slowed her step, not wanting to trip on the uneven cobbles.

"Lady Wycliff? Are you here?" she called out in a tone that she hoped disguised her own. "The book-sellers all appear to be closed?"

Something scraped over the cobbles up ahead, and Hannah clutched the cloak tighter at her throat. Her heart hammered and would surely burst through the spell keeping it frozen in time. A shape detached itself from the shadows and padded toward her. Even in the low light, she made out the form of a large dog. No, a hound with glowing red eyes.

For a second, relief surged through her, then it drained away. Wycliff was behind her, not in front. But as it neared, this hellhound didn't look right. It wasn't as large as her husband, nor did it have the same wispy, red-tipped fur made of smoke.

Another hellhound? And if not, what? She swallowed the lump in her throat. "Nice doggy," she rasped.

A second shape emerged from the dark, taller and broader than Wycliff, but not of the same monstrous dimensions as Frank. Hannah stepped back and turned her face into the covering of the hood. "Oh. Excuse me," she muttered and turned to walk away.

"Stay right there, missy, or I'll unleash the hound

on you. One word from me and he'll drag you to Hell," the figure said, gesturing to his canine companion.

The hound padded closer and issued a low growl.

The clouds parted above, and a sliver of light wormed between the buildings. Silver flickered over the hellhound and it shimmered like a summer heat haze. In the middle of the hound, Hannah glimpsed a much smaller and more corporeal dog. Hannah's mage silver ring tingled a warning. Not a hellhound, but the illusion of one.

"I must go." Hannah stretched out her hand to ward the man off.

The fake hellhound growled, but a much deeper response came from the inky night. The man lunged at her and Hannah cried out as the assailant grabbed her outstretched hand and pulled, expecting her to tumble toward him. Instead, Barnes popped out of the end of her sleeve and clutched tight to the man.

"What?" In the second it took him to realise her hand had not come off in his, she ducked to one side.

The attacker tried to shake off the hand, except Barnes refused to let go, squeezing the man's fingers for dear life.

19

"Stop her!" the man commanded the hellhound illusion, and it circled around behind Hannah.

She searched the night and found the other set of glowing red eyes close by. A much larger hellhound stepped forward, its head low as sizzling drool fell from its long canines.

"Bloody hell! He's outdone himself this time. Hold the filthy dead thing there while I freeze it," the assailant commanded as he battled Barnes. With his free hand, he waved a small vial.

Emboldened by the presence of Wycliff, Hannah pushed back the hood of the cloak. "You'll not burn an Afflicted tonight."

"My master says otherwise." Working the stopper off the vial with his fingers, he threw the contents at her.

Hannah flung up her right arm and the deep blue liquid splattered over her hand and sleeve. She gasped at the icy touch and suddenly her fingers wouldn't obey her command to shake the drops free. Heat flared from her mage silver ring and raced across her skin. With a soft *poof*, the liquid burst into nothing and she could move again.

Meanwhile, the attacker managed to peel off the mitten that Barnes clung to and tossed it to the ground. Refusing to give up the fight, Barnes launched himself at the man's ankles and started climbing his leg.

Wycliff trod closer to Hannah, his head swinging back and forth, and she feigned a fearful expression as he approached. It wouldn't do to ruin their ruse by stroking his smoky fur.

Frank appeared and swiped one enormous hand at the smaller hellhound. His fist passed through its insubstantial fur and connected with the creature wearing the disguise. The fake hellhound emitted a high-pitched whine and shook itself. The illusion fell away to reveal a wiry white and brown terrier that glanced up at its master and then ran, bolting away into the night.

"I don't need you, you mangy cur!" He gestured to Wycliff. "What are you waiting for? Attack!"

The fierce hellhound obeyed. Wycliff lunged and bit into the man's side. He screamed in pain as hot canines pierced his flesh, his body flung one way and then another as Wycliff shook his head. Barnes still clung to the man's leg but couldn't advance past a bent knee.

"Stay. Safe," Frank intoned to Hannah as he stood

between her and the fight. Although it was rather one-sided as the assailant struggled to escape the hell-hound's grip. A sickly sweet smell drifted through the air and hoarse cries punctuated the night.

"I promise to stay out of the way if you assist Wycliff." Hannah peered around the stitched-together man. She drew an acorn from her pocket, pressed the stalk until it clicked, and then tossed it into the air. The acorn popped and turned into a pale blue globe that hung in the air and provided blue-tinged light over a twelve foot radius—enough to illuminate the fight.

Frank drew back his arm and struck the other man on the chin. The attacker's head snapped back, and he staggered sideways, but Wycliff held him in place in his monstrous jaws.

"Who are you?" Hannah demanded from the safety of a bookseller's doorway.

Frank uttered a low growl and lunged, smacking the man above his nose with his forehead. This time, the arsonist's knees buckled, and he dropped to the cobbles.

Wycliff wrenched his head to one side and pulled his teeth free of clothing and muscle as the man fell. "Taylor," he said over his shoulder.

"You *know* him?" Hannah moved closer, but kept out of arm's reach.

"He's the Bow Street Runner who has been assisting my investigation." Wycliff prowled closer and set his massive front paws on the man's chest. Saliva dripped from his fangs onto the prone man's torn coat. Each droplet sizzled as it hit fabric and skin. Frank stood on Taylor's feet and Barnes scrambled up his torso to stand on his chest at full alert.

Taylor struggled to worm his body free of the creatures holding him down. "You?! Did that dead mage turn you into her lapdog?"

"Who are you working with?" Hannah crept closer, but kept Wycliff in front of her. She surveyed the fallen man. He tried to bat at Wycliff, but the smoky fur scorched his hands. On his mittenless left hand, she noted an odd blue mark by his thumb.

Wycliff hunched his shoulders and shifted more weight into his front paws, pressing on Taylor's lungs. "He was working with Nash. But who pulls your strings?"

Taylor barked a short laugh. "I'm not telling you. Call yourself an investigator, you've learned nothing!"

"I found you," Wycliff growled.

Taylor turned his face, and his fingers scrabbled at the cobbles. "Filthy Afflicted. They are all going to be rounded up and burned."

"They live peaceful lives. Snuffing them out is a terrible crime," Hannah said.

"Peaceful?" Taylor laughed. "They're murderous monsters who steal the brains of honest folk. That was my cousin they slaughtered at the Harriers six months ago. We wondered why the authorities wouldn't let us see her, and burned her body right quick, they did. But

I've talked to Nash and I reckon you knew, didn't you? Those toffs cracked her head open and scooped out her brain like she were a boiled egg." Taylor pushed off the cobbles and flung out an arm. He hit Barnes, sending him flying across the lane. Wycliff body slammed Taylor back to the ground.

"I'm sorry for your loss, but you cannot blame every Afflicted for the actions of two. You will be punished for your crimes, just as they were." Hannah scanned the dark lane for Barnes, and to her relief, the hand righted himself and scuttled back into the circle of light.

Taylor scoffed, then wheezed as Wycliff pressed harder on his lungs. "I'll never be punished. I'm not doing anything wrong. Haven't you heard? You can't murder a dead thing."

"There are many different types of justice, and you will be judged," Hannah murmured.

Wycliff opened his jaws and snapped, latching on to the man's shoulder and upper chest. Taylor screamed as flesh sizzled and burned. The hellhound worked its head back and forth as cries turned to groans and pleas. Then the hound stepped back, dragging a shadow from the physical form as though he pulled a tablecloth free of a table. Taylor's body went limp on the cobbles and the cries were silenced.

Barnes trotted over and flicked the body with his index finger in a gesture that resembled a kick. Then he scuttled over to the discarded mitten and claimed it for himself.

Hannah bent down and picked up hand and his trophy. "Well done, and thank you for your bravery." She placed a kiss on the backs of his knuckles.

Hannah stayed clear as her husband threw the shadow toward another dark shape that drank the light from the acorn.

"One last thing," Wycliff said. He padded close to the remains and bowed his head. His fur stood to attention and the red tips glowed brighter. A flash burst from him and jumped to the body. Hellfire encircled it and orange flames leapt high.

The hellhound shook itself and the fur fell away to reveal Wycliff. He held out a hand to Hannah. "There is nothing more we can do here. Let's leave before the curious are drawn by the flames and the smell."

AFTER RETURNING TO THE CARRIAGE, they collected Miss Knightley and drove her home. Wycliff walked her to her front door, then Frank took them back to Westbourne Green. They found the Miles household awake and lights blazing in the windows. Seraphina had been alerted through Hannah's ring. They gathered in the library, where a pot of hot chocolate waited.

"You found him, then?" Seraphina asked as she poured chocolate into the cups.

"It was Taylor, the Runner. I thought him useful in the investigation, but he was probably sticking close to control what I knew." Wycliff took a seat next to

Hannah. "His hellhound was a terrier wearing an illusion."

"What did you do with him?" Sir Hugh asked as he settled into an armchair.

Wycliff huffed. "Dispensed justice. He will not seize another Afflicted."

"Did you notice his hand? He had an odd blue mark here." Hannah rubbed a spot between her thumb and forefinger.

"A mark?" Wycliff pulled his notebook from a pocket and flipped through the pages. "Like this one?"

Hannah pressed to his side and studied the drawing. "Yes. That's it."

"Peters had the same tattoo on his left hand. That cannot be a coincidence. It might be some secret society," Wycliff said.

"Might I see that?" Seraphina asked.

Wycliff turned the notebook toward her, and she sucked in a breath. "Here is the evidence you sought. That squiggle is a monogram of the initials J and T. James Tomlin. He marks everything he owns, so Taylor and Peters must have been in his employ. I knew he disliked me, but I never imagined his hatred ran so deep he would extinguish others to reach me."

Wycliff tossed the notebook to the side table. "Now that we have confirmed the identity of the mage behind this, what do we do about him? We have only delayed his plans, not stopped them. He will find another like Taylor to do his dirty work."

"Or worse. He will inflame the mob. We cannot protect all the Afflicted," Sir Hugh said.

Hannah remained silent for a long time, her fingers curled around the mug in her hands. "We may not be able to stop Lord Tomlin, but we can remove potential victims from his reach. It is time for us to walk the dark path."

"Hannah—" Wycliff rasped.

She placed her mug on the table before her and held up a hand to stop his protest. "We must journey to the underworld. All of this could be halted if we come back with a cure. Or, at the very least, with some answers."

"Or we could come back with nothing." He softened his tone. "Or fail to return at all."

Sir Hugh cleared his throat. "Should you fail in your mission, I will lose my entire family and the very reason for my existence." Here he paused and reached out to take Seraphina's gloved hand in his larger one. "I have held my silence, as I know it is not my journey to take. But sometimes, despite the risks and odds being piled against you, you must take that step regardless. My only comfort is that the three of you will be together."

Tears moistened Hannah's eyes. Her father would lose them all, but still saw the benefits to their dangerous journey. She faced Wycliff and raised a hand to his cheek. "We do this together."

He let out a ragged sigh. "Together," he whispered.

"Catch a few hours' sleep. We do not know what awaits us." The words drifted from Seraphina with a soft tone.

Hannah couldn't argue with her mother's suggestion. Even though she would journey with Wycliff, part of her wanted a few more hours with him while her soul still resided in her body, and her heart pumped in her chest.

THE COUPLE SLEPT late that morning. Or didn't sleep. Once they had exhausted themselves physically, Hannah lay with her head on Wycliff's chest, listening to his heartbeat. He stroked her hair and told her tales of the *rapscallion's* childhood at Mireworth, as rain fell outside.

Some hours later, the family gathered in the library, the weather reflecting their mood. Storm clouds rolled across the countryside and darkness had fallen prematurely. Sheba and Barnes sat on the rug by the fire. Timmy huddled in a corner, his arms wrapped around his slight frame. Hannah chose the settee, while Wycliff stalked to the fireplace.

Seraphina wheeled herself to one side. "Amongst my readings, I have found a clue which I think explains how the Afflicted remain animated. The Egyptians believed that when the physical body, or *khat*, becomes a corpse, it creates a link between the soul and earthly remains. There are two forms of the soul, known as the *ba* and *ka*, but I won't bore you with the differences between the two. What is pertinent is that the *ba* form can journey between the afterlife and the corpse. However, the *ka* form has to reunite with the body each night in order to sustain it, otherwise it deteriorates."

Hannah leaned forward as she grasped the meaning in her mother's story. "Sustain it? Do you think the Afflicted suffer rot because their *ka* has not returned to the corpse?"

Seraphina nodded. "It seems a likely explanation. I suspect the *ba* is tethered to the physical remains, which is what Wycliff can perceive as the hound, and keeps us animated. We don't know how Dupré formed this curse, but I believe he corrupted an ancient Egyptian rite. What if his twisted magic has trapped the *ka* somewhere? If it cannot return to our remains to give us sustenance, we decay on our feet."

"But even if this *ka* returned to the Afflicted's body, wouldn't you still be dead?" Wycliff asked.

"Yes. It is not a cure, but might alleviate the worst of our symptoms if we discover a group of trapped *ka* in the underworld." Seraphina wheeled closer to Hannah. "And the demand for pickled cauliflower might decrease."

"The time for questions is over. Let us seek answers." Hannah tightened her grip on her hands to steel herself. While most of her was not afraid, a tiny sliver of doubt murmured, *What if...?* She shut out the voice. Now was the time for boldness.

"How long will this take?" Wycliff asked. He stood

by the fire, leaning against the mantel, his arms crossed and his hands clenched around his upper arms. Fire and pain burned in his dark eyes and Hannah couldn't look at him directly, or tears would well up in her own.

"Hours, at most. Hannah was close to death when Sera first performed the ritual. Our girl will not live to see out the day," Sir Hugh answered.

"Now, Mother, and let the storm break free." Hannah reached out and took her mother's hand. Seraphina loved storms and often turned her face to the rain, letting it soak her veil to drench her skin. Hannah thought it would be a marvellous way to die, out in the rain under a lightning-lit sky. Or had the powerful mage summoned the storm so the very sky would mourn the death of her daughter?

"Stretch out, please, Hannah." Seraphina gestured to the settee.

Hannah turned upon the cushions and lay down. Wycliff broke away from the wall and hovered near her head. His Adam's apple bobbed up and down as he swallowed.

"Don't touch her, Wycliff, not yet," Seraphina warned.

He nodded, but stayed silent.

Hannah closed her eyes as her mother rested one hand on her head. The other she placed over her daughter's heart. She murmured the reversal spell to free Hannah from the time lock that held her frozen. The familiar hand tightened around her heart, but this time when her mother uttered the last word, the pressure remained. Her blood turned to lead in her veins and sluggishly pulsed through her body.

"It is done," Seraphina said as she removed her hands.

The words drifted to Hannah through water, her mind having difficulty processing what they meant. Her entire body ached and breath came short in her lungs. Her body fought against the intruder, now released from its prison and rampaging through her. Panic surged up her throat. She didn't want to die, but she must.

"How do you feel, Hannah?" her father asked.

She opened her eyes, Wycliff now beside her. He wrapped his arms around her and helped her to sit up. She wet her lips, which had become dry. "I...ache."

"I'll not leave you," he murmured. "What do you wish to do?"

She didn't know. Thoughts wouldn't form properly. Like a puzzle broken apart, nothing would fit together to create a sentence. The image of a chicken appeared in her mind with its unblinking stare. Were they tucked up safe from the storm? Perhaps she should check.

Hannah rested one hand on the arm of the settee and leaned on it to stand. The floor undulated under her feet as though she walked across the surface of a turbulent river. The fist squeezed tighter around her heart and the organ fought for each beat. Hannah sucked in a breath as her vision swam and black dots danced before her eyes.

"Wycliff?" Only one certainty remained firm in her

dying mind. She needed her husband's arms around her.

20

Wycliff couldn't look as the mage removed her spell and pushed Hannah toward death. He loved his wife with a fierce passion that would endure beyond death, but he didn't have the strength to see it unfold. He closed his eyes and his chest tightened as he swallowed unshed tears. He would be Hannah's strength, her rock in her last moments. Then he would be the first to greet her soul when it separated from her form. But the pain of losing her shredded him.

"It is done," Seraphina said.

Only then could he open his eyes and be at her side, helping her to sit up. Hannah sat immobile, her head bowed. Her father enquired how she felt, but she shook away the question and muttered something about the chickens. Using the arm of the sofa, she levered herself up like an invalid. Then she turned, a lost look in her eyes, a sheen of sweat on her brow.

"Wycliff?" Her tone was soft, with a worried edge.

He caught her as her knees buckled, and swept her into his arms. Her eyelids fluttered shut. One trembling hand went to his chest.

"Should it happen this fast?" He held Hannah to his chest as he stared at her parents. He thought he had hours to prepare, to steel himself against what would come, but she had slipped away within minutes.

"The curse has fought my magic for two years and, I fear, laid an ambush for this day." Seraphina wheeled her chair around the settee.

"The glade," Hannah murmured against his shirt. "I want to die in the glade."

The words punched him in the gut, and he nearly fell. *I want to die in the glade.* He bit back the cry of anguish that roared in his veins. He wouldn't lose her, he reminded himself. This was temporary only, so that she might walk beside him on the journey to come. He would restore her to life. And if he could not...then he would dwell in the underworld with her. Whatever happened, they would be together.

"The glade, then," he whispered and kissed her forehead. Her body warmed in his embrace as a fever burned through her, yet at the same time chills wracked her limbs.

"Let the storm free," Seraphina murmured as she held out her arms to Sir Hugh.

The older man glanced at Wycliff, his eyes bright with tears. The large surgeon let free his grief for his dying daughter. His gaze fixed on Hannah, slumped in Wycliff's arms. Not only would he lose his daughter this night, but his wife would also journey beside her.

Wycliff carried his precious burden through the house, down the rear stairs, and into the forest. Percy the peacock emitted his shrill cry and shadowed his footsteps, the harem of peahens following. Sheba, carrying Barnes with two fingers twisted in her collar, shot ahead to lead the way. Snatches of wind tugged at Wycliff's hair and clothing, but the trees bowed out of his way.

Timmy hurried from the library to join them, jumping over ferns in his path. While Wycliff cradled his wife, Timmy fetched the blankets and pillows from the hidden storage box and laid them out by the water. A grim darkness spread over the city even as time nudged toward midday, so the lad activated the few lanterns scattered around the glade. The soft yellow light encircled Hannah and Wycliff.

Wycliff knelt and lowered Hannah to the blanket, positioning a pillow under her head. She stirred and opened her eyes for a moment. She touched his arm and then it fell away. Sweat slicked her skin and her lungs drew air in shallow gasps.

With nothing more he could do, Wycliff fussed with the blanket, smoothing out the edges. He listened to her ragged breathing that seemed to match the irregular burble of the water. He cradled her to him and waited. Timmy sat on the grass, clutching the spaniel to his chest. Barnes perched on the lad's knee.

Sir Hugh carried Seraphina out to the peaceful

glade and set her down in her flower-covered bower. Roses bloomed with a buttery glow around her as the mage murmured soft words. The temperature warmed and the wind fell away, and while they could watch the storm above, only a few tepid droplets dampened their skin. The creatures of the forest joined their vigil. Birds clustered along tree branches. Hedgehogs gathered at the base of a tree. Fireflies darted about. Percy and the peahens bedded down close to Hannah's feet.

Wycliff took Hannah's hand in his and couldn't tear his attention from her face. He wanted to command her to fight the curse, but knew she would not. The next step required her to die. She would give her life in an attempt to save the other Afflicted. Overhead, the storm broke. Thunder crashed and a single flash of lightning cracked across the clouds. Hannah drew one deep breath...and sighed. Her life ebbed away as the rain pelted the earth.

Minute after minute, Wycliff waited for her to inhale again. Yet she remained still in his arms.

Timmy crept forward and sat beside Wycliff. The lad's shoulders shook as silent tears rolled down his face.

"Now, Timmy," Wycliff said as he stroked Hannah's hair back from her face.

The lad reached out and placed one hand on the side of her neck. After a long silence, he sobbed, "She's gone."

Wycliff curled over Hannah, a keen rising in his chest. He thought he had known pain when a hellhound latched on to his throat and simultaneously tore and cauterised his flesh. But that agony paled compared to the white-hot barbs that pierced his heart now. Tears cast the world in a mist. He loved her beyond death.

Thunder shook the trees in answer to Wycliff's cries. Wind howled through the branches, but only the faintest breeze touched them under the magical umbrella. With an effort, he remembered their task. To take the journey ahead, he first had to let Hannah go. He lowered her to the blanket and placed a kiss on her still warm lips.

Then he let Timmy take charge. The lad spread another blanket over her immobile body and knelt beside her to begin his vigil.

Wycliff rose and grabbed hold of the sorrow and despair as the hound flowed over him. So fixated was he on Hannah's physical form, it took him a moment to register her spirit. Her soul stood next to her lifeless body, gazing down upon it. A warm yellow glow shone from her. Hundreds of fireflies formed her gown and clustered in her hair. She vibrated with beauty and he sucked in a breath at the sight of her.

She turned and smiled at him. Then Hannah reached out and stroked his smoky fur. "We do this together, Wycliff."

He nudged her hand with his muzzle and choked back a cry.

From the bower, Seraphina murmured words that set a chill racing over his fur. On the last syllable, thunder crashed and jagged lightning danced over the night sky. The silver thread that connected the mage's soul to her body snapped, and the ends drifted to the grass and shrivelled up into nothing. The mage's body fell into Sir Hugh's arms and he cried out her name.

Her elegant soul leaned down and kissed the top of her husband's head.

"I entrust you with all I love in this world, Wycliff, and pray you bring them back." Sir Hugh stared at him, anguish written all over the man's face as he lost both wife and daughter. Unable to see their souls, he surveyed their physical remains, now bereft of animation.

Wycliff nodded. He had no words of comfort to offer the grieving surgeon. He struggled with his own sense of loss at Hannah's death, even though her soul stood next to him. Seraphina moved to stand on his other side, her soul possessing the limbs missing from her physical body.

"Keep hold of me. I do not know what will happen," he instructed their two souls.

Each woman reached out a hand and touched his shoulders. He called to the void and a path opened between the trees, the inky darkness pulling him as though it were magnetic. One cautious step at a time, the group began their journey. The dark swallowed them, as though they walked into the centre of the storm. Silence enveloped them and the rain ceased. The forest disappeared and Wycliff saw only a black ribbon laid over midnight velvet. One foot in front of the other, he walked. Whispers raced over his skin, but they merely seemed curious about his companions. At least the void hadn't demanded his wife as sacrifice.

A golden shimmer surrounded them, emanating from the women's souls. Wycliff didn't know if they walked for hours, days, or mere moments. Every step was identical to the previous one, with no scenery to mark their progress. Then tiny dots broke away from Hannah and Seraphina, and fireflies swirled around him. He snapped his jaws at the bright spots in irritation. One dot merged with another, then another, to create a large glowing ball that shot away.

The sphere of fireflies hovered in the distance, the light pulsating and growing. As they neared, it encompassed them and Hannah gasped. Her fingers tightened on his shoulder as they stepped through the ball of light and into the underworld.

Hannah closed her eyes against the stab of brightness as the cloak of darkness drew back from around them. The glare subsided, and she opened her eyes and sucked in a gasp at the landscape laid before them.

"Duat," she whispered, and took one step forward on the golden ground.

Sand under her feet turned to lush green growth as it rushed to meet a winding river. The water a pure blue, shadows played over its surface and hinted at creatures in its depths. More rustling reeds and grasses interspersed with pastel pink flowers on the other bank gave way to a wide, paved road. In the distance was a towering temple, with a city spread out beyond it until its buildings merged with the horizon.

"Hannah," Wycliff murmured beside her.

She turned, and her eyes widened. He had grown and changed. His smoky, fire-tipped fur was now a silky black so intense, it shimmered blue under the sun. In size, he stood as tall as she and large enough to ride like a pony, each upright ear bigger than her hands. His eyes were a deep amber that glowed with hidden warmth. Around his neck was a wide gold collar inscribed with hieroglyphics, and from it dangled a golden ankh.

"Does the light hurt your vision?" She ran a hand over his fur. No longer did it dissolve under her touch. In the Duat, it was made corporeal.

He shook his head. "Here, my vision seems normal. You and your mother have also changed."

When Hannah stared at her mother, she gave a sob of joy. Seraphina stood as Hannah always remembered her. Tall and slender, her chocolate hair with sun-bleached ends loose around her shoulders. Blue eyes bright with intelligence. Her skin had never been a fashionable alabaster, but bore the golden caress of the sun from time spent outside with neither bonnet nor parasol. Both of them were dressed in a gown that combined the current Empire fashion with images from ancient texts—a simple linen dress that fell to their feet with gold cord wrapped around their torsos.

Seraphina opened her arms, and Hannah hugged her.

"You do not know how good it feels to stand on my feet after my years in that chair. Nor how pleased I am to see your face without the veil misting my vision. But we must not be distracted. We have a purpose to fulfil." Seraphina stroked Hannah's hair.

Hannah pulled back and wiped her face with the heels of her hands. "Then let us go to the temple. Does that not seem the best place to begin our search for answers?"

They walked toward the river, where a jetty stuck out into the water. A barge tied there bobbed up and down with a gentle movement. Dark shapes drifted past and a pair of eyes and nostrils emerged as a hippopotamus snorted water and then paddled downriver.

"Doesn't this look much like the tiles in the grand entrance at Mireworth?" Hannah asked as they approached the barge. She plucked a delicate pink lotus bloom and inhaled the soft fragrance. Then she tucked it behind her ear.

"Yes. But how is it possible that a scene from Duat was created in the house?" Wycliff's fur rippled over muscle as he walked.

"I suspect Kemsit might have had a hand in that." Seraphina held out her bare arms and let the sun caress her skin.

An odd tingle ran over Hannah's skin, and someone whispered her name. She turned toward the sound, but found no one there. Odd. Her sandal caught on something and the tingle rippled over her foot. Bending down, Hannah picked up a chunk of glass or crystal. Some two inches in diameter, it appeared almost translucent except for a silver wisp swirling inside it.

"How beautiful," she murmured. It warmed her hand and reminded her of her mother's magic. How odd.

"What have you found, Hannah?" Seraphina asked.

"A piece of glass. I am sure it called my name, and it tingles like your magic." Hannah held it out for her mother's inspection.

"How odd. But I am sure we will find many odd things here." Seraphina smiled and gestured to the river.

Hannah tucked the glass into a pocket of her gown and thought no more of it, as she followed her mother.

They walked along the jetty to the barge, the only way to cross the river. Painted in brilliant hues of gold, red, and blue, its deck was scattered with cushions large enough to curl up on. A canvas awning stretched above and created shade for those resting below. As they boarded, the man at the helm bowed to Wycliff and then issued orders to his oarmen.

A faint breeze cooled the air and carried with it an array of odours. Hannah picked out the sweetness of flowers, a hint of spice, and the sharp tang of citrus. Their journey across the river to the other side didn't take long enough—she wanted to float down the river and soak in the peaceful atmosphere. Then she remembered her father and Timmy, keeping watch over their physical forms in the glade.

"How easy it would be to forget the living world and stay here," she murmured.

"Many souls choose to remain here, rather than journeying on to the true afterlife," Seraphina said.

On the other side of the river, more men appeared and swung a gangplank over before making the barge secure. As they disembarked, the helmsman bowed again and smiled at them.

"Do you think they do that to everyone, or should we read something into it that they bow to you?" Hannah asked her husband.

Wycliff's head rose even further on his massive neck and shoulders. "Maybe it's the gold collar that marks me out as important?"

Hannah absorbed their surroundings. Some people flowed toward the temple. Others tended the crops in fields by the river. A few fished in small boats. The afterlife in the Duat resembled life by the Nile. She wondered if the crops were still prone to the vagaries of the weather and the annual flood of the Nile, or did death remove some of that unpredictability?

"How will we find Dupré?" Wycliff sniffed the air. He stared at a group of people and they jumped back out of his way.

"We ask whoever is in charge. We are assuming the French mage is even here. For all we know, there might be different versions of the afterlife and this one is tailored to us." Seraphina rubbed her hands together and sparks flickered over her skin. "Interesting. My power is stronger here. Even the air energises me and pleads with me to use it."

"You are a shadow mage and this is your realm. Could your increased ability allow you to create a cure here for the Afflicted that Wycliff could carry back?" Hannah asked.

"I feel as though anything is possible here. Keep your eyes open for any Afflicted we recognise. Finding a *ka* in Duat would confirm my theory that the two parts of the soul have been separated from their physical form," Seraphina said.

"Does that mean you might encounter your own if you are currently inhabiting your *ba*?" Hannah wondered how she would keep them all straight and how the two might be merged into one again.

"I don't know. We need to find someone who does." Seraphina gestured to the temple with its soaring stone columns.

They walked the road laid with bricks of a golden hue—so well laid, Hannah doubted a hair could slide between them. The road was easily wide enough for three chariots to pass each other. One approached, the sides painted cream with a vivid blue pattern. The horse's coat shimmered like copper, as though made of beaten metal. The man holding the reins possessed bronzed skin, a muscled bare chest, and a fine linen kilt around his hips. He saluted to Seraphina as he trotted past and winked at Hannah.

"Oh, my," Hannah whispered. A lady never saw such displays of half-naked men in London unless she were smuggled into the bare-knuckle fights. The cadavers that found their way to her father's laboratory or the dissection lectures didn't compare to a living specimen.

"It's probably an illusion like the one I wear, and his physical form weighs more than a hippopotamus," Wycliff huffed.

Hannah ruffled her hand through her husband's fur and stifled a laugh. Did a hint of jealousy stir within the enormous hellhound? "Nothing is more magnificent than you, dear husband, in any form—but particularly unclothed."

Seraphina snorted and then coughed. "There are some things a mother does not need to hear, Hannah. Although I am delighted by how much you two love each other."

The hellhound's shoulders shook with a mostly silent snicker and a gush of good humour flowed through Hannah. Around them, people wandered in many different directions. Some struck off from the road and walked across the glittering sand. Others were in charge of oxen, pulling carts laden with wares in pottery jugs or wooden boxes going to or from the city.

As Hannah watched the people conducting their afterlives, one face tugged at her attention. The older woman with grey hair tied in a neat bun wore a sad and lost expression. She plucked at her sapphire-blue gown and kept stopping people to ask them something. Each passer-by shook their head and carried on, and the old woman shrank more into her body. Her eyes widened as she watched the massive hellhound approach, then her gaze wandered over Seraphina and the woman gasped. "Lady Miles!"

Seraphina halted and tilted her head at the other woman.

Hannah knew that voice, but it had been two years since she had last seen that face more recently covered in a heavy black veil. "Lady Albright?"

21

THE WOMAN SOBBED and rushed toward them, skirting around Wycliff. She grabbed Hannah's hand. "Oh, Lady Wycliff. How pleased I am to see you and your mother. I do not know what is happening, or where I am."

Hannah bit her lip. Relief surged through her that Lady Albright had journeyed to the afterlife and wasn't trapped in the cemetery. But how to explain the rest?

"This is the afterlife, but it is not the one we are raised to expect," Hannah said in a soft tone. Then she pulled the older woman to one side of the wide road. Large stones with hollowed-out tops were regularly positioned along the road, like benches placed in a garden. Many were covered with brightly coloured blankets. They sat on one draped in green, yellow, and cream stripes.

"I do like this blue gown. I cannot remember the

last time I wore such a shade." Lady Albright smoothed a hand over her dress.

Wycliff stretched out on the ground, his colossal head on massive paws, and eyed the people milling around them.

Seraphina declined to sit; having regained her legs, she preferred to use them.

"Lady Albright, do you remember what happened to you?" Hannah asked.

Confusion crossed the older woman's face. She scrunched up her eyes and sucked in her bottom lip. "It all seems so vague. Like a dream. My cousin and I had a disagreement. I decided if I was not welcome under her roof, I knew where no one would remark upon my presence. The maid picked me some snapdragons from the garden and tied them up with ribbon. I took a hansom cab out to Bunhill Fields to visit..." Her voice trailed away.

Hannah squeezed her hand. "To visit Henry."

With a nod, Lady Albright looked away and wiped a tear from her eye. The passage of years could never diminish a mother's anguish at losing her child. Hannah glanced to her mother, busy crafting dragonflies in jewel tones and setting them free to buzz around them. What had it cost her mother to free the spell that had killed her child? "Do you know what happened next?"

"Dark came quicker than I expected. There was a lovely man who arrived at the same time as me. He said he was a Bow Street Runner, and he offered to escort me to the mausoleum. He lit a lantern to show the way." Lady Albright held out her hand and a sapphire-blue dragonfly alighted on her palm.

"Taylor," Wycliff barked from his spot at Hannah's feet.

"As we neared the mausoleum, he pulled something from his pocket and threw it at me. I remember cool liquid seeping through my gloves and gown. Then I could not move and...oh...how it hurt." Her shoulders heaved, and she shuddered at the memory. The dragonfly flitted away as she dropped her face into her hands. "Then everything went blindingly white, and I screwed up my eyes. When I opened them again, I stood here, at the end of the road by the river."

"I'm sorry to make you remember such a horrid thing. You are beyond anyone's ability to hurt you now." Hannah placed a hand on the other woman's arm.

"But where am I? I do not understand what is happening. Am I in Hell?" Lady Albright shook free of the memory to focus on more immediate concerns.

"This place is called the Duat. It is where souls go after they have passed. You can stay here if you wish, or there is another place that is like Heaven. I think that is why many people are heading to the temple." Hannah assumed that inside the temple, the souls had their hearts weighed. Or at least, she supposed the ceremony occurred there, given what she had read in books.

"I don't know if I am ready yet. It is so nice to feel the sun on my skin and I've not worn anything but black for so long." Lady Albright put on a brave face. "Wait—you said souls come here after they have passed? Oh, Lady Wycliff." Her eyes widened as she realised Hannah was also dead.

"I am fortunate. I have journeyed here with both my husband and my mother." Hannah rose from the seat.

"That...beast...is *Lord Wycliff*? That would explain rather a lot." Lady Albright scrunched her sandal-clad toes away from the reclining hellhound.

"I will come back for you, Lady Albright, but we must carry on to the temple." Hannah worried about the other woman, alone in the afterlife.

But she only smiled. "Oh, you go ahead, dear. I feel much better now that I know you and your mother are here too. Since I am truly dead this time, I imagine I can wait for some time."

Seraphina cupped her hands together and shook them. Something within her grasp clinked. Opening her palms, she held several golden coins. With a shake of her other hand, a sapphire-blue pouch materialised. The coins were dropped into the pouch and she held it out to Lady Albright. "Here, buy yourself a treat from one of the stalls. You can eat whatever you desire here."

"Oh, really? I would love to eat an orange again. Do you think they have those?" She took the pouch and clutched it between two hands.

"I am certain of it. Here is a fruit vendor now." Seraphina gestured to a man pushing a wheelbarrow along the road. Brilliant oranges sat next to bright green limes, and vibrant red apples nestled beside blood-red plums.

They left Lady Albright exclaiming over the fruit and trying to decide what to purchase, and continued toward the temple. The structure increased in size as they neared, the pillars soaring to easily a hundred feet above their heads. Pools of glittering blue water ran along either side of the entrance and fish flashed between the plants. Palms spread their fronds and offered shade to the people who sat beneath and chatted. Others carried baskets and were selling wares or food.

Hannah thought everyone happy and content with their place in the afterlife, but the more she looked, the more shadows she saw darting at the corner of her eye. Some people were draped in tones of grey and stayed out of the sun. They cast furtive glances around them and scuttled deeper behind buildings and rocky outcrops when she tried to look directly at them.

"Souls who do not want to be judged," Wycliff said when he followed her line of sight to a cloaked figure peering from behind a column. "My urge to hunt them down and drag them to the temple is the same one I experience walking through Bunhill Fields."

"An instinctive reaction, perhaps?" Did the afterlife use hellhounds, too, to ensure the souls of wrongdoers did not escape justice?

She paused by a pool to watch the fish playing hide and seek among the reeds. A voice that whispered her name seemed to come from under the water. Curious,

Hannah brushed her hand along the surface, and as she skimmed over a water lily, a chunk of glass wedged itself between her fingers. Pulling it free, she held it up to the light. A pale rose in colour, inside it a wisp darted like that inside the clear piece she'd found earlier.

A niggle took up residence in her mind, whispering that the coloured crystals were important. Or perhaps she had developed magpie tendencies in the afterlife and simply wanted to collect pretty things. Either way, Hannah placed the pale pink crystal in her pocket with the other and continued up the steps. They halted at the entrance to the temple.

"It's beautiful," Hannah murmured in wonder.

Even the most talented artist would fail to capture the full grandeur of the interior. The paintwork glowed with a metallic shimmer, the colours more vibrant than anything she saw in the living world. Huge murals covered the walls. Egyptian deities fifty feet tall looked down upon their subjects. Pots large enough that Frank could hide in them contained palms and ferns with deep green foliage.

"This will confuse the Christians," Seraphina said. "Although I suspect the aspect changes depending on one's core beliefs. We expected the Duat and so that is what we found."

"But what of Lady Albright? She expected to find Heaven. Unless the curse somehow ties one's soul to this afterlife," Hannah said.

"We are all bound together in many ways." Seraphina stopped before a mural that depicted a mage crafting a silver orb between her hands. People sat at her feet, their upturned faces awash in the glow.

They followed a central aisle, where a queue of people formed. Before them was a raised platform with an altar that appeared identical to the one in the scroll Seraphina had found. The goddess of truth and justice stood behind her scales, her feathered arms easy at her sides. The scales were modest in size compared to everything else around them. The brass gleamed in the low light. In a pan on one side of her scales lay a glistening white feather. The other waited for the heart of the soul wishing to journey on. A man prostrated himself before the altar, perhaps unable to watch as the scales dipped from side to side, finding their balance. They came to a halt, the heart weighing heavier than the feather.

"You are unworthy," Ma'at intoned.

The soul cried out. The man flung up his arms, his hands outstretched either to defend himself or plead his case. A creature lunged from the shadows. Monstrous jaws snapped up the heart from the scales and gulped it down. The soul's cries were cut short as he crumbled to the floor and dissolved, his soul form now no more than dust motes spinning on a ray of light. Then even they disappeared.

"Ammit," Hannah whispered as the creature retreated to the shadows. "But where is Anubis?"

"Heel, my hound," a loud voice commanded.

Wycliff emitted a grunt, and his body turned involuntarily to the right. He ground his jaws and snapped as his paws slid over the stone floor. His long nails grated on the smooth stone, trying to find purchase.

"Wycliff!" Hannah cried, and rushed to his side.

"My master calls." He growled and snarled as though someone reeled in a chain attached to his ornate collar.

Seraphina cast a glowing orb and flung it into the air. It spun for a moment, then flew to one side of the raised platform.

Hannah nearly tripped when her mother's light revealed who had called Wycliff to his side. Only her hand on Wycliff's fur allowed her to keep her balance.

Before them stood a towering man with the head of a jackal. Some eight feet tall, he possessed a chiselled torso of ebony skin stretched over tight muscle. Around his hips hung a cream linen kilt edged in gold. Golden bracers inset with blue and green gems encased his forearms and were matched by a collar around his neck.

Anubis.

"You dare to cast magic in my realm?" Anubis roared at Seraphina. He snapped out one arm that held a staff and a narrow beam of red shot toward the mage.

Seraphina crossed her wrists and then gestured with one hand. The beam crumpled like an autumn leaf into a hundred tiny pieces that floated to the floor. "This is my realm, too."

Anubis laughed. "So it would seem. At last, my hound brings me the missing shadow mage. It has been too long since one served at my side."

A woman stood beside Anubis. Hair like a raven's

wing fell down her back to her waist. A Horus eye was drawn in heavy black around her eyes and her lids were painted with gold. She wore a gown similar to the clothing of Hannah and her mother, but the gold cord made an intricate pattern as it criss-crossed her torso. She regarded them with the hint of a smile on her full lips.

Anput, wife of Anubis.

Wycliff sat on his haunches before the god of the underworld. "Why was I created?"

Anubis leaned toward Wycliff and inhaled, his large nostrils flaring. "You are familiar. I once granted his life to a man who smelled like you, at my shadow mage's behest, but there is also a whiff of Kemsit about you."

"He is the descendant of de Cliffe. Is that why your hounds did this to him?" Hannah stepped forward, but one hand still gripped Wycliff's fur.

The fearsome god swung his head to Hannah and narrowed his eyes. "Who are you?"

"My daughter."

"My wife." Seraphina and Wycliff answered simultaneously.

A scream halted Hannah's response, as another soul tipped the scales. She glanced over as Ammit lunged and snapped the heart between her jaws. A shudder ran down Hannah's spine. She understood why some chose to stay in the Duat, rather than present themselves for judgement only to be found unworthy.

"I journeyed here beside my husband and mother,"

Hannah replied, steeling her spine to meet Anubis's inky gaze.

A smile tugged at Anput's lips. "It appears your hound married the daughter of your shadow mage. Kemsit would be pleased."

Anubis frowned, and his grip shifted on the staff.

"Why did your hounds create Wycliff? And after you answer that question, I want to know what being a shadow mage entails." Seraphina walked to the base of the dais. Sparks rippled over her skin as magic coursed through her.

Anubis pinched the bridge of his jackal nose and walked backward to his throne. He dropped onto the curved seat. Reclining sphinx created the arms and each spread a winged arm to form the back of the chair. The god of the underworld tapped long fingers on a sphinx head as he glared at them. "De Cliffe promised me his heir to replace a hound, in exchange for his life. Kemsit journeyed with him to that cold and wet isle to ensure he kept his promise."

"One of mine for one of yours, a bargain struck, the tower endures," Hannah whispered. She ran her fingers through Wycliff's silken fur. "It wasn't an exchange, but a promise. De Cliffe gave his descendant to become a hellhound."

Wycliff snarled and jumped to his feet. He snapped at his master. "Where is my choice in this?"

Hannah stroked the fur rising along his spine. She understood his anger, but events that day had shaped her life, too. "If you could undo that day, Wycliff, would we ever have crossed paths? We are chess pieces upon the board of life, are we not, Mother?"

The pony-sized hellhound heaved a sigh and sat back down. "You are right, Hannah. I would change nothing, if to do so would mean we never met."

Anput grinned and stood next to her husband. "Your fate, hound, was sealed long ago. But I think the outcome is satisfactory, is it not?"

"Why were your hellhounds prowling the living realm? One has never been seen since, except for Wycliff here." Seraphina crafted her own curved seat from the air and sat at last. Then she crossed her legs and uncrossed them, before placing her feet flat on the ground.

"The hounds were called forth when the shadow mage ritual was invoked. They were sent to find her and escort her here, but they returned alone. It took de Cliffe's heir to bring you here." Anubis gestured with his hand.

"Like my husband before the hellhounds, my mother did not consent to becoming a shadow mage. Her life was snuffed out by another, a man called Dupré, who perverted the ritual to create a shadow mage." Hannah borrowed bravery from the presence of her mother and husband. The longer she spent in the temple before Anubis, the more her curiosity emerged.

"Is this true?" Anubis barked at Seraphina.

"Yes. This living mage brewed a most heinous poison. First, he tested it on me, then he unleashed it on England—our country, where Kemsit's remains rest.

Three hundred innocents lost their lives. But he used spells he found in Egypt without understanding their effect. We rot upon our feet. Only consuming the brain of another keeps the decay from consuming us." Seraphina pushed off from her chair and paced before Anubis, something she had not been able to do for two years. The linen of her gown flowed around her legs like water. "I cannot imagine that you intended your shadow mage to exist in such a perilous state."

Anubis rolled his shoulders and tossed his staff to the ground. "My shadow mage does not decay. Your *ka* should give your physical form the sustenance it requires from the Duat, to keep that form intact. Your body must remain well preserved to serve me in the living realm."

Seraphina paused and faced the god with a faint smile. "Yet that is our predicament. Those struck down by this curse should be relieved of that horror, if we cannot restart their hearts and restore them to life. We believe something stops the *ka* from returning to the *khat* each night, and that it is tied to the evil magic Dupré cast."

Pride flowed through Hannah at how her mother tackled the god of the underworld without flinching.

The dead mage continued, "We seek his soul, which may hide here. His hands are covered in the blood of innocents and if we know how he cast this curse, we may be able to undo it. Or free the *ka* so our bodies no longer deteriorate."

"You stand before me and speak of bloody hands?

Yours are dripping with it, shadow mage." Anubis swiped the air and blood fell from Seraphina's hands and dripped to the stones at her feet.

She shook her hands, and the blood vanished. Then Seraphina straightened her spine and stared at the god. No easy feat when he stood eight feet tall and upon a dais. "I stood on a battlefield and defended my soldiers against a charging enemy. Dupré sneaked into the bedchambers of women and snuffed out their lives in a cowardly manner. We are nothing alike. If you expect me to serve you, you first need to stop my body from rotting."

Then her mother turned and walked back to her seat. There, she inspected her fingernails. Hannah glanced from shadow mage to god. As Anubis went to rise, his wife placed a hand on his shoulder.

"Your mage's request is reasonable," Anput said. "Let them find this soul. He should answer to you, husband, for twisting our sacred rituals to his own ends."

Anubis nodded. "Very well. You may hunt him and drag him before me."

"How do we find one among so many?" Seraphina stood and gestured to her chair, which winked out of existence. A handy skill, Hannah thought. She was growing tired of all the walking and standing.

Anubis barked a laugh, and it echoed around the temple until it seemed a hundred jackals laughed in response. "This is our realm, and our hellhound is before you. His purpose is to seek out the foul souls who conceal themselves. Place your hand on his head and give him the name of the one you would have brought before you."

Seraphina did as instructed and rested her hand between Wycliff's large ears. Then she whispered, "Dupré."

22

THE NAME ECHOED through Wycliff's skull and reached a crescendo, as though he had stuck his head between a pair of cymbals at the exact moment they crashed together. He shook his head to disperse the ringing in his ears, and the noise faded to a single faint note. He turned. The sound shifted and now came from outside his head.

He brushed himself against Hannah in a farewell caress, inclined his head to the mage, and then took off at a run. People scattered out of his way, and he bounded down the steps in a single stride. Hitting the sand, he closed his eyes and drew a deep breath. He filtered through the noise of startled souls, circling birds, and vendors selling their wares.

The clear note pulled him in one direction, toward the bustling city. He set off at a lope; the sand disappearing under his paws as he ran. A breeze ruffled along his back and cooled his fur. The gold ankh on his collar swung back and forth, splashing bright light over his feet.

The city reminded him of those he'd seen during his time in the army. Red-tinged mud-brick houses were crammed close to one another and dotted the rise of the land. Many had flat roofs where the occupants slept at night to take advantage of the cooler air. Washed clothing in sunny yellows, fiery reds, and vibrant blues was strung between buildings and created flapping flags. As he slowed his pace to accommodate the press of people, Wycliff pondered the ordinariness of an afterlife where you still needed to do laundry.

Pausing at a crossroads, he lifted his head to find the tone. The steady pitch came from his right and the rolling hills behind the city. Trotting along the busy roads, Wycliff observed that he generated two different reactions in people. Some reached out to stroke his fur as he passed and murmured greetings, others shrank and hid.

A group of children ran along the packed-dirt street, kicking a ball between them. That made him pause. For some reason, he hadn't expected to see children in the Duat. But then, death did not discriminate on the basis of age or status. Death took everyone, whether you were prepared or not.

Onward, the ringing tone pulled him. The houses lay farther apart on the outskirts of the city, and soon he made his way through scrub and scraggly plants. The hill loomed before him and a dim shadow at the bottom indicated a depression or cave. The noise between his ears pinged every time he stared at the dark spot.

Wycliff shook his head as the tone increased in pitch with each stride he took toward the entrance. He sniffed, catching a ripe, unwashed aroma. Then silence fell in his skull as the sound vanished.

"Found you," he whispered as he stood on the line between light and dark.

The cave ran back into the hill for several feet and created a space similar in size to a large parlour. A lantern burned near the back and highlighted the room. Shelves and a table were pushed to one side. Everything seemed constructed of crooked and misaligned wood, as though built from sticks and branches rather than milled timber. Or made by someone unused to using his hands.

A man sat on a roughly constructed bed. He appeared to be somewhere in his sixties, with silver hair and a bushy beard laced with silver. He was dressed in simple linen trousers and an overshirt, both stained with sweat and grime, the original cream now a dingy brown. Neither man nor clothing had been washed in some time. Wycliff had found the source of the sweaty stench.

Books and scrolls were scattered around the man's feet, and an open one rested across his lap. He held his hands over the pages and muttered under his breath. Over and over he rubbed his hands. The incantation became louder, and then he slapped his hands together.

Nothing happened.

The man swore and tossed the book to the dirt floor to join the pile of others. At which point he noticed Wycliff and jumped to his feet.

"Magic not working?" Wycliff asked as he stalked closer.

"I am the strongest mage in all of France and Europe. I commanded powerful forces when I last stood in Egypt at my emperor's side. My magic should work in this hellhole, too." Dupré's attention darted to the exit behind Wycliff.

"You *were* a powerful mage. Now you are dead and your power passed to another." He took a step closer to the mage who had crafted the curse that took Hannah's life. In his mind, Wycliff imagined setting fire to the man and watching him burn. But that wouldn't drag the cure from his lips. Despite his gut reaction at the prospect of seeing the creator of the Affliction suffer, he had to bide his time. Wycliff expected his rage to turn his vision red, but this close to the man, his veins chilled instead.

Some people didn't realise that ice burned. Most lads got their tongues stuck at some point in their youth, or laughed as another boy licked cold metal or a chunk of ice. The ground under Wycliff's paws cracked as the earth froze. White slivers raced away from his pads. His fur tinkled with the music of frosted leaves.

"Why are you here, dog? Go away and leave me to my work." The mage waved a hand at him, as though shooing a chicken out of the way.

What Wycliff wanted was to hear the man scream

in agony and beg for his life, but when he reached out for the void, it didn't appear. He wondered if it only worked as a conduit between the living realm and the Duat. That seemed inefficient to him. How was he supposed to dispatch an evil soul he had ferreted out of its hiding place?

"You are summoned to the temple. I am to fetch you." Wycliff's words turned to snow and drifted to the floor.

"I am not interested. I am staying here with my books. Somewhere in here is the spell I need to transport me back to France." Dupré shuffled sideways, edging toward the opening of the cave.

"This is not a request." Wycliff padded closer and bared his canines. Saliva froze and turned into stalactites hanging from his jaws.

Dupré lunged and snatched up a chair at the end of the bed. He swung it and wood smashed into Wycliff's head.

Fool. The flimsy chair broke apart as though it were made of twigs. All it did was annoy him. Wycliff snapped and latched on to the mage's arm.

The man screamed as his flesh iced over. He jerked and struck out with his other hand, but his warm palm stuck to Wycliff's frozen side. Wycliff took a step toward the light and dragged the mage with him. The mage's sandals scuffed over the dirt as he tried to dig in his heels, and he threw his weight backward. The flailing man was no impediment at all to the pony-sized hellhound, rather like a child trying to stop a determined horse. Part of Wycliff was disappointed; he wanted more of a fight. Perhaps Lady Miles would invoke a stronger reaction in Dupré.

He blinked as he emerged into the daylight with his prisoner and heaved a sigh. It would be a slow trip back with the man's arm wedged in his jaws. At that point, Wycliff discovered Dupré didn't appreciate the value of silence. The mage ranted, raved, swore, and then pleaded nonstop.

Wycliff pondered turning his cold fury into blazing rage and seeing how the mage who had created the Afflicted enjoyed a good inferno. But that might not go down well with his wife, her powerful mother-in-law, or the god of the underworld, who all waited for him. That led him to contemplate Anubis's employment terms. There weren't enough hours in the day already to satisfy the demands of Mireworth and his role as investigator, without having to sniff out recalcitrant souls for Anubis.

HANNAH WATCHED the massive hellhound run from the temple and wished her husband a safe mission.

Anubis stepped down from the dais and gestured to Seraphina. "Come, shadow mage, there are spells I need you to reinforce around my temple."

A coy smile flitted across Seraphina's face. "I haven't decided if I want the position yet. What happened to Kemsit?"

Anubis frowned and glanced back to his wife, as though expecting her to deal with this troublesome member of her sex. "She grew weary and journeyed to the Aaru."

"What happened with de Cliffe in Egypt that he struck a bargain to give up his descendant to be your hellhound?" Hannah asked. Since they had the attention of Anubis, who better to ask about the secrets hiding at Mireworth?

The god of the underworld emitted his barking laugh. "I will only tell my shadow mage that tale, once she takes up her position."

Well, that wasn't fair. Hannah shot her mother a pleading look—the one that usually allowed her an extra book at the store, or an hour longer to read before bed.

"Since you have opened negotiations...I will become your shadow mage when you restore my daughter to life," Seraphina threw out to the imposing god.

Hannah nearly called out *and yourself*, but bit her lip. Logically, if her mother's heart beat once more, she would no longer be a shadow mage. The implications stuck in her throat—a child's innocent life would be cut short. The boy who inherited her mother's powers on her passing could not exist if Seraphina lived. He would die to restore her power.

Anubis crossed his muscled arms, and his ears twitched. "Come. I have a ward that holds back the void that is cracked. Fix it and I will consider the fate of your child."

Seraphina brushed a hand over Hannah's cheek. Worry flitted behind her eyes. "Will you be all right on your own?"

"Yes. I want to observe the ceremony here, then I have something I might do while we wait for Wycliff." An idea gnawed at her, and this presented an opportunity.

Relief flowed over her mother's face, and Hannah sighed at how she missed the range of expressions concealed by the veil. "I shall see what information I can extract from Anubis while I repair his ward."

Hannah sat on the dais at the feet of Anput. The goddess reclined on a gilded chaise while a man waved a massive ostrich feather fan above her. On closer inspection, Hannah noticed Anput's unusual headdress depicted a jackal recumbent upon a feather. The symbolism struck her as combining the feather of truth used in the weighing ceremony and her husband's role as overseer of the souls in the afterlife.

"Did you fear marrying a hellhound?" Anput asked.

Hannah turned the question over in her mind. At the time they were wed, she hadn't known of his other form. Before she had glimpsed Wycliff's true nature, she might have been afraid. Now she only saw the soul of the man she loved. "No. The outer form does not cause me fear, for I love what dwells within." Many would run screaming from the scarred face of Frank, but the monster possessed the gentlest of natures.

"You are wise for one so young." Anput regarded Hannah with a thoughtful gaze.

Hannah gestured to the brass scales. "The scales do not judge a person's exterior, but the deeds and thoughts that dwell within the heart."

The goddess made a noise in the back of her throat and smiled, like a teacher pleased a student had answered a question correctly. Hannah watched the ceremony until her bottom grew numb from sitting. Then she stood and walked from the temple and back down the stairs. On the busy road, she searched the faces, trying to find the familiar one they had passed on their way into the temple.

There, off to one side, sat Lady Albright with an orange in her hand. She peeled the citrus and stacked the rind beside her. Judging by the size of the pile, she had consumed more than one orange since Hannah had last seen her.

"Lady Albright, if you have had your fill, would you join me in the temple?" Hannah asked.

"Very well. I have so enjoyed eating fruit again." As she stood, a woman came along and swept up the peel into a basket and carried it away. Lady Albright's attention drifted to watch a group of children at play. "I suppose this place is not so bad, but..."

"You miss Henry?" Hannah finished.

"Yes. My dear little boy. How I miss his laughter

and bright smile. But he was snatched from me far too soon." A tear glimmered on her lashes.

"Many souls are content to stay here, in the Duat. Others move on to a place called the Aaru. I believe that is where you will find Henry." While Hannah didn't know for sure, instinct told her the innocent child would have gone to the golden place ruled by Osiris. Given all the poor woman had suffered, especially at the hands of her uncaring husband, surely she would be judged worthy of continuing her journey to join her child?

"Can I go there, too?" Lady Albright's eyes widened with eagerness.

"Yes, I believe you can." Hannah drew the woman closer as they walked up the central aisle of the temple. People parted around them. Some bowed their heads as Hannah passed, probably because they had last seen her accompanied by a hellhound and a shadow mage. Before the altar, people milled around waiting for their chance to approach. While it was no doubt rude to cut ahead of the others, Hannah didn't have an eternity to wait. When one soul was dispatched and its form disappeared, Hannah stepped forward and pulled Lady Albright with her.

With a bow, she addressed Ma'at, who stood in front of her scales. "This woman has led a good and honest life. She is ready to journey to Aaru to be reunited with her loved ones."

"The feather will determine her fate." The goddess

of justice and balance waved them closer, and the single ostrich feather in her hair nodded.

At that point, Hannah realised that poor Lady Albright had no idea of what would happen to her. The Egyptian ceremony was rather different from having a quick chat with Saint Peter at the Pearly Gates. She tightened her grip on the other woman's hand. "This will not hurt, I promise. Look at me and tell me about Henry. What made him laugh the most?"

"We had a puppy. How they loved one another." The woman's eyes were unfocused as the memory played out in her mind. At that moment, Ma'at reached out to pluck Lady Albright's heart from her chest. The goddess's fingers eased through the soul's form and removed the organ.

Hannah stayed by the older woman's side as the goddess placed the heart on the scales. The feather rested on the other side. The two sides played a game of seesaw, one side up, the other down. Hannah bit her lip, certain in her own heart that Lady Albright would be found worthy. She let out a sigh as the scales levelled off in perfect balance.

"This soul is worthy. She may journey to the Aaru," Ma'at announced. Then she picked up the heart and returned it to Lady Albright's chest.

A golden doorway opened beside the scales with a glowing path so similar to the one Hannah had walked with Wycliff, and yet so different.

"Is that it, is it over?" Lady Albright whispered to

Hannah. She dared a glance downward at her chest, but no visible sign of the process remained.

"Yes, it is done." They walked closer to the light.

A small shape shimmered within the golden glow. Lady Albright sobbed, "It's him! Henry!"

She turned to Hannah with tears in her eyes and hugged her. "Thank you, Lady Wycliff, for all you have done."

Lady Albright stepped onto the golden road and walked through the glowing doorway. Her form took on the same yellow hue as she knelt down and embraced the child. The light encircled the pair, and then floated away as though a thousand fireflies took flight.

Hannah wiped a tear from her eye. While she could not save Lady Albright in the living realm, she had brought her peace in the afterlife. As she turned, she met the gaze of Anput, who watched her with keen interest in her eyes.

23

A COMMOTION ERUPTED at the temple entrance and drew everyone's attention. People cried out and pushed themselves to the pillars as the hellhound strode down the aisle. The stone crackled under his feet and ice rippled away from him. Those who were too slow to move toppled and flung out their arms as their sandals slid away from them on the slippery layer.

From the hound's jaws dangled a man's arm, the rest of him limp and dragging between Wycliff's legs, the body skating along on the layer of ice. The mage kept up a stream of curses that made Hannah's ears redden.

Before the dais, Wycliff spat out the mage. Then he shook himself and with a soft *whump*, fire raced over his body and the ice dissolved, leaving a puddle of water around his feet. That then turned to steam and Wycliff stood in a warm mist until it drifted upward.

Hannah waited until the puddle evaporated before

going to his side. She stared at the captured mage, who challenged her expectations. She thought she would see the visage of evil...but he looked like a grandfather with grey hair and a long grey beard, a rotund belly, and laughter lines in the corners of his eyes. He also possessed a colourful line in curses that would make a sailor blush. Not to mention an aroma similar to rotten fish.

"I have had to listen to that the entire way back," Wycliff muttered. "Not to mention he tastes as bad as he smells."

Seraphina stepped from behind a column, the obsidian god at her side. The fallen mage glanced over the god of the afterlife as though he were of no importance, but the woman at his side made him turn beetroot red.

"You! I should have known such an abomination would reside in this Hell," Dupré spat. "Not that it matters. We are all powerless here and there is nothing you can do to me now."

Seraphina laughed. "You might be powerless. I am not."

As she approached, she rolled her hands together and then flung them out. A ball of silver light shot toward the downed mage and encircled him. Seraphina waved her hands like a conductor and threads broke loose and wrapped themselves around the man's hands, feet, arms, and legs. Then she drew her hand upward like a puppeteer and commanded her marionette into an awkward position.

"Impossible! How are you doing this?" Dupré demanded as he struggled against the bonds.

"You made a mistake any mage learns as a child—don't cast spells you don't fully understand. You corrupted the shadow mage ritual of Anubis. While you killed me, you left me animated in the world of the living. You made me a creature of the underworld, and I draw my power from this realm." Seraphina pulled the strands tighter against her enemy's form and with a swipe of her hand, spread his arms wide as though he were chained to an invisible wall.

"A dead mage is a creature of evil!" he hissed.

"Evil is not defined by life or death, but by your actions. *You* are the loathsome creature. You created this curse, and you will tell me how to reverse it and restore your victims to life." Seraphina flicked a finger and a tiny bolt of lightning shot along a silver strand to zap the prisoner.

The French mage gasped, and his head snapped forward. Then he drew a deep breath and steadied himself. He looked Hannah's mother dead in the eye. "There is no cure. I made sure of that to ensure your end was prolonged and painful."

"No," Hannah whispered.

With no cure, the Afflicted would be at the mercy of Lord Tomlin and every frightened man who sought to protect his brain. How long would they endure as the country turned against them? She doubted the Afflicted would last a year. They had mere months at most. They would be forced to flee England and roam the world, always one step ahead of those who hunted them. Her knees buckled and Wycliff dipped his weight to support her. Hannah fisted his fur as she met his amber gaze, despair already settling inside her. "We cannot be cured."

Wycliff knelt and lowered her to her knees. Hannah pressed her face to his side and inhaled his smoky aroma. They had pinned all their hopes on extracting a cure from Dupré. Her tears evaporated against his warmth. What would they do now that all hope was lost?

"Together, Hannah, beyond death," Wycliff murmured as he nuzzled against her.

His words reminded her that she was loved, regardless of whether she possessed a pulse. She steeled her spine and despair drained from her to be replaced by determination. She had journeyed to the afterlife to find relief for the Afflicted, and she refused to return empty-handed. Hannah climbed to her feet and kissed Wycliff's furry muzzle. Then she turned to face the man whose actions had stolen her life.

"You killed innocent people, then left them to suffer all over again as their bodies rotted." Hannah tried to reconcile the man's genial appearance with the blood running from his hands.

"We were at war. Things were done." He shrugged and had the audacity to stifle a yawn as though they bored him.

Hannah took a step closer. Wycliff nudged her side, offering his protection should she need it. She stroked his fur. The man before her was now power-less, stripped of his magic and his life. Events of the past two years crashed into her mind. She remembered the lives lost, the horrors she had witnessed, the help-lessness as they laboured to find a cure. All because of this man.

She let go of Wycliff and advanced on the mage. If she had been a man or a mage, she would have demanded justice be extracted from his hide. "This was not war, or the clash of one army against another. You used twisted, evil magic and created a poison that stole into the parlours and bedchambers of hundreds of people and snuffed out their lives like a thief in the night. You struck at them in the one place they should have been safe—their homes."

"Who are you but another dead thing? Shoo, little fly, go bother someone else." Dupré tugged against the bonds holding him upright and muttered a spell that turned to empty words.

Wycliff growled, and Seraphina narrowed her gaze and sent another lightning bolt rippling through the lines. The French mage twitched as spasms of elec-tricity surged through him.

Who was she? A mouse who could roar. Rage flowed through Hannah. Here, immobile before her, was the man who had murdered her mother and set free the poisoned powder that had stolen three hundred lives. Only the intervention of Sir Ewan Shaw had stopped a far larger tragedy from unfolding. Dupré had created enough of the poison to take thousands of

English lives. Even more damning, he didn't exhibit a single shred of remorse for his actions.

"You cast the shadow mage spell without my permission and transformed this woman against her will." Anubis prowled around the twitching mage.

"He should be judged, husband." Anput gestured to the brass scales.

Hannah shook her head and clenched her hands into fists. "You should not foul the scales of justice by weighing his heart. If I could, I would pluck it out myself and toss it to Ammit!"

Anput stepped forward and took Hannah's clenched hands in hers. "Then do it. We give you our permission to take this worthless being's soul and feed it to the void."

Anput stroked Hannah's knuckles with her thumb, and a tingle brushed over her skin. Could she do such a thing? Emotions collided inside her. She worked alongside her father to save people and ease their suffering. For years, she had studied books and always took the quiet route through life. Here, now, was her opportunity to step out of the shadow and deliver justice for the Afflicted.

Yes, she could do this. For the former Lady Albright thrown into the gutter by an uncaring husband. For Miss Knightley, spurned by her fiancé and left alone to her fate. For her mother, taken from Hannah and her father. And for herself, her heart stilled as she died in Wycliff's arms, robbed of their future together.

Hannah strode over to stand before Dupré. "You asked who I am. I am *justice*."

She reached out her hand. Her fingers touched the grimy linen covering his chest. In her mind, she visualised the placement of his heart, if he even possessed one. She recalled how easily Ma'at's hand had slipped into Lady Albright's chest, like a hot knife through butter.

She pushed, expecting resistance from skin and muscle and the odd weight that ran up a scalpel during an autopsy, but found none. Dupré gasped as her hand disappeared into his chest. An odd, gelatinous feeling rippled over her knuckles, as though she demolished a jelly. Logically she assumed that since they were in the Duat and both souls, it was not unlike two ghosts colliding and one passing through the other.

"No. Stop it. You cannot do this." Dupré's eyes widened and he tugged furiously at his bonds. He curved his spine, trying to arch his chest away from Hannah's reaching hand.

Hannah ignored his twitching and concentrated on her task. Her fingers found a solid object, and she grabbed hold and pulled. The man's heart popped free of his soul form and Hannah held it aloft. Unlike the dark red hearts of those she had witnessed being judged, this organ emitted a black ooze that seeped between her fingers.

"Rotten to your very core," Hannah said. Then she tossed the sticky object to Ammit.

The goddess snapped her crocodile jaws and

caught the treat. Instead of swallowing it in one gulp, she held it between her long teeth.

Dupré screamed and his knees gave out. He slumped against his bonds, and only Seraphina's silver net kept his arms outstretched and his torso upright. "No! Please! I'll do anything!"

"Anything? Cure the Afflicted." Hannah stared him in the eye and waited. This was his last chance, if a cure existed.

The old man gasped and shook his head. Tears rolled down his cheeks—shed for himself. "I cannot. But give me time...perhaps...one day..."

Hannah turned and walked to Wycliff. Sliding one hand through his fur, she nodded to Ammit. The Eater of Hearts bit down slowly. One long tooth at a time pierced the rotten organ. Hannah shuddered when it appeared the goddess relished the disgusting taste in her mouth, the black ooze sticking to her teeth and forming droplets at one corner of her jaws.

Dupré writhed on the ground, begging for mercy. When all her teeth had lacerated his heart, Ammit closed her lips and swallowed. The mage let out a single blood-curdling scream and then his soul form exploded with a soft *pop* and turned into ash. The pieces drifted to the ground but never touched it, each winking out of existence.

Anput smiled at Hannah. "Now it is your turn."

Hannah swallowed the lump wedged in her throat and her fingers curled deeper into Wycliff's fur. "No. I do not want to be judged. I will return to the living realm with Wycliff and my mother."

"You are dead and your soul stands before us. You must be judged if you are to continue your journey." The goddess walked toward Hannah.

Wycliff growled and Seraphina took up a warrior stance, a ball of light sizzling between her outstretched palms. "No one touches my daughter."

"Stand aside, shadow mage. Heel, hound," Anubis called and tugged on an invisible lead.

"I'll not leave her side!" Wycliff snarled and snapped.

Hannah held out her hands, but didn't know how to help him as the goddess advanced on her.

The hellhound planted his massive feet. His entire body resisted the god's command until a *crack* whipped through the air and he surged backward onto his haunches.

"What?" Anubis rose from his throne. "You would both defy your master?"

"You are not my master. I answer only to the woman I love and you will not take her from me." Wycliff curled his gigantic frame around Hannah.

Seraphina stood on the other side of Hannah and raised a shimmering sphere around them. "You made me an offer, Anubis. I will serve as shadow mage on the condition you restore my daughter to life."

Anubis barked in laughter that echoed around the temple. "You are a worthy shadow mage. This child must be extraordinary that she commands the loyalty of my hound."

Anput placed a hand on her husband's arm. "He loves her, husband. They have a unique bond. Think how they could *both* serve us in the world of the living."

Anubis grunted and rubbed his jaw. "There is potential in what you say, wife. Let this one be judged. If she is worthy, she may choose between the Aaru or being restored alive to the earthly realm."

Hannah placed her hands on either side of Wycliff's face and stared into his amber eyes. "I will do this. You and Mother need to return to Papa. He cannot lose us all." She swallowed her fears as pictures flowed through her of all that could have been and now never would. Only a few moments ago she had plucked out Dupré's heart as anger rolled through her veins. Those actions would stain her soul. If she were judged unworthy, then so be it. She would have an eternity in the void to contemplate her mistakes.

Wycliff rested his face against hers. "You are worthy, Hannah, and we will return together."

Seraphina cast her daughter a worried glance. "Are you sure?"

Hannah kissed Wycliff's nose and then hugged her mother. "Seeing you again, as you once were, makes everything worthwhile."

Seraphina lowered the shield and kissed Hannah's forehead. Then, with slow steps, Hannah walked to Anput. The goddess pressed her hand to Hannah's chest. She couldn't look and kept her gaze fixed on

Wycliff. A hollow feeling swirled inside her as the goddess pulled free her heart and carried it to the scales. Hannah dropped to her knees and flung her arms around Wycliff's neck. If Ammit ate her heart, at least the last thing Hannah touched would be Wycliff.

The scales made a faint ting as they tipped one way and then another. Hannah buried her face in her husband's fur, unable to watch as her crimes were counted against her. Seconds passed. Would Ammit take her quickly in one snap, or draw it out like she had with the mage?

"You are as worthy, Hannah, as I knew you to be," Wycliff murmured in her ear.

Bravery failed her. Hannah peered through his fur and glanced at the scales. Sure enough, her heart sat in perfect balance with the feather. She gulped in relief and tears of joy misted her vision. "We can all go home."

Anput plucked Hannah's heart from the pan and returned it to her chest. Then she walked to Anubis' side. "Do they not remind you of us, husband? As the hound is your servant upon the earth, so his wife could be mine. They are the balance the living realm needs— one to find foul souls to feed to Ammit, the other to help the worthy to the golden path of Aaru."

"A most excellent idea, wife." Anubis waved his hand, and the assembled people clapped and cheered.

Anput removed a chain from around her neck, from which dangled an ankh. She placed the necklace over Hannah's head. The gold warmed against her skin and a slow tingle ran through her body. "This will allow you to travel the realms with the hound. When you return to your physical form, touch the ankh and say these words to restart your heart." The goddess whispered a phrase in Hannah's ear in an unknown tongue. The words swirled through her and took up residence deep inside her.

Ma'at approached and removed a golden bracelet from her arm. She snapped it around Hannah's left wrist. "This will allow you to reach into this realm and hold my scales."

Seraphina hugged Hannah. "At least we have you restored, even if we cannot free the others trapped in the curse."

"Trapped," Hannah whispered the word. The weight in her pocket reminded her of the pieces of glass. She drew out the objects and cupped them in her hands. "I found these on our walk here. Each called to me in a different voice. This one"—Hannah held up the larger, clear piece—"reminds me of you. The pinkish one calls to mind Miss Knightley."

Seraphina took the bigger lump from Hannah's palm. A wisp swirled around and around, creating a soft ball of pure white. "There is something trapped within that hums a tune that resonates through me."

Anput took the rose-coloured one and cupped it in her palms. She closed her eyes and bent her head over the object for a moment, then nodded. "Our servant is right. This rock contains a *ka*. The curse the evil one cast trapped the divine spark within."

"Can I return this to the person it belongs to?" Hannah glanced at her mother as she asked the question.

"Yes. Touch this to the person's heart and the *ka* will be free to nourish the physical form once more," Anput said.

Wycliff grumbled. "More work to do, and now we have drawn Hannah into this."

Anput wagged a finger at Wycliff. "When you have freed the *ka*, you will have your reward for your service, hound."

"What does that mean?" Wycliff stayed by Hannah's side.

Anput held the pinkish crystal to the light, the spark within doing a slow rotation. "Once the *ka* is freed, it will no longer have a use for its prison. You may have the rock that trapped it."

The hound blew out a long sigh, and Hannah bit her lip. She could well imagine Wycliff's private thoughts at being told he would be rewarded with a brightly coloured piece of glass. While a monetary reward would go a long way toward restoring Mireworth, it lightened Hannah's heart to know that at least two of the Afflicted would be free of that aspect of the curse that saw them rot.

That line of thought left her with more questions. "With the *ka* once more able to nourish their forms, does that mean they will no longer require the other form of sustenance?"

"As long as the *ka* journeys to the Duat to energise

itself here and returns to the *khat*, they will not require anything else." Anput placed the object back in Hannah's palm.

"You will be restored, shadow mage, once your daughter releases your *ka* to you in the living realm," Anubis added.

Joy flowed through Hannah. Her mother would no longer rot. Then she thought through the wider implications. There were possibly some three hundred Afflicted, and she held the *ka* of only two. "I need to find the others."

"This is your gift, Hannah. You can sense the magic the curse used to trap their *ka* here in the Duat. That part of our soul must be taken prisoner in the days between when we die and arise as the Afflicted." Her mother cupped her face and placed a kiss on her forehead.

Even with her ability to sense magic in use, the idea of finding so many stones in the land of Duat was akin to finding a particular grain of sand on a beach. It might take her years to locate them all. "But we cannot stay too long here to find them. What of Papa?"

"You may return to the Duat as you need, or when we require you, so long as you walk the path with the hound." Anubis stalked back to his throne and seated himself. He waved his hand and the weighing of the hearts resumed.

Hannah made a decision. "We will search for the rest of the afternoon, then return to Papa."

They spent a few hours searching the land between

temple and river. Back and forth they paced, Hannah halting when a tingle raced over her skin and Wycliff digging in the dirt. As Osiris completed his journey across the sky, she clutched a basket filled with a kaleidoscope of coloured glass, each in a different hue, all containing a trapped *ka*.

"Let's go home," Hannah whispered.

24

THEY RETURNED the same way they'd arrived, back across the river to the inky doorway. Wycliff clutched the handle of the basket in his jaws. Hannah curled one hand in Wycliff's fur as they stepped within, the other gripping Seraphina's hand. Eventually, the darkness of the void gave way to the velvet of night. The lanterns were bright spots around the glade. Sir Hugh cradled his wife in his arms in the bower. Timmy sat vigil beside Hannah's form.

Wycliff placed the basket on the ground beside her body.

"Wycliff! Are they with you?" Sir Hugh called.

"Yes. We have all returned," Wycliff replied.

The surgeon sobbed his gratitude.

Hannah was staring at her body, wondering what to do next, when a gentle tugging pulled her down until she hovered above her form. Her soul eased back into her physical remains. The necklace around her neck glowed brightly as the parts of her were brought together. Hannah rubbed at the spot where the ankh rested against her skin and whispered the words Anput had murmured in her ear. A single vibration boomed through her and she sat up with a gasp as air whooshed back into her lungs.

"She's back!" the lad cried.

Wycliff shook himself free of the hound and kissed her. As he pulled back, worry tugged at his eyes. "Did Anubis keep his promise?"

Hannah held out her right arm to Timmy. "Am I alive or dead, Timmy?"

The brave lad swallowed and took her arm. His fingers gripped her wrist and his eyes widened in wonder. "You're alive."

"Alive? Is it true? Did you find a cure?" Sir Hugh asked.

Seraphina stirred in his arms as her soul settled back inside her.

"Of sorts." Hannah plucked the clear chunk of glass from the basket and approached her mother.

Sir Hugh helped his wife to sit up. Hannah placed the crystal over her mother's heart. Light burst from the stone and burrowed into her mother's skin.

Seraphina raised her veil and before their eyes, her mother's complexion, its flesh and eyes already restored, returned to its sun-kissed warmth.

"Sera," Sir Hugh sobbed his wife's name.

"That's not the only remarkable thing." Seraphina lifted the hem of her gown and wiggled her toes.

"Your legs!" Timmy exclaimed.

Joy rushed through Hannah. Her mother might still be dead, but she would dance with her father again. The crystal cooled in her fingers. Without the spark of the divine, it returned to a clear state. When light from the lantern struck it, rainbows burst across the glade.

A laugh erupted from Seraphina. "Do you know what you hold, Hannah?"

She held it up. On close inspection, it did hold a remarkable array of reflections inside it.

"While I am not the expert my dear friend Kitty is regarding these matters, I believe, dear Hannah, that you are holding a diamond," her mother said as she pulled up her gown to let her husband examine her legs.

"The crystals turn to gems when the *ka* is freed?" Hannah's jaw dropped as she stared from the basket, to the object in her hand, to Wycliff's chiselled features.

His eyes widened, then he too burst into laughter. "Anput did say we would be rewarded for our service. For once, events might have gone in our favour. If these do indeed turn into precious gems, then we will be handsomely rewarded for our endeavours."

Hannah burst into tears and flung her arms around Wycliff's neck. Then she kissed her husband most soundly. They had travelled to the underworld and back, and now had their entire lives before them.

THE NEXT DAY, Seraphina settled herself in the bathchair and dropped the veil over her face. After days of bickering among themselves, the mage council had finally agreed to meet her. The council occupied a stout, round building on the outskirts of London. Magic prickled around her as each new mage added their own touch to the structure.

"Ready, my love?" Hugh asked her, a hand on her shoulder.

She tilted her cheek to his hand. "Yes. Let us set the cat among the pigeons."

Hugh grasped the iron rings and pulled, opening the heavy double doors.

Lady Miles wheeled her chair into the opulent chamber. England's mages met in a room more fit for a sultan's palace. Soft orange silks draped the walls. Around the edges of the room, sofas in forest green were piled with vibrant blue cushions.

A round table dominated the centre of the room, inset with a mosaic of blues, creams, and sage green. Within that was a clock face ten feet across. Twelve high-backed chairs encircled the table, each sitting at a point on the clock. Only six chairs were occupied. Three mages had yet to reach their majority. Of those three, two served their apprenticeships to another mage and one, the child who had inherited Seraphina's living powers, would live a normal childhood until the age of five. Three other adult mages were in far-flung corners of England and hadn't returned for the meeting.

Lord Pendlebury, the oldest mage and therefore the

council's Speaker, nodded from his chair. "Lady Miles, you wish to address this council."

She wheeled herself closer. Some of the mages angled their chairs toward her. Mage Tomlin narrowed his gaze and his lips thinned to mere lines, like those of a petulant child.

"I once sat amongst you," she began.

"And now you should be six feet under," Tomlin muttered under his breath.

The man's horrid temper knew no bounds. Seraphina would enjoy putting him in his place. "Then a curse crafted during the war stole my life and that of some three hundred others. We were rendered undead, and rot stole along our limbs."

"The Affliction is a terrible curse that cannot be undone. This council and all of England grow concerned over what is required to sustain your existence. What is needed for a few cannot be outweighed by the concerns of the many. A permanent solution must be found," Lord Gresham said.

The others muttered in agreement.

Seraphina smiled, not that they could see it under the veil. "I agree. How fortuitous that I have returned from a journey to the underworld and have brought back a cure. My daughter and Lord Wycliff will visit each of the Afflicted to dispense it. Some of them may decide to remain undead, but I can assure you, gentlemen, those Afflicted will no longer rot, nor will they need any sustenance."

A gasp went around the room as the mages digested her meaning.

"They will neither rot nor require any form of sustenance?" Lord Gresham clarified.

"They will not. That should put an end to this needless panic." She rested her hands in her lap.

"The Afflicted will become *immortal*?" Lord Pendlebury leaned forward in his chair and a bright light lit his eyes.

Seraphina shrugged. Funny how men showed keener interest once they realised immortality was at play. "I do not know for certain. Ask me that question again in a hundred years."

"If this is true, we will be able to reassure the population that any harm you pose has now passed," Lord Pendlebury said.

"It should also put an end to the horrible burnings of the Afflicted by mage fire. I hear the arsonist became a victim of his master's potion." She stared at Tomlin.

"Are you trying to imply something?" he hissed at her.

She grinned behind her veil. "I'm sorry, was that too subtle for you, Tomlin? I am well aware that yours is the hand controlling these events, and that you set out to expunge my fellow Afflicted from this earth." Her voice hardened. "Call off your dogs, or I will unleash my hound." She didn't bluff or threaten. Wycliff would enjoy pulling the mage's soul free of his body.

Tomlin pushed back his chair and slammed his fists

on the table. "I will not listen to the rantings of a dead thing. You have no proof and your presence is an offence to this council."

Seraphina stared at the man who had once been much in favour at court. "Justice may be delayed, but she will never be denied, Tomlin. No matter how powerful you think you are, you cannot escape death. The day will come when you step from this realm and into mine and I promise you, I shall be waiting. I wonder if your heart will be as rotten as that of Dupré."

"Dupré? You have seen him?" Lord Pendlebury asked.

She nodded. "He was hunted down in the afterlife, his heart torn from his soul form and fed to Ammit the Eater of Hearts and Devourer of the Dead. How he screamed as he pled for mercy."

Seraphina raised her veil and the men before her gasped. She had the exquisite pleasure of an unobstructed view as the colour drained from Tomlin's face. Let him spend every day of the rest of his life in the futile search of a way to escape her reach.

Then she stood. The men before her pushed back their chairs, excited chatter breaking out among them as the legs her husband had once had to remove appeared, fully restored. She chuckled to think how they were so easily fooled. While she sat in the chair, she had dangled her legs in the underworld until she needed them. She had latched on to the idea after seeing how Wycliff disappeared when he placed a large paw on the black path. All she had to do was open a path beneath her chair.

Tomlin leapt to his feet and gestured to her. "See! She is an evil thing! We must burn her before her evil infects all of us."

"Ah. *Burn the witch*. Long has that been the rallying cry of ignorant, frightened men." Seraphina walked around the table. As she moved, she changed her plain linen shift into a gown of vibrant green and sapphire-blue that swirled into peacock feathers.

"Events are somewhat extraordinary, Lady Miles. Surely you can understand our concern that you have retained your power after death and have now regrown your legs," Lord Pendlebury said.

"As I said, the cure will restore the Afflicted." She paused at the chair where once she had sat. A peacock was carved in its high back. With a finger, she traced a wooden feather with the eye in its centre. "Over the centuries, we have lost our way. Once, we embraced two types of magic. Now you practise only one, and are afraid of the other. You wield magic from the living realm. I am the embodiment of the magic that dwells in the afterlife."

"You tapped into something evil," Tomlin snapped, but he was hushed by the mage beside him.

"Darkness is not evil. Just as light is not necessarily good. Everything must be in balance. Light and dark. Life and death. I am a shadow mage. You must set another chair at the table, gentlemen. England has twelve living mages and one dead one. A shadow mage will sit amongst you...again." She carried on walking her circuit around the table.

"Again?" Lord Gresham repeated.

"I suggest you scour the mage records. A shadow mage called Kemsit came to these shores in the twelfth century and she was not the first to tread English soil." Seraphina smiled and brought her hands together over her stomach. The men before her had much to learn, and with her intervention, the next generation of mages would be far more enlightened.

With a rose-coloured crystal in her reticule, Hannah embarked on her own journey. Frank took them to the address and waited outside. The maid showed Hannah into the parlour, Wycliff on her heels. The room had changed in appearance from that occasion when she had asked to see a bloodstained dress and Wycliff had moved the name *Emma Knightley* up on his list of possible suspects in a horrible murder.

Paintings once again graced the walls and occupied their shadows. Even the woman in question had altered, and she greeted Hannah with a genuine smile and not reserved suspicion.

"Lady Wycliff." She stood and bobbed a curtsey in greeting.

"Miss Knightley." Hannah took her friend's hands and glanced at Wycliff. How to proceed? Recent events were still so new and her abilities untested. First,

Hannah had to restore the woman's *ka* before she tried anything else.

"Please, be seated. I hope you are well?" A tiny flicker of sadness raced behind Miss Knightley's eyes with the question. Her heart had stilled two years ago, but Hannah's now beat stronger.

"Yes, thank you. I have come here today to restore something of yours." Hannah drew aside her skirts as she sat, then pulled the pink crystal from her reticule.

Miss Knightley leaned forward, a frown between her brows. "I do not understand. That piece of glass is not mine, although... How odd that it stirs a feeling of ownership as I look upon it."

Hannah held the object between her thumb and forefinger. The spark within turned loops. "What is inside is indeed yours. This holds the spark of the divine that is missing from your soul. While giving it back to you will not restore you to life, it will remove your symptoms."

"I'll still be dead?" Miss Knightley's shoulders drooped and sadness flitted behind her gaze.

Hannah's fingers tightened on the tiny prison. She offered a placebo rather than a real cure. "Yes. But you will no longer rot, nor will you need your particular sustenance. You can eat whatever you like, or nothing at all."

The other woman nodded. "That is better than nothing, I suppose. How does it work?"

"I have only to place this over your heart." Hannah waited for permission.

At the nod to proceed, she held the crystal to the bodice of the other woman's gown, over her heart. The shard warmed in her fingers as Hannah thought of the underworld. The flash of pink erupted from its prison and disappeared between the fibres of the gown. Removing her hand, Hannah glanced at the crystal and wondered if there was such a thing as a pink diamond.

"I know you are disappointed not to be fully cured. During our journey to the underworld where we found your missing spark, I was taught another avenue that would restore your heartbeat, but it is not without its risks." Hannah reached up and touched the notch at the base of her throat. Much like Wycliff's hound form, the heavy necklace bestowed on her by Anput shimmered against her skin, waiting to be called forth. A similar feeling encircled her left wrist, where the bracelet gifted to her by the goddess of justice and balance rested.

Miss Knightley's eyes widened. "You speak in riddles, Lady Wycliff. While I am grateful to no longer have to ingest that...cauliflower...please tell me plainly. Can I be cured entirely of this horrid Affliction?"

Hannah rubbed the ankh between her fingers. "Yes, there is a way. If you are willing. Your heart will be weighed against the feather of Ma'at, who is a goddess of truth, justice, and balance. If you have lived a good and honest life, you will be given a choice. You can either sever your connection to this realm and journey to the afterlife, or it is within my ability to restore the breath of life to your body and your heart will beat once more."

Miss Knightley gasped. "Truly?" She rose and walked to the window and silence stretched before she turned with worry pulling at the corners of her eyes. "And what if I am found unworthy?"

"Wycliff will consign your soul—which keeps your physical form animated—to a darker place," Hannah whispered.

"Hell." Unshed tears shone in Miss Knightley's eyes. "But Lady Wycliff, I have not led an honest life. I have deceived those I love. I have taken money to slice my flesh for the entertainment of bored nobles. I—"

Hannah left the sofa to take the other woman's hands. Wycliff remained silent, standing guard by the fireplace. How horribly would this interview have gone if he had conducted it? He probably would have started by telling Miss Knightley she was going to the void unless her heart weighed less than a feather.

"Do you trust me?" Hannah asked.

Miss Knightley bit back a sob and nodded.

"It is my opinion that you have indeed led an honest life. You have been tested by your circumstances, but love for your family has been your guiding light." Hannah drew her back to the sofa, and both women sat. "But you can remain as you are. You do not have to take the next step."

The other woman sat with slumped shoulders. "The dead have no rights, though. I cannot hold property, or marry."

"No. You will need a protector when the time comes that your parents are unable to fulfil that role." Hannah's mother had no idea how long they would exist in their restored state. Possibly, they would create a new line of Immortals like Doctor Husom. They should start a club if that were the case, so they were not lonely as the centuries ticked by.

"Do it. Let us have a conclusion to this matter." Miss Knightley drew herself up and a hint of determination crept into her gaze.

Hannah closed her eyes and called on her underworld form, letting the spirits of Anput and Ma'at guide her. When she opened her eyes, Miss Knightley's soul stood behind her, ghostly hands resting on the back of the sofa.

"Do not be afraid." Hannah rested one hand on Miss Knightley's chest, then she reached inside the woman and withdrew her heart.

Soul and physical form gasped in unison, then Miss Knightley fell back against the arm of the sofa.

Hannah used her left hand, with its golden bracelet, to reach into the underworld and pull forth the scales. The silver feather waited on one side and she placed the heart on the other. The pans rocked, as though the two items were on a seesaw. Hannah held her breath, willing the scales to reach equilibrium. Then the two sides levelled out.

"You are worthy, Miss Knightley. Now you have a choice to make." Hannah replaced the heart, so the woman would be whole for the next step. The scales shimmered and returned to the other realm.

A golden line drew itself from ceiling to floor and split apart. Light spilled into the room as though the sun shone through a window. Beyond, a flower-filled meadow beckoned.

Miss Knightley's soul turned to Hannah, while her physical form remained prone. "Am I to go through?"

"If that is what you wish. Or you may return to your life, free of the Affliction. Your heart will beat in your chest and whatever happens from this day forward, your life is fully yours to live." Hannah wagered with herself what the other woman would choose.

The soul shook her head at the golden doorway. "I would reclaim my life. I do not wish to leave my parents to grieve my passing, and I am not so old that I might not yet find happiness for myself."

"Very well." Hannah touched the ankh at the base of her throat with one hand and rested her other hand on Miss Knightley's chest. She whispered the words entrusted her by Anput and a golden thread flowed down her arm and through her fingertips into the other woman.

Miss Knightley's soul drifted back over her physical form and sank into it with a sigh.

Hannah let go of her and glanced at Wycliff, grateful that his other form had not been needed. If Miss Knightley's heart had weighed more than the feather, the hellhound would have grabbed the heart in its jaws and fed it to Ammit, who resided in the dark void.

The clock ticked, and snatches of noisy London drifted through the window. Miss Knightley drew a sharp breath and sat bolt upright. One hand went to her chest, her eyes wide. One loud breath was followed by another as she held her hands out before her and turned them over. Then she placed one over her chest.

A tear rolled down her cheek as she turned to Hannah. "Thank you," she rasped. She flung her arms around Hannah and hugged her.

While the women embraced, Hannah slipped the pink gem into Miss Knightley's pocket. It would fetch a tidy sum that would change the other woman's life.

Hannah wiped a tear from her own eyes. It lightened her heart to know that one woman had been rescued from the curse and restored to her life. The first of many, she hoped, as word spread among them. Stories of the cure would fill the newspapers with joyous tales rather than horror.

"Mother! Father!" Miss Knightley jumped to her feet and ran to the door, calling for her parents. The older Knightleys fell into the room. How coincidental that they happened to be leaning on the parlour door.

"Whatever is it, Emma?" her father asked.

"Lady Wycliff has cured me. Feel. My heart beats once more." She took her father's hand and pressed it to the side of her neck.

Mrs Knightley burst into tears—she always had been prone to fits. "Thank you, Lady Wycliff. However can we repay you for restoring our beloved daughter to us?"

Hannah patted the older woman's arm. "I am glad that I could finally ease Miss Knightley's suffering. I look forward to seeing her at many a ball next season."

Mrs Knightley stammered, "That would be lovely, but, well, we shall see."

Hannah smiled. They would indeed see. Miss Knightley deserved a chance to find happiness, and Hannah knew exactly who to ask to ensure that happened.

The new Duchess of Harden.

Wycliff offered his arm, and they left the Knightleys to celebrate. "Where to now, Lady Wycliff?"

Hannah tapped her reticule, where her mother's diamond lay concealed. "A jeweller. I rather think that Christmas at Mireworth this year will be the best one of my life."

THE END

Hᴀɴɴᴀʜ's ᴊᴏᴜʀɴᴇʏ has reached its conclusion, but are you curious about where it all began...?

Tournament of Shadows
Book 1: Opening Gambit

They thought to use her as a pawn... but she plans to take control of the game...

Sᴇʀᴀᴘʜɪɴᴀ Wɪɴʏᴀʀᴅ ɪs ᴀɴ ᴀʙᴏᴍɪɴᴀᴛɪᴏɴ—ᴀ female mage. Those who control her life treat her as little better than a zoological exhibit, and constantly point out the inferiority of her magic. She doesn't know why she was allowed to live and expects every day to be her last. When the chance comes for freedom, Seraphina seizes it.

When her guardian is murdered, suspicion falls on the young mage. Is this the opportunity the shadowy forces need, to terminate the experiment of letting a female mage live?

The brilliant young surgeon Hugh Miles is tasked to determine cause of death and aid the investigation to find the murderer. Can Seraphina place her trust in Hugh, or will her life be over before she ever really lives?

Buy: Opening Gambit

History. Magic. Family.

I do hope you enjoyed Hannah's latest adventure. If you would like to dive deeper into the world, or learn more about the odd assortment of characters that populate it, you can join the community by signing up at:

www.tillywallace.com/newsletter

ALSO BY TILLY WALLACE

For the most complete and up to date list of books, please visit the website

https://tillywallace.com/books/

Available series:

Tournament of Shadows

https://tillywallace.com/books/tournament-of-shadows/

Manner and Monsters

https://tillywallace.com/books/manners-and-monsters-series/

Highland Wolves

https://tillywallace.com/books/highland-wolves/

ABOUT THE AUTHOR

Tilly writes whimsical historical fantasy books, set in a bygone time where magic is real. Her books combine vintage magic and gentle humour with an oddball cast. Through fierce friendships her characters discover that in an uncertain world, the most loyal family is the one you create.

To be the first to hear about new releases and special offers sign up at:
www.tillywallace.com/newsletter

Tilly would love to hear from you:
www.tillywallace.com
tilly@tillywallace.com

facebook.com/tillywallaceauthor
bookbub.com/authors/tilly-wallace

Printed in Great Britain
by Amazon